LBD

Live & Fabulous!

by
grace dent

g. p. putnam's sons
new york

ACKNOWLEDGMENTS:

Huge thanks to all of the usual suspects . . .

Thanks to Sarah Hughes and all the brilliant Puffin people for their support and patience as LBD II rolled along and real life occasionally got in the way.

Thanks to the fabulous Adele Minchin.

Eternal gratitude to Caradoc King, Vicky Longley, Rob Kraitt and Linda Shaughnessy at AP Watt.

Massive thanks also to John Rudolph and the U.S. Penguin team, who believed in the LBD from the very first word (and even made raunchy pink thongs to prove it).

Finally, thanks to Jon Wilkinson for enduring my incessant moaning and numerous show-biz tantrums.

You're all great—it wouldn't be half as much fun without you.

G. P. PUTNAM'S SONS, a division of Penguin Young Readers Group. Published by The Penguin Group.
Penguin Group (USA) Inc., 375 Hudson Street, New York, NY 10014, U.S.A.
Penguin Group (Canada), 10 Alcorn Avenue, Toronto, Ontario, Canada M4V 3B2
(a division of Pearson Penguin Canada Inc.)
Penguin Books Ltd, 80 Strand, London WC2R 0RL, England.
Penguin Ireland, 25 St. Stephen's Green, Dublin 2, Ireland (a division of Penguin Books Ltd.)
Penguin Books India Pvt Ltd, 11 Community Centre, Panchsheel Park, New Delhi - 110 017, India.
Penguin Group (NZ), Cnr Airborne and Rosedale Roads, Albany, Auckland, New Zealand
(a division of Pearson New Zealand Ltd).
Penguin Books (South Africa) (Pty) Ltd, 24 Sturdee Avenue, Rosebank, Johannesburg 2196, South Africa.
Penguin Books Ltd, Registered Offices: 80 Strand, London WC2R 0RL, England.

Library of Congress Cataloging-in-Publication Data
Dent, Grace. LBD : live and fabulous / Grace Dent.—1st American ed. p. cm. Sequel to: LBD : it's a girl thing. Summary: Now fifteen years old, Ronnie, Fleur, and Claude, with Fleur's sister as their chaperone, are having the time of their lives at the Astlebury music festival when Fleur suddenly disappears while crowd surfing. [1. Music festivals—Fiction. 2. Rock music—Fiction. 3. Sisters—Fiction. 4. England—Fiction.] I. Title. PZ7.D4345Lb 2005 [Fic]—dc22 2004005508 ISBN 0-399-24188-4
10 9 8 7 6 5 4 3 2 1 First Impression

for **bob watts**
and **veronica mccormack**—

who took me to Glastonbury when I was thirteen.

contents

Chapter 1

the curse of
the flaky buttmunch

"So can I take your name, please?"

"It'sh Ronnish . . . ," I tell the nurse, sniffing back tears, smudging foundation on the keypad of my mobile phone.

"Ronnidge?" confirms the nurse.

"No, Ronn-eee . . . I'm Veronica Ripperton," I say meekly.

"Okay . . . and is that Miss or Mrs. er, Flipperhorn?"

"Ripperton," I repeat, dabbing my eyes. "Look, this isn't about me anyway. It's about my, er, *friend*. Well, he's my boyfriend. I need to know if he's in your emergency ward."

"Can I take his last name?" replies the nurse.

I can hear pages being flicked and a long, faint exhale of breath. As the nurse begins searching her logbook, I catch sight of my sorry self in the living room mirror. What a fright.

It's 7 P.M., Friday night, and I, Veronica Ripperton, am pacing the floorboards upstairs at the Fantastic Voyage pub. I'm wearing my most fantastic "makes yer boobs look like a proper rack," pale pink, clingy T-shirt (now mascara stained) and my intensely snazzy "entire month of pocket money in one card swipe" denim pencil skirt (now covered in snotty bobbly tissue bits).

Despite braiding my hair and applying Light-Reflecting Bronzing Powder since 3:30 P.M., on sound assurance from *Glamour* magazine that it would give me "that blissed-out San Fran beach babe look," it pains me to say I look more like a sun-burned, depressed Martian. Or a "South American swamp don-key," as my tactful friend Fleur would probably say.

Obviously I'd be more destroyed about the above if my life wasn't in tatters anyhow.

"Steele. He's called JIMI STEELE," I tell the nurse. "Try look-ing at the lists for your special fracture unit . . . or . . . oh my God . . . what about the intensive care ward!"

My voice is beginning to choke up.

"*Uggghh* . . . he might even be DEAD," I whisper. "Actually, could you put me through to the morgue after this, please?"

"That won't be necessary," replies the nurse firmly. "Now, what time did this accident happen?"

"Accident? Ooh, well, I'm not totally sure there's been one yet," I say, truly hoping I don't sound like a complete idiot. "It's just that I heard an ambulance go wee-wahing down the high street about ten minutes ago . . . and my boyfriend Jimi . . . well, he's almost two hours late to pick me up. We're going to the Blackwell School Summer Disco, you see."

Even deeper sigh from the nursie.

"Tuna on whole wheat will do for me. Actually, Julie, just green salad," says the nurse, blatantly chatting with a passing colleague.

"And I've called his mobile phone, but it went straight to voice mail. It must have been smashed in the horrific impact of the car pile-up," I babble on and on. "He's a skateboarder, you see, and he's always doing really dangerous, death-defying stunts and . . . er, hang on, are you ordering your dinner!?"

"Mmm," admits the nurse. "I've been here since seven A.M. and I've only managed to grab half a yogurt and a handful of M&Ms. My damn phone won't stop ringing."

"Ooh, er, sorry about that . . . ," I mutter.

"But I'm listening at the same time," says the nurse. "Death-defying stunts, you say? Wonderful. Well, I'll no doubt be sewing his vital organs back inside him at some point soon then. But, fortunately for you, his name's not down on my, er, guest list tonight."

The nurse chuckles at her own little joke.

"He's not there? Oh, brilliant. That's totally ace!" I say. "So do you have the numbers of any other emergency wards that I could call?"

"Veronica, who on earth are . . . ," interrupts my mother, Magda Ripperton, materializing before me clad in what can only be explained as a bizarre, multicolored . . . jeez, and this pains me to say it . . . jumpsuit. You know, like overalls that mechanics wear, but fitted around the ass with a silver zip up the center. The zipper is undone a few inches, revealing a generous glance of mother cleavage.

Nooooo. Please, God. PLEASE say she wasn't outdoors dressed like that with her boobs hanging half out. Not near the school?

Magda's long, thick brown hair is scraped up into a high ponytail with mad, static chunks escaping at the fringe, pointing skyward. Her cheeks are glowing, which may be connected to the posh boutique shopping bags she is clutching in each hand.

3

Since my mother got herself into the pudding club last year (Pregnant at the age of thirty-eight—can you believe it?), she has begun residing in a parallel fashion universe where vile clothes are gorgeous and vice versa. I blamed it on her hormones and weight gain (By nine months Mum was almost big as Luxembourg. She had her own flag and everything), and thought once she gave birth she might calm down. But I was so wrong. It simply gave her more mobility to shop.

"Who are you speaking to? Who's in the hospital?" Mum is shouting.

"I'm on the phone. Go away!" I snap back.

Magda's brow is creased. She can tell I've been crying. Suddenly she's grabbing at me, trying to snatch the phone from my hands.

"*Pggh,* just give me that phone," she bleats. "Has there been an accident?"

I try shooing Magda away, but as an entity, she is highly un-shoo-able.

It's like being charged by an ill-tempered, colorblind octopus.

With a crafty pincer movement, Operation Jumpsuit Terror liberates the phone from my right hand, leaving me opening and closing my mouth, waving my arms like a synchronized swimmer.

"Yes, hello, Magda Ripperton here," Mum says, switching to her hoity-toity posh phone voice. Grrrrrrr. "Veronica Ripperton's mother speaking. What is occurring here, if you please?"

Mum listens to the nurse, her face turning slightly pale.

"Oh, right, she did, did she?" Mum sighs, shaking her head. "Mmm, uh-huh . . . Jimi Steele? Oh, yes, I know him very well . . . ," Mum says, in the tone of someone recalling an intimate fungal infection. Her nostrils are flaring.

"Well, Staff Sister Jacqueline, I apologize profusely for Veronica. Her father and I are having her head examined next week. It's an ongoing problem. Good evening to you."

Mother presses "hang up" on the phone.

I narrow my eyes at her. She sneers back.

"I'm not even going to comment on that," lies my mother blatantly. "Just please tell me you haven't got the Missing Persons Bureau on Jimi Steele's case too. Or Interpol?"

"You don't understand," I sigh dramatically.

"Cuh," Mum splutters, managing to communicate in the space of one grunt that:

1) She understands only too well . . .

2) . . . that Jimi, my prize flaky buttmunch of a boyfriend, has gone AWOL on a very important night indeed and she thinks . . .

3) . . . I should have dumped his sad "pants-far-too-big-for-him" ass months ago for one of the "plenty of other fish in the sea" swimming about out there.

Fine . . . if I wanted to swap the most beautiful boy at Blackwell School for a haddock.

"I hate you," I tell her, glancing at my watch. I am soooo going to miss this party.

"No, you don't," she replies.

"I *do* hate you," I assure her, sighing even more deeply. "I hate the world."

"Well, I *love* you anyhow," Mum replies cunningly.

"Bleuggh," I reply.

Mum and I gaze at each other in silence. I check my phone again for missed calls. Zilch. Nada.

Downstairs, crowds of beer-heads are making their noisy way into the Fantastic Voyage, spilling out into our newly built beer garden, enjoying the hazy June start-of-the-weekend feeling. Travis, our Aussie bartender, is wrestling crates up from the cellar and flirting with the girlie customers.

The smell of Jimi Steele *not* arriving to take me to Blackwell Disco hangs pungently in the air.

"Sooooo," announces Mum, peering at me. "Aren't you supposed to be with Claudette and Fleur shaking your thang tonight? You've been at hysterical point about this for weeks, haven't you?"

"Hmmphgh," I say, plonking down and picking up a copy of *Your Baby Monthly,* feigning engrossment in a feature on inverted nipples.

Mum may have a small point there.

My very own all-girl cosmic fighting force, Les Bambinos Dangereuses, or the LBD as we're universally known, have held hair/body/clothes summit talks every single night for a fortnight to debate the Blackwell end-of-term disco. It's the indisputable social event of the year! Well, so far anyway. We've spent eons yaddering about which outfits made our boobs look perkier, our booties look peachier and our upper arm skin look less like corned beef. Then, after a zillion outfits were tried, Fleur Swan even made Paddy, her dad, digital-camera her sashaying up and down the stairs in her top five choices, just to make an "informed decision."

Suffice to say, Blackwell Disco, is . . . or was . . . a big deal.

"And I'm gathering that Crown Prince Retard was escorting you there," says Mum.

"Don't call him . . ."

"Sorry, *sorry*, I mean Jimi."

Mum mimes "buttoning her lip," but as ever, her will to speak is too strong. "Right, let's go!" she barks, grabbing her car keys off the coffee table.

"Fix your makeup, missy, you look like a disgruntled panda. I'm driving you to Blackwell myself. Call Claudette Cassiera now and tell her we're en route."

"But . . ."

"Lovely Claudette Cassiera *is* going, isn't she? And *that* Fleur Swan? Well, unless Paddy sent her to the nunnery like he threatened to last week. That poor man . . . his nerves must be shot to pieces."

"Yeah, they're *both* going. But you don't understand, Mum," I begin. "Jimi said he was going to come here and pick . . ."

"Oh, spare me," grunts Mum.

"So I can't just go, Mum," I argue. "He wouldn't let me down! He must have had an accident or . . ."

"Ooh-hoo! He'll be having an accident when I get ahold of him," scoffs my mother, miming squeezing someone by the throat. "At least I'll make it look like an accident."

Oh, dear.

"Right, Cinderella?" Mum says, clapping her hands. "What you need is a good dance, blow the cobwebs away."

"Not going," I say sulkily.

"Ooh, I quite fancy a rave myself," Mum says, not at all joking. "I might pop in for a leg stretch when I'm dropping you off. Y'know, say thanks to Mrs. Guinevere for resurrecting Blackwell Discos. I'll see if that miserable old headmaster Mr. McGraw fancies cutting a rug."

I feel faint.

"Ooh, Ronnie, y'know, since I had Seth, y'know, I feel like I've got a fresh lease on life."

Mum begins gyrating her bum from left to right, waving her hands.

Wonderful: My entire world is obliterated and she's doing the Macarena.

"Will they play any Tamla Motown?"

"No," I say through a very small mouth.

"Any reggae?"

"You're not coming in."

"I'm going if you don't," Mum bribes.

Then Mum notices the tears starting to run down my face. She stops shaking her rump.

"Aww, Ronnie, come here," she says, sitting down beside me and wrapping her arm around my shoulder. "I know how you feel. It's crap. Being stood up is really crap."

"Where can he be, Mum?" I ask.

"Oh, he's just out there. Somewhere. Being a jerk," says Mum, tickling my neck.

"You don't think he's dead?"

"No, Ron. The smart money says he's absolutely alive."

"The night's ruined," I say bleakly.

Over the last ten months, I have learned some harsh lessons about the realities of keeping, training and maintaining a boyfriend. Sometimes it really sucks. I mean, what flaming excuse in the *entire world* could that great farthead give for standing me up tonight?

And this after an entire *330 days* of quacking on that I'm a "total babe" and "absolutely hilarious." Oh, and he gets a "dead weird feeling inside whenever he sees me."

("Hoo-hoo! I get that feeling sometimes," hooted Mum when I told her. "Usually after eating brussels sprouts . . .")

Pah.

Because if boyfriends care so much that they can slaver on soppy stuff like that, how can they hurt your feelings so much?

Correction. How can they hurt your feelings so much AGAIN?

"Because when it comes to most men, Veronica," says Mum sagely, "you'd be better off with a sock puppet."

I tend to take Mum's man advice with a pinch of salt. She always refers to her marriage to Dad as "a drunken bet gone too far."

(For more wisdom refer to the appendix.)

Then suddenly, we hear some footsteps on the stairs.

JIMI STEELE! HOSANNNNNA!!! LET'S PARTY!

Er, not quite.

"Ahoy, ladies!" says my father, Lawrence "Loz" Ripperton, proprietor of the Fantastic Voyage, appearing in the doorway with a vast grin plastered across his face. My five-month-old baby brother, Seth Otis Ripperton, is strapped to his chest in a powder-blue papoose, snoozing.

"Howdy!" chirps Loz. "Ah, it's good to see the womenfolk of the Fantastic Voyage all present and accounted for."

My father has somehow missed that while his daughter is sobbing, his wife is dressed as an insane parachute commander.

"We menfolk have been to a meeting," Dad says, patting Seth's tiny head.

I look at Dad with total bemusement. "You've just attended the Garstang Brewery summer finance general meeting with Seth strapped to your front in a pastel papoose?" I ask witheringly.

"I know!" says Dad proudly.

What is happening to my life? Here is a man who, until a year ago, wouldn't drink a wine cooler in public for fear it made him look "a bit gay." Now he's waltzing about like Mary flipping Poppins.

It's a world gone mad, I tell you.

I want my old, predictable parents back.

This is yucky.

Everything these days pivots around the desires of Seth Ripperton.

Night and day. Day and night. It's like they've converted to an obscure religious cult, worshipping a fourteen-pound pink lump. And don't get me wrong, Seth is totally, like, the most gorgeous baby you have ever seen. I mean, he's far better looking than some of the freaky-looking things you see on the high street, but right now, he never does anything remotely newsworthy aside from cry, poo, cry while pooing, sleep. (He still manages to squeeze poos out while snoring, don't worry.) No, I tell a lie: Very recently he's begun sitting upright with his head lolling about like a helium balloon.

There was never this fuss when I was a child.

Oh, no, believe me.

When Loz and Magda brought me home from the maternity ward, they simply pushed my buggy into the backyard and left it beside some old Garstang Pale Ale crates. I was raised by a family of benevolent passing owls. All I ate was mice and worms till I was eleven, which raised eyebrows in the school dinner hall when I got my packed lunch out.

No wonder I get stood up on a Friday night.

"You have a very vivid imagination," sighs Flight Field Marshal Magda, standing up and unhooking Seth from Dad. "I remember hugging you at least twice," she adds dryly.

"Hee hee, the orphanage kept sending her back, didn't they, love?" chuckles Dad. "They knew we were still alive. They kept spotting us, pulling away in the car!"

Ooh, my sides.

ꙅend in the reinforcementꙅ

BRRRRRRRR BRRRRRRRR

At last my phone rings!

I swoop toward it, in a rugby tackle move, praying it's not Nana calling me to discuss what she had for her supper. However, the screen reads:

LIAM ANSWER?

Why's Liam "Blackwell bad boy but dead nice really" Gelding calling me?

I press "Yes."

"Hello?" I say.

"What do you mean, hello? How, hello?" begins Fleur "Operation Shock and Awe" Swan, sounding excessively cross. "Right, this better be good, Ronnie. Very good indeed. This party started almost two hours ago! I've been asked for, like, two songs already . . . And Carson Dewers in lower sixth has bought me a Coke and asked for my mobile number! Where the flipping heck are you, butt crack?"

"I'm . . ."

"Look, just tell me you're just walking in the front door now, or I am going to burst an artery. Just tell me you're almost here."

"Mmm . . . er wah . . . well, I'm at home . . . ," I begin, but talk is futile.

"You're still at hoooooooome!? Claude, CLAUDE . . . she's still at home! At home!" shrieks Fleur.

"No way! Is she okay?" I hear Claude ask in the background.

"I was waiting for . . . ," I begin.

"The Fusia mobile phone network has been down, like nationally, since six P.M., did you know?" shouts Fleur. "We couldn't get a signal until now. Everyone's on Fusia except Liam, who's on G5 Network. He just turned up, we just borrowed his phone . . ."

"I'm on Fusia too," I try to say.

"So where are you?" shouts Fleur again. "I've seen Jimi trying to call you loads of times too. He's got a Fusia phone, hasn't he?"

"What? Jimi is at Blackwell?!"

"Yes, Jimi is at flaming Blackwell. He's been here for an hour with Naz and Aaron. Everyone's here."

"But . . . whatttttt? I've been . . ."

"He's over at the other side of the hall now. I'll just go and get him . . ."

I can hear Fleur begin to move through what sounds like a pretty hectic crowd.

"But he was picking me up!" I say, getting all blubbery again.

"He was what? Picking you up? Tonight?! He was picking you up from the Voyage. So you're there waiting? *I knnnnnnnnnnew it!*" Fleur has reached eruption level.

"Is that Jimi?" asks my mother, also sounding rather cross.

"No, it's Fleur," I mouth, keeping extra tight hold of my phone.

"Let me speak to her," instructs my mother.

"Back off!" I say, swatting her away.

"Oh, dear, is this another Jimi Steele misdemeanor?" says Dad, opening a jar of pureed apple and prodding Seth awake with a spoon.

"Leave it, Lawrence," snaps Mum.

"Hoo-hoo! What's the poor bloke done to you all this time?" chuckles Dad.

"Right, he's crossed an LBD line this time. There will be repercussions," snarls Fleur, moving up on her prey. "Oi, Steelo, what do you think you're doing, standing up my best mate?"

Fleur sounds very irate. I wouldn't mess with her.

"Er, what? She's . . . ," I hear Jimi's husky voice begin.

"Speak to her, not me, loser," shouts Fleur, slinging the phone at him.

"Ronnie!" begins Jimi.

It just feels great to hear his voice. *Gggnngn.* I'm such a sap.

"Why aren't you here, Ron? I was meeting you here after six-ish and . . .

"Owwwwwww, Fleur, that hurt! Ronnie, your friend just kicked me! Owwwww! My shin!"

"Fleur, stop kicking Jimi," I hear Claude saying rather half-heartedly.

"We were meeting HERE at the pub," I say. "We said we'd go together."

"Did we . . . ?"

"You said you were going across town to look at that sec-ondhand skateboard you saw in the *Local Daily Mercury.*"

"Yeah," says Jimi, "and you said time would be tight so I'd not have time to pick you up then."

"Nooooooo, you great useless sack of poo! I said time would be tight, but I'd *wait for you to pick me up.*"

Why does he never listen?

"Oh," says Jimi.

"Oh," I say.

"Sorry, Ronnie," Jimi says meekly. "I got a bit mixed up . . . But hey, just come anyway!"

"I can't get in after eight P.M.! That's McGraw rules. No entry after eight P.M.," I yell.

"Damn. You're right . . . you can't."

"Right, time's up with that phone, Steelo," I hear Liam

Gelding complaining. "Three other people want to make a call . . . I can make some money here."

"Ronnie. Gotta go. I'll call you later," says Jimi.

Then the phone goes dead.

I feel like someone's just punched me in the stomach.

"Ready to rock?" asks Mum, jangling her keys.

"Mmm," I sigh. "Can't get in after eight. Phone networks were down and . . ."

And then I start crying again. Big proper tears.

"Awwwww, love. I'll sort it out," says Mum. "Do you want me to go down and argue with Mr. McGraw?"

No, I do not. I'd rather take all my clothes off and run around the school ground with my bottom blowing in the breeze. That would be less embarrassing.

"Nah . . . I'll just stay here." I sniffle.

Mum, Dad and I all stand in silence. There is nothing left to be said. I wish I'd never been born.

"Hey, Ronno, we're ordering in tonight!" announces Dad, somehow imagining that crispy kung pao chicken changes anything.

"And a DVD?" suggests Mum. "We can get a movie out too."

I know they're just trying to be nice, but I wish they'd both shut up.

"Oh, Ronnie, don't take it too badly. It's just one night," says Mum, beginning what seems like a long meaningful speech. "I mean, you're only fifteen, and there'll be stacks of other nights-out to come."

I stare at her crossly.

"Believe me, I had a lot of nights go bottoms up like this when I was a kid. And well, I look back now and giggle about it, 'cos, well, it's all part of growing up and . . . *OH MY GOD, LOZ,* loook!"

Mum is pointing frantically at Seth, perched in his vibrating baby chair.

"Loooooook, Loz! Look at Seth! Seth's picking his nose!! He's picking his nose! He's never done that before, has he!?"

"Ha ha! Go on, my son!" shouts my absolutely elated dad. "Pick us a winner, Seth!"

"Ronnie, Seth's picking his nose! How great is that?" laughs Mum.

And at that point, I decided to spend the Friday night of Blackwell Summer Disco in my boudoir. Alone.

~~~~~~~~~

the party that never was postmortem

"*Pggh,* cheer up, Ronnie, it wasn't that good anyway," instructs Fleur Swan, perched on her bed in LBD Headquarters on Disraeli Road, dabbing menthol toothpaste on what is ripening into a juicy love bite beneath her left ear. "Now, did anybody notice if scarves were 'In' or 'Out' for summer?" she says. "Claudette, chuck me *Glamour* magazine."

That'll teach Fleur to chop her blonde locks into a raunchy bob, I think with small satisfaction. *She's never going to hide that hickey.*

"Scarves are totally last season," I say crossly. "So's looking like you've been attacked by a killer weasel."

"Declan *is* a bit like a weasel, isn't he?" groans Fleur. "But it all happened so fast! One minute I was dancing and the next minute . . . well, we were properly snogging!"

Fleur flaps herself with one carefully manicured hand.

"Oh, that was sooo hilarious!" hoots Claudette Cassiera, bouncing on Fleur's futon, her ebony plaits jiggling gleefully. "Especially later on when that other lad Mikey asked you to dance, and you said . . . er, ahem, cough . . . splutter . . ."

Claude has noticed my dark countenance.

"Well, actually it wasn't that funny," Claude corrects herself. "It was more . . . er, *boring.*"

I sigh deeply.

Fleur called this emergency Saturday morning LBD meeting to cheer me up. It is *not* working.

"Exactly, Claudette, the whole night was *très* dull," agrees Fleur, "thanks to *that* Jimi Steele. It felt dead weird without you there, Ronnie."

"Too right," says Claude with a half smile. "We missed you, Ron."

"Ta," I say quietly.

"So anyway," says Fleur, prancing across to her tangerine-colored iMac and flicking the mouse to online, with a whiz and a crash as the modem dials up, "I've gathered us here today for a very important discussion . . ."

"Uh-oh, it's going black in the middle already," Claude interrupts, helpfully pointing at the hickey.

"Well, we'll make my neck bite point of order three, shall we?"

"Point three?" I say with a jolt. I've been on top of Fleur's cream suede beanbag for more than an hour now, wallowing in misery thinking about Jimi Steele. "Did I miss two?"

"Excellent question, Veronica," says Fleur. "Sorry to wake you up there . . . well, point one is obvious: Jimi Steele."

"Boo, hiss!" says Claude, cupping her mouth theatrically.

"Exactly. That so-called boyfriend of yours, Jimi Steele. We are very displeased at his behavior, Veronica," announces Fleur.

"*Pggghhh,* me too," I whisper. "I'm not speaking to him."

"Ever again?" says Fleur hopefully.

"Well. Not since last night anyhow," I mumble.

I'm omitting to mention Jimi's twenty-two missed calls since 10 P.M. last night I've been dying to pick up.

And the increasingly frantic voice messages he's left. One of which sounded like he was blubbering.

(I want to ring him back so much.)

"Good. You've not spoken to him! Freeze him out!" says Fleur gleefully. "My mum once blanked Paddy for an entire month and she got, like, a BMW convertible at the end of it."

"Yeah, Ron, you should hold out for a pair of Rollerblades at least," says Claude dryly.

I knew I could trust the LBD to take my side, but it doesn't make me feel any more certain what to do.

"So you think I should dump Jimi over ruining Blackwell Disco?" I say, already aware of what Fleur's answer will be.

"Yes. Immediately," she says, without consideration. "This is just one of a laughable catalogue of offenses the toad has inflicted upon you. *Can him.*"

"Thank you, Fleur," I say, turning to Claude. "Cassiera, your turn."

Claude pauses, ever the cautious bambino. "Mmm . . . dunno," she says. "He certainly needs to be taught a lesson. I'm sure of that."

"*A lesson!? Pghhh,*" huffs Fleur, flicking her mouse around her mouse pad, mesmerized by the flashing screen. "Ooh, hang on a second . . . wooo-hooo! Claude, pass me that blank CD, please. I've just had an e-mail from Mad Mavis in Chicago."

Fleur's breathing seems to have gone all wonky.

"Mad who?" says Claude, rooting among the cacophony of magazines, makeup packaging and candy wrappers that makes up Fleur's desk.

"Mavis," repeats Fleur, clearly totally elated. "Oh, she's just this crazy Spike Saunders fan in Chicago. I chat with her in the Spike web chat rooms. She's just tipping me off that the new Spike CD *Prize* is up as a file share on RippaCD.com! It's not out in the UK or in the USA for *six* weeks yet!"

"That's illegal!" frowns Claude.

"Oh, shut up! Spike won't mind, we're his friends!" laughs Fleur, waving at a poster on her wall featuring Spike stripped to the waist, slightly sweaty.

"We met Spike only once, Fleur," I say gently, recalling the admittedly wild, but once-in-a-lifetime occurrence that happened a year ago. "We're hardly his best buddies."

Fleur rolls her eyes, then stares at several "signed" letters from our hero tacked up among the bum and pec montage above her bed. The treasured letters, replies to Fleur's fan mail (plus a bizarrely real-looking thank-you note for her last Christmas gift) have been wafted under our noses by Fleur on many, many occasions. Of course, Fleur doesn't just reckon

Spike remembers us, she actually thinks he quite fancies her too.

Obviously, Claude and I *know* the flipping letters are just photocopies from his fan club secretary, but you've got to humor Fleur sometimes. She's not overly furnished with "living in the real world" skills.

"And downloading Spike's CD illegally helps him, er, how?" says Claude, teasing Fleur. "Please tell us, because I'm intrigued."

"Huh! I'm only making one copy!" Fleur grumps, frowning at the timer on her screen as the MP3s download slowly. "Flipping broadband dial-up! I'm changing ISPs this week. This is so slow it's unreal. Anyway, I'll e-mail Spike straightaway afterward and tell him it's being hosted on RippaCD.com. Then he can get his lawyers onto it."

Claude and I stare at Fleur, trying to keep our faces straight.

"And I bet he replies too!" Fleur persists.

Claude shakes her head in disbelief.

"Anyway, back to Jimi—that's what we're here for, aren't we?" Claude says, turning to me seriously. "Now don't get me wrong, Ron, I like him, I mean, he is dead lovely most of the time."

Claude's being fair as ever . . . but I sense a "but."

"But, the great poosplash has just ruined the biggest LBD shindig of the year. He thinks you're quite happy to fritter your life waiting about for him."

"Hmmm," I say.

"Pah!" Fleur says. "The selfish loser reckons you've nothing better to do than play second best to his flipping skateboard . . .

which, may I remind you, is essentially just a child's toy. He's in the lower sixth form, for crying out loud! When's he getting a car so he can at least drive us to gigs? *Pgggh?!* I mean, what is the point of him? He's neither use nor ornament, as my granny would say."

"And he's just too flaky," adds Claude. "He should have double-checked about the Blackwell Disco arrangements. Then we wouldn't be having to cheer you up, would we?"

"S'pose so," I mumble.

They can discuss Jimi all they want, I think to myself, *but they don't know him like I do. They don't know about all the funny conversations and in-jokes we have. Like the one where we text each other pretending to be lost elephants . . . like . . . MURRRRRRRRRRRR! . . . or about how he taught me to be excellent at chess on the huge life-sized chess game Dad's installed in the pub's new beer garden. And how we play backgammon together for money (he owes me £6.50). Or how we sometimes hint that we'd like to be kicking about together when we're old and gray.*

And yes, I know that sounds totally berserk, but sometimes I think I do.

And then he spoils it by being an earth-shatteringly thoughtless berk.

"Well, *whatever,*" says Fleur, holding up her hand in a "speak to my wrist, it's got an answering machine" sort of way. "All I'm saying, Ronnie, is that you need to take the reins. The ball's always in his court these days, and he's holding all the cards. It's time you battened down the hatches and took the bull by the horns."

"We're still talking about Jimi here," Claude assures me, deadpan.

"We certainly are, Claudette. Veronica here is in serious peril of becoming one of those drippy chicks who puts her life on hold for a boy, and we, the LBD, have a duty to stop it."

"Ronnie," chuckles Claude, covering her mouth with her hand in surprise, "you're turning into Sharon Spittle!"

"Noooooo! I'm not turning into Sharon Spittle!" I moan, clutching my head.

Sharon Spittle is a Year 11 girl who has been engaged, like, three times already. And every time, she asks Edith the android school secretary to change her surname in the class register. Then she prances around showing off a gaudy ring that usually comes out of an amusement arcade until her finger goes green. Cringe. Sharon once fell in love with Ataf Hussein in the sixth form and began appearing at Blackwell in a full Muslim burka. The girl is an absolute horse's ass. A total prize numpty.

She's the sort of dweebish, bed-wetting mutant who . . . rings emergency wards on Friday night to find her boyfriend.

Oh my God, I'm turning into Sharon Spittle!

"That's it, then, new LBD legislation has been passed: Blank Jimi Steele. Blank him for a month!" chants Fleur.

"A month's about long enough, Ronnie," shrugs Claude.

"Okay. A month it is." I smile, feeling extremely empowered. I switch off my mobile phone and put it in my bag.

"Which brings me neatly to point two," says Fleur, grabbing a Post-it-note-stuck copy of *New Musical Express* magazine. "Now wait for it . . ."

"Go on, I'm on the edge of my beanbag," I say dubiously.

"Two words, a hundred and twenty thousand people, forty-eight hours of LBD fun, one fantastic way to annoy the bejesus out of Jimi Buttmunch Steele," chirps Fleur with a highly mischievous grin, "blows Blackwell Disco and that little fête we held last year right out of the water. Ta-da! Astlebury Festival!"

Fleur opens the mag at a double-page advert for Astlebury, happening the last weekend of July. Less than two weeks away.

"Oh, God," mutters Claude. "Fleur, we agreed . . ."

"Astlebury Festival?" I say. *"You want the LBD to go to Astlebury Rock 'n' Pop Weekender?"*

"Yes!" says Fleur.

"Now Fleur," I begin, almost as if I'm talking to my mad old nana. "Have you forgotten what happened *last year* when we asked our parents about Astlebury?"

"Uh-huh."

"We didn't go, did we?" I say very slowly.

"Pah, a minor setback," scoffs Fleur. "Look, girls, I know we agreed we'd not bother asking this year, blah, blah, blah . . . but behold! Our friend, honorary LBD member, pop god and all-round kind of swoon Spike Saunders is headlining the second night! Oh, and Final Warning are playing too."

"That's Jimi's favorite band," I say with a slight evil grin.

"And there's a twenty-four-hour dance tent this year too!" Fleur squeaks.

"And an unsigned bands stage! Ooh, I bet loads of gorgeous musician lads hang around that one! And there are tickets left, I've checked!"

"God, how annoyed would Jimi be if we all went, eh?" mutters Claude. "That would be soooo ace." Then she checks herself and tries to be sensible.

"Fleur, do you realize," Claude asks, adjusting her specs with her finger, "that a psychiatric symptom of insanity is asking the same question again and again but expecting a different answer?"

"Uggh, eh?" says Fleur.

"Okay, more simply . . . Fleur, the LBD won't be allowed to go. Just like last year," says Claude. "Ergo, you're insane."

"*Ergo*, that's a maybe," argues Fleur, "but you're forgetting something crucial, Claudiebuns. Last summer, when the LBD asked to go to Astlebury, something totally fantastic and unforgettable happened. We ended up having a huge fabulous adventure and meeting Spike Saunders! Ooh, can you not see, girls?! It's our *destiny* to ask again."

"She's got a point, Claude," I say, warming to the idea. "But you do both know that my uncle Charlie doesn't work for Spike anymore, or even work in the music business at all, so it's a bit different this time."

Fleur and Claude nod their heads thoughtfully.

"But hey, it wouldn't hurt to ask our parents," I say, feeling suddenly maverick. "And besides, I'm well up for another LBD jamboree. I think it might just show Jimi who's wearing the trousers in this relationship too."

"You're not kidding," smiles Claude.

"Well, that's our second point of order then," says Fleur. "We begin applying pester power to our parents about Astlebury forthwith! Oh, this is going to be so great, girls! Everyone say we're agreed!"

"Agreed!" Claude and I chorus, not quite believing our own ears.

"Who needs Blackwell Disco, bambinos? We're off to Astlebury!" giggles Fleur, suddenly clutching her neck. "Jeez, I better get this battle scar covered," she says. "I'm gonna ask Paddy right away! Well . . . the second he gets home after his anger management class."

The best thing about Fleur Swan is, she'll never truly know just how funny she is.

"Good a time as any!" concedes Claude, giving Fleur a big thumbs-up before lying back on the bed and covering her head with the *NME* magazine.

BLACKWELL SCHOOL MEMORANDUM—
FOR THE ATTENTION OF PARENTS/GUARDIANS

DATE: Tuesday, 13 July
SUBJECT: End of Term
FROM: Mr. McGraw, Headmaster

Parents and guardians of Blackwell pupils are reminded that summer term ends this <u>THURSDAY, 15TH OF JULY.</u>

Much as I acknowledge that this is a joyous time of year for pupils, ever indicative of high spirits and youthful japes, please let me stress that any repetition of previous years' shenanigans <u>WILL NOT</u> be tolerated.

Any pupil straying the boundaries of acceptable innocent fun into the realms of wanton, evil tomfoolery <u>SHALL BE PUNISHED ACCORDINGLY.</u>

Can parents/guardians please note that the following items <u>ARE EXPRESSLY FORBIDDEN FROM BLACKWELL SCHOOL:</u>

* EGGS * FLOUR * WATER PISTOLS * ALL PETS *
INDELIBLE INK MAGIC MARKERS * SCARY CLOWN MASKS *
STINK BOMBS * FIRECRACKERS * GHETTO BLASTERS OR ANY
GENRE OF "SOUND SYSTEM" * ALCOHOL * CATAPULTS *
PEASHOOTERS OR ANY OTHER BLOW WEAPON *
BUTTERFLY KNIVES * SMOKE BOMBS *
SHURIKAN THROWING STARS * NUNCHUCKS

NB—Blackwell staff reserve the right to frisk pupils suspected of carrying contraband items.

Finally, please let me take this opportunity to wish you all a jocund summer and also sincerely thank everybody for a pleasant term. I'm certain it was as rewarding and inspiring for the pupils as it was for myself.

<u>MR. MCGRAW</u>

Chapter 2

the happiest days
of my life

Oh, thank you, God. Another term practically over.

I absolutely, totally and utterly hate school with every fiber of my being. I hate the hideous uniform, with its hideous gray A-line skirt with kick pleats, and the fetching blue woolen sweater that makes me look like a big shapeless blue and gray splodge. Oh, and not forgetting the snazzy white ankle socks, the most unflattering hosiery choice possible for my chunky ankles and goalkeeper calves. Of course while I look like a barrel on feet, Fleur Swan carries off the whole idiot garb with stylish aplomb. The fact that she's almost 85 percent long brown, toned leg doesn't do her much harm. Claude, incidentally, doesn't mind the Blackwell uniform, because "having her clothes chosen for her every day gives her more time to learn."

Yes, she did actually say this . . . the big book-ogling freak.

But uniformphobia is only the beginning. I hate pretty much everything else about Blackwell. I hate being yelled and harangued at 7:15 A.M. to "get out of my pit" by my drill sergeant mother. I hate arguing with her every single day over the fact that I don't want to eat yucky poached eggs or vile bran cereal eleven minutes after opening my eyes. I hate then being absolutely ravenous by 9:30 A.M. (wishing I'd eaten the bran-poo flakes) and then having to sit through double French while Madame Bassett witters on about delicious-sounding *croque-monsieurs* and *gateaux de chocolate*. I hate being shoved out into the yard at break when it's drizzling because school rules decry pupils sitting in the classrooms. So the LBD loiter glumly around the back of the gray bird-cack-splattered gym to find shelter from the elements, then get shoved away by teachers because it's a hideout for smokers. So we trudge to the far end of the lower-school yard, where we're shouted at again because pupils are now barred from "frequenting within twenty meters' radius of the school pond." (This new rule emerged after Royston Potter threw Sebastian Smythe, a sensitive Year 8 ballet enthusiast and amateur puppeteer, in among the algae every day for a whole week. Eventually Seb began wearing a lemon Speedo to school and pirouetting in himself, just to cut out the middle man.)

Sometimes I feel as if the LBD spend our entire Blackwell break times being chased round and round the ranch confines like depressed ankle-sock-wearing big game.

And I hate that if you're not excellent at sports and you're not promising at math or English, or on the other hand you're not a total freako uniquo who disrupts lessons by setting fire to desks and punching staff, you start to feel sort of . . . well . . . invisible. Oh, and I hate, hate, hate those belligerent thickos who work in the P.E. department, like Mr. Patton, who has hairy shoulder tufts poking from under his yellowing T-shirt and thinks we all don't know that he's dating that cafeteria worker with the eczema who always picks her nose. *Bleeeeee!*

I hate worrying which corner of the school my lessons will chuck me in, and dreading bumping into any of Blackwell's many vile school bullies who are always armed with a nasty remark or sneering glance. And, yes, this does mean you in particular, Panama Goodyear and your snooty ghoulish gang. Jeez, why are newspapers filled with such tragic deaths, yet bogdwellers like Panama never chance upon a runaway combine harvester?

I hate some of the teachers so much that I actually smirked, yes, *smirked* when one of them fell down the science block stairs and fractured his collarbone. In my defense this was Mr. Graves, who wears a beige car coat, always has white phleggy bits in the corners of his mouth and . . . this is the grudge I hold . . . once read out *to everyone in my* applied science *class* a note I passed Claudette asking to borrow some lunch money. All the boys called me Parasite Ripperton and threw pennies at me for a week.

I hate being yelled at to "WALK, DON'T RUN" all the time. Even when I am flipping walking!

And being told, "The bell is for me, not for you" at the end of every lesson. I hate assemblies where we get moaned at for half an hour about our "shoddy uniform standards." And school trips that are always to somewhere rubbish like the local radioactive power plant, monastery ruins or forgotten seaside towns so we can study their now-obsolete fishing industry.

Suffice to say, I hate school. If it wasn't for Fleur and Claude . . . well, I don't know how I'd cope.

• • •

"I've really, reeeeeally hated school this term, Mum," I tell Mum matter-of-factly as we stare at each other over the breakfast dishes, picking sleep snot from our eyes. "I'm not going today."

"Of course you hate school," says Mum dryly, pausing to make a face at baby Seth, who's slavering all over himself in his chair. "Only weirdos like school. I'd be more worried if you loved it."

Mum does this reverse psychology thing a lot. It's sort of un-nerving.

"This got anything to do with *that Jimi*?" says Mum.

"Nah." I sigh.

Thank you, Mother. That's a record twelve whole minutes awake before I've been reminded about the Jimi scenario.

"You see, I don't need to go today anyway, it's the end of term. All the lessons have wound down now. It's not like it's *compulsory*," I moan.

"Really?" says Mum.

"Yeah. It's like, y'know, *flexitime*. I've gone almost all year, y'see? Even when I've been ill and stuff . . . so I get today in lieu."

"Ahhhh, right," coos Mum. "Well, you just get yourself back to bed then. I'll bring you a cup of tea after I've done all the housework, fed Seth and supervised the lunchtime shifts."

"What? Really!" I shrill, getting all excited.

Mum looks full of glee now.

"Nooooo! Of course you can't! You're going to school with the rest of the ankle biters!" she erupts, laughing like a demented horse. "Ha ha, *flexitime*! I've heard it all now. Get your bag packed, twinkie, you're off to school. I'm spending some quality time with my son today. I estimate I've got about three months left before he starts back chatting to me too—I'm going to enjoy it!"

Huh! It's bad enough that my mother pranced around town for nine months with a massive stomach, meaning everyone at school knew beyond doubt that she and Dad are still, ugggghhh, y'know, "doing it" *(bleeeeeeee!)*, but now that Seth's born, she's blatantly giving the little infiltrator preferential treatment! I wish I had a child psychologist to tell all of this to. I am sooo totally being mentally abused. And as for Seth, well, I can't wait until he's twelve so I can give him an extra-big revenge wedgie. Obviously, for now, I'll just let him be cute and stick pureed fruit in his scalp, as that seems to make him happy.

"Pghhhhgh," I huff, changing tack, clutching my stomach. "But I can't go to school. I feel sick."

"So do I," retorts Mum, laughing. "Come tonight, I've got your miserable face to look at for six entire weeks. You! Mooching about, telling me you're bored on repetitive play and tapping me for money. I'm as sick as a bleeding parrot."

At this millisecond, it occurs to me that there is no more suitable conversational junction to ask Magda about the LBD's jaunt to Astlebury Festival. I've been procrastinating over this for four days now, as every time I see Mum she's either knee-deep in poo and diapers or downstairs pouring pints or cooking bar meals till almost 11 P.M. while I watch Seth. There's no point in asking Dad, as all decisions have to be rubber-stamped by Her Highness.

But hang on . . . surely Magda has just specifically said that

31

she wants to see less of my miserable face? It could be gone for almost four whole days!

"So Muuu-huum," I begin, using my singsong voice, the traditional opening bars to me wanting something.

"Yep, what do you want from me now?" Mum predicts over her shoulder, clearing half-eaten eggs into the rubbish bin. "And before you begin, Veronica, go easy on my nerves. I don't know if you've heard, but Cassie and Kiki, those brain-dead bimbos I was foolishly calling waitresses, finally quit their jobs last night. I am officially a woman on the edge of something murderous. I mean . . . Grrrrrrrrrrrrr!"

Mum throws her head back and sort of roars, by way of illustration.

"Errrr, ooh . . . ," I mumble.

"Ibiza! Flipping Ibiza! They've only gone and got jobs in a beach disco! And, well . . . that's it! *Au revoir!* No notice! Nothing. Vamooooosh! I've got no staff left! Well, except that useless Aussie idiot Travis, and to be frank, if he calls me Sheila one more time, I'm going to stick his didgeridoo intimately where the sun doesn't set and . . . ooh, well, I could almost explode."

"Oh, dear."

"Yes, *oh, dear!* This is not good for my post-natal blood pressure, Ronnie. Why is the world filled with annoying cretins? I'm soooo angry. God, y'know, Ronnie, I think if anyone gives me any hassle today, I'm simply going to whip off my varicose vein support tights and strangle them!"

"Mmm . . . right," I say, biting my lip as Mum crashes cupboard doors, being that sort of angry where she laughs a lot with big, wide, scary, unblinking eyes.

That's the worst kind. She's gone to the bad place.

"But anyway, tootles, enough about me," Mum says, crashing open the dishwasher and producing a large sharp bread knife. "What did you want to ask me?"

The knife's edge glints in the early morning sunlight.

"Mmm . . . y'know, it doesn't really matter," I say, being as flaky as the LBD always accuse me of.

"Oh . . . well . . . are you sure?" asks Mum, pausing a second from chucking plates into their rack with wild abandon.

"Yeah, I'm sure. Gotta go anyway, Fleur and Claude are here. See ya later, loonytoons," I say and blow her a kiss.

"Ta ta for now," says Mum, catching it and smacking it to her cheek.

"Hey, and face-ache . . . enjoy your last day at school, eh?"

"*Gnnnnngn,*" I groan.

♪pecial e♪cort

Fleur Swan is propped against the black knight on the oversized chess set near the back gate of the Fantastic Voyage, madly texting, with digits o' fury, whichever lad it is this week on her top-of-the-range mobile phone. Fleur is always texting. She prefers to deal with most people outside of the LBD employing sentences of approximately three words or less. And even then, those words will be abbreviated to an unintelligible mess of numbers and symbols that not even Claude can decipher.

This conversational brevity gives Fleur more time to focus on her ambitions, namely

1) To marry "Duke of Pop" Spike Saunders,

2) To feature in the "Beyond the Velvet Rope" party section of *Red Hot Celebs* magazine and

3) Her ongoing life quest to find unchippable gold nail varnish.

You've gotta have dreams.

Today Fleur (34-22-34) is wearing her Blackwell uniform with the skirt turned up at the waistband, shortening it elegantly at the knee. Her love bite is expertly hidden with industrial-strength concealer gloop while her legs are newly shaven then moisturized, sporting an all-over even tan. Fleur's crisp white shirt is tailored neatly into her waspish waist, and her hair looks like she should be cavorting through fields of spun wheat in a shampoo ad. She really hacks me off sometimes. I, in contrast, have a creased blouse and odd socks. I very quickly hazarded using some eyeliner before I left the house and haven't had a chance to comb my hair yet. Roughly speaking, I look like an aging goth rocker on the last leg of an eighty-date "No Sleep Till Moscow" world tour.

Sometimes the penchant to attack Fleur with my school bag just for being so flipping gorgeous is especially virulent.

" 'Bout time, slowpoke," Fleur smiles. "Thought you were a no-show."

"Me too! Hurray, you're here!" says Claudette in the midst of cleaning her specs. Today Claudette looks like . . . well, just like a girl who could adorn the cover of the Blackwell School prospectus depicting a wonderful example of a model pupil. All bushy tailed and eager of manner in a nicely pressed uniform.

"Hmmm, sorry, girls," I say sheepishly. "Look, let's go, shall we? Let's get today over with."

Claude and Fleur didn't always come to collect me for school every day. However, as my attendance became slightly more "erratic," the LBD decided I needed extra incentive. I actually cut out only once, but they seemed to think it was a real big deal. I don't recommend cutting, by the way; it quickly transpired that hiding by myself in the local municipal library from 9 to 4 was even more tedious than double algebra. Not glamorous and wild-childish at all. Sigh. That's the problem with hating school: I haven't quite worked out where I want to be instead. Oh, and Magda doesn't know about any of the above (as you may have guessed by the fact that I'm still in possession of a head).

"So," says Fleur, putting her phone into her bag, "what did your mum say?"

"What?" I say, playing stupid.

"Your mum . . . about Astlebury? You promised to ask her last night."

"You *did* ask her, didn't you?" says Claude, raising a quizzical eyebrow.

"Yesss, of course I've asked her," I lie blatantly, as it seems like the easiest thing to do. Look, I've been awake only thirty-eight minutes! I'm not proud! You try tackling the wrath of these two demons when you're half asleep.

"Yeah, 'course I asked her. I did it just then, er . . . just before I came out—that's why I'm late."

"And!?" trill Claude and Fleur in stereo.

"She . . . er, said that she'd . . . think about it and get back to me."

"Poo. That's totally rubbish," says Claude glumly. Then she checks herself. "Ooh, sorry, Ron, no offense to your mum and that. We could just do with getting a move on. The tickets are, like, ninety-five percent sold out. We're really leaving it late now."

"I know, I know," I sigh.

"And, look, I don't want to be the harbinger of doom here but . . . ," Fleur says, sounding slightly rattled, "but . . . oh, nothing, it's not important."

"What?" I say, grabbing her arm, stopping her.

"Tell us, Fleur," says Claude.

"Oh, it's not that bad, it's just *irritating*," frowns Fleur. "You see, I heard yesterday that Panama Goodyear and her moron disciples already got sorted for tickets . . . they're all going to Astlebury."

"Wah? Ugggggggggh!" I groan. This news feels like an ax between my shoulder blades. "But . . . but . . . noooooo! That's so unfair! Are you sure?"

"Yep," nods Fleur. "I walked back from school with Liam last night. He's a surprisingly good source of gossip for a bloke."

"Oh, well, that's just great, isn't it?" huffs Claude, pursing her lips smaller than a rat's ass as she speaks. "And I suppose Panama's daddy's lending them his Land Rover to drive down in, is he?"

"Hmmm," says Fleur, rolling her eyes. "You mean the

£60,000 bad boy with the cast-iron rhino repellent stuck on the front?"

"*Pghh* . . . 'cos Mrs. Goodyear needs that diesel-guzzling safari truck to get to Safeway and back, doesn't she?" I hiss. "Flipping eco-fascists."

"Huh, well, 'Crush anything in our path' is the Goodyear family motto, isn't it?" tuts Claude. "They need that rhino prod to scoop away peasants."

The LBD have agreed on many occasions that bitching about Panama is a waste of time and just playing into their hands . . . but sometimes it's just so flipping necessary.

"So, so," I say, taking a deep, steadying breath, "are all of Panama's clique going? What about Abigail? And Leeza? And what about Zane Patterson!? Old orange-faced Zane must have got his nose into this one, has he?!"

"You've forgotten Derren," sighs Fleur, naming a particularly loathsome individual who flounces around Blackwell with a Prada sweater wrapped around his shoulders and spray-on pants that you can virtually see the outline of his nether dangly parts through. Derren spends all day sneering and jeering at anyone not as aesthetically blessed as himself.

"Y'know, I think I actually hate him," says Claude, clasping her hand in front of her mouth at the outburst. "Er, mmm, in a good-spirited Christian way, of course."

"You've not heard the worst bit yet," Fleur winces. "Apparently Panama's dad bought all five of the gang tickets as a little present. Liam reckons another of the Goodyear's great-uncles has died, leaving them even more cash and property. He reckons they actually own most of Wales now."

"Right, enough! *Enouggggh!*" says Claude, pushing us all along. "I don't care about them anyway. It's us we need to worry about. We need to get permission from our folks and our own tickets *tout de suite!* Oh, and that means *really quick,* for those of us who've snoozed through French all year," deadpans Claude, looking straight at me.

"Hmmm," I sigh, trudging along beside her. Astlebury seems a million miles away now, in a distant fun-filled cosmiverse.

We turn the corner to Blackwell Road, at the top of which lie the school's playing fields and red-brick buildings. Quickly we notice something gooey splattered all over the pavements. Eggs.

"Eggs!" shouts Claudette.

"Yak!" sneers Fleur, stepping over oodles of shell and sticky mess.

"Uh-oh, here we go . . . ," I groan, with a sense of impending doom.

In the distance, I spy more smashed eggs, and recognize a Year 7 kid trying to climb out of a large trash can, where he's been deposited by his friends. The air's becoming hazy, and a floury taste is coating the back of my throat. On the floor a smashed-up bag of self-rising flour is being pecked by a disappointed pigeon.

"Watch out!" shouts eagle-eyed Claude as another egg propels through the morning air toward us, narrowly missing my head and splatting the blazer of a lad coming up behind us.

"Gonna get you, retard!" squeals the kid, pulling out a water pistol and running past, drenching my back.

Ker-splllllat! goes another egg, narrowly missing Claude's head and landing by my feet.

The LBD stare at it, then carry on walking in silence.

It's going to be a very long day.

"So what did Paddy say then?" I ask Fleur as we walk through Blackwell's black wrought-iron gates. "You were commencing Stage Two hasslement last night, weren't you?"

Fleur shakes her head a bit, then raises her little snub nose huffily skyward. "Hmmm . . . well, news isn't good," she confesses. "Remember I first asked him on Monday when he was in his study? Y'know, ringing and e-mailing all his James Bond Society web-nerd buddies and all that dead important stuff he gets up to in mission control?"

"Yeah, he said he needed time to think, didn't he?" I say.

"Mmm, sort of. Actually, to be more specific, I showed him the *NME* advert, and said we all wanted to go to Astlebury Festival, and he looked at it, then he sort of stared at me for a bit . . . and then he started crossing his eyes and dribbling . . . then he began slapping his forehead and rocking backward and forward in his swivel chair, shouting, 'Saskia! Saaaaskia! Agghhh, it's all happening again! I've fallen through an anomaly loophole in the time-space continuum! The events of last year are replaying and I'm powerless to stop it. Harness the laser! Agghhh! Hellllp!' "

Fleur carries on walking, not even cracking a smile. I can't help sniggering. He makes me laugh, Paddy Swan . . . well, for a grown-up anyway.

"He is verily a comedic genius," Fleur says witheringly. "So anyway, I pestered him again last night, and this time he claimed he needed time to 'research the proposal.' Pah! *Research?*"

"What sort of research?" I say. "Does he want to check if

there are segregated male and female camping facilities? Snogging police? What?"

"Huh. More likely that the fascist pig clearly knows that ever since Carmella Dupris confirmed she's headlining on Saturday night, tickets have almost sold out. There's a countdown running on the official Astlebury website."

"Oh, surely he's not that clued in," says Claude.

"Huh! Well, I've been snooping on his Mac and Astlebury.com is bookmarked on his Internet favorites. I've got him sussed . . ." Fleur flicks her blonde locks and rolls her eyes. "I absolutely loathe him," she concludes.

"Awww, no you don't," says Claude. "And besides, Fleur, try not to lose your rag just yet, 'cos if we get the go-ahead, we're going to need his credit card to book the tickets. I mean, who else would trust us to pay him the cash back?"

Claude's right. Paddy might be a right royal James Bond–obsessed pain in the butt, but he's stuck his neck out for us before. The crazy fool. "S'pose so," mumbles Fleur.

We walk through the main gates heading for the central entrance, joining the happy throng of 1,000 other inmates gearing up for their final day of term. The stench of rotten cabbage and decaying animal is ripe in the air: end-of-term stink bombs, I hope, although it could be a delicious dining hall stew being reheated for the final time before being frozen for autumn term. In the main cloakroom, Deputy Head Mrs. Guinevere and Ms. Dunn the scatty religious studies teacher are prowling the floors wearing looks of perpetual suspicion. As we pass the back of the administration corridor, past Mr. McGraw's office, I spot our headmaster's beaky, depressed nose poking through the blinds, surveying the brewing end-of-term disorder.

"Anyway, Claude," I say as we reach our homeroom, "how's it hanging with Mrs. Cassiera? Does it look hopeful?"

"No. Still waiting," frowns Claude. "Only now, she says she's going to ask 'him upstairs' what he thinks she should do. What with Astlebury being such a potentially dangerous place and, y'know, with it being my first time at a pop festival, she needs some 'divine guidance.' "

"Who lives upstairs?" says Fleur, looking confused. "Is your uncle Leonard staying? Does that mean you and Mika are sharing a room again?!"

"She means God, you great numpty," I say, shaking my head. Claude's mum is *très* religious. She's got a hotline straight to heaven . . . y'know, a bit like the pope. Well, except I imagine the pope probably asks God dead important stuff like, "Why, oh Holy Father, do the Ethiopian orphans suffer so much?" and probably not random trivia like, "Will it rain next week for the Ghanaian Methodist Church chicken cookout?" or "Should I have a demi-wave on my hair for Sandra's wedding or just buy a big flamboyant hat?"

The Lord, Gloria Cassiera often says, knows all within this kingdom, as well as the next.

"Oh, well, flipping great," says Fleur dramatically, sashaying through the classroom doors and finding her seat. "That's us totally stuffed then. Let's just forget it all, should we?"

Claude says nothing. She just thins her lips.

As I pass, I poke Claude in her flat belly and wink, as if to say, "Ignore Miss Huffypants, Claude, we're all in the same boat here."

Claude winks back, as if to say, "I know, don't worry about me. Oh, and by the way, Ronnie, I'm still hopeful. We could still go."

I really want to believe her.

arrivals

No matter how much I stare at the clocks during double English, the hands won't shift around any faster. We're spending the last lesson before summer break comparing our creative writing assignments, although in reality this has mainly been Mr. Swainson, our English teacher, dissecting and applauding Claude's "stunning composition," or, as I see it, 900 words of pretentious codswallop titled "Arrivals."

"Claude's work brought a tear to my eye," bleats Swainson, dressed in his trademark sludge-colored suit jacket worn with faded denim jeans that he tries to pass off as trousers. "It was so moving!"

Claude bristles with pride.

"Bravo," I mutter, by now on the verge of stabbing myself to death with my pencil.

At some juncture, in the eyes of the Blackwell staff, I can't pinpoint when exactly, Claude Cassiera made the leap from everyday pupil to Blackwell royalty. I think they had a crowning and anointing ceremony that day I was cutting. It's all very weird.

"You see, the female lead character in Claude's story woke up one day and found she'd laid a egg," coos Mr. Swainson. "And when the egg hatched, it was an identical version of herself, wearing the same school uniform and everything!"

"Wow!" gasps the entire front row. "That's really clever!"

"It worked on so many levels!" confirms Mr. Swainson. "So I had to give Claude the class's only A star."

Another A flipping star? *Gnnngnn!*

I don't know what I'm more angry about: the fact that Claude got an A for basically rehashing one of the mad dreams I told her about when my mother was pregnant, or the fact that I got only a C for my quasi-pathetic ramblings about a madcap badger.

"The theme was supposed to be 'new life,' you great clot!" hisses Claude.

"Well, no one told me that!" I grumble.

"I told you," snaps Claude. "It was written on the board too!"

Claude's narked because she knows I was too busy moping about Jimi to pay attention to such trivialities.

"If you just tried a bit, you could get A's too!" huffs Claude, sounding exactly like a less fun-loving version of my mother.

Thankfully, the lunch bell resonates through the building, meaning I can escape.

"Gotta go, I've got an appointment," says Claude, squeezing my shoulder reproachfully. In a flash she's got her bag and gone, I'm not sure where. The teachers probably want to carry her shoulder high around the yard or something.

I pack my bag moodily and trudge off toward the dining hall to eat cheap cupcakes with Fleur.

As I turn into the middle-school corridor, I get the most peculiar sensation.

I just know Jimi Steele's waiting for me.

I know it before I actually *know it,* if you know what I mean. My radar picks him up, his eyes drilling into me. There's an unmistakable way Jimi holds himself, with his shoulders back and his hands in his pockets, propped up against the Year 10 notice board, his big bag with his art projects in it over his shoulder.

My stomach lurches.

"All right?" Jimi says, wincing a bit, as if he's expecting a smack, either verbal or physical.

"Oh, hello," I say, trying to be curt, while trying desperately not to smile. Somehow a small grin fights its way past my molars.

We stand staring at each other while a posse of Year 7 kids wanders past nudging each other, whispering and grinning.

Ugh. Does everyone in this entire school know we're in the middle of rough patch? It seems so.

And why didn't I make more of an effort to look nice today?

Jimi, of course, looks his typical seriously windswept yet gorgeous self. A tad tired, perhaps, but still dead sexy in a pale blue baggy T-shirt with stripes and his slate gray oversized jeans with the ripped left knee. A small amount of sandy hair is protruding from his T-shirt top.

Sigh.

"Nice chest wig, wereboy," I say dryly.

Jimi chortles slightly bashfully. "Ugggh, I know, it's getting worse, isn't it," he moans. "Naz says I look like a strategically shaven chinchilla."

"Hmmm . . . ," I say, wrinkling my nose. "Naz has a salient point there. There *are* depilatory creams for your sort of problem, y'know?"

"Mmm . . . well, if it begins to grow on the backs of my hands, I'll look into it." Jimi smiles, holding up both of his hands like big claws.

We gaze at each other.

There's a small awkward silence.

"You look good today," he says, a tiny bit resentfully.

"Do I?"

"Yeah . . ." He nods. "Well, y'know . . . you just look like you."

Jimi looks majorly upset now. With a small amount of prodding I could probably get him blubbing. But the stupid thing is, I don't want to make him feel any worse. In fact I want to wrap my arms around him right then and tell him that . . .

Woooooh, hang on! This sort of airy-fairy girlie behavior will not do at all! There's a good reason I'm not talking to this nincompoop. I must, must, must remember that.

"So anyway, Jimi," I say slightly officiously, "what exactly can I do for you?"

The change of tone seems to startle him. "Errrr? Well . . . I . . . ," he says, grappling around for something to say.

" 'Cos I gotta go," I say, beginning to move past him. "I'm meeting Fleur, y'see?"

I'm just calling his bluff, really.

"No, Ronnie, hey, don't go!" he says, grabbing my shoulder gently. "Look, babe, I've come to talk to you. Y'know, about stuff. This is so stupid! And you won't pick your flipping phone up!"

"Well, I'm not just dropping everything to speak to you now," I huff. "I've got plans."

"Oh, c'mon!" Jimi pleads, grabbing for my hand. "Look, let me buy you lunch?"

I stop in my tracks. Despite being highly principled, I'm broke and hungry. "By lunch, do you mean actual *lunch* lunch?" I ask witheringly. "Or do you mean buy me a pie and let me sit on a wall watching you sprain stuff?"

Jimi rolls his eyes. "No! I mean actual, proper, real, sit-down, knife-and-fork lunch." Jimi smiles, rooting around in his brain for a venue. "At, er, Ruby's! You like Ruby's, don't you?"

Gnngnn . . . I *looooove* Ruby's! It's a fab little cafe just off the high street where all the coolest sixth formers go. The hippies who own it sell amazing organic cakes and play break-beat CDs and hip-hop.

He's not making this very easy, is he?

Jimi cups my cheek with his hand, looking a little more scamp-like.

"C'mon, Ron," he says, "just one little lunch, eh? I've got loads I want to say to you. What could possibly go wrong?"

I look at him sadly. It's very difficult to reject lunch with a lad who has long blond eyelashes, a perfect snub nose and a fab bum that just won't quit.

But Fleur will kill me if I say yes. This does not fit into the "blank him for a month" regimen.

"I don't think it's a good idea, Jimi," I say eventually.

The firmness of my tone makes Jimi rather exasperated. "Oh,

look, Ronnie, just stop it! I'm not leaving things up in the air like this!" he says emphatically. "Why have you always got to be so annoyingly stubborn?"

"Huh!" I huff, taking a deep breath, ready to begin illustrating why I feel "stubborn" when two familiar voices interrupt my rage.

"Wooooo-hoooh! Head for the shelters!" whoops Aaron. "Think we've got World War Four breaking out here!"

"Ha ha!" snorts Naz. "Get your tin hat on!"

"*Pgghhh,*" I huff, eyeing Jimi's two best friends disdainfully. "You mean *World War Three,* Aaron. There have only been two actual world wars so far."

Aaron looks a bit confused; he begins counting on his fingers. "So what was that last Middle East one?" he asks. "That was, like, fairly big, wasn't it?"

"It's not the size of the war," I sigh. "It's the amount of countries involved in it, like when . . . Look, hang on, I don't want to discuss this. Can you two just bog off, please, we're talking?"

Aaron starts laughing even louder now. "Ahhhh . . . still in the doghouse, are we, Jimi?" he snortles, rolling up a copy of *Fireboard* magazine and smacking Jimi over the head with it.

Jimi's previously kindly expression has stiffened to a frown since Dumb and Dumber showed up.

"Coming to get some lunch?" asks Aaron.

(He's not exactly inviting me along too, it should be noted. Saying that I'll probably just get in the way of all those grrrreat fart stories they always tell.)

"Give us a minute, lads?" says Jimi, waving them away, turning to me rather grumpily. "Look, are you going to start acting like a normal human being and come for lunch with me or what?"

"I beg your flipping pardon?" I growl back.

Naz and Aaron chortle wildly at Jimi's cheekiness.

"Okay, obviously not," Jimi grunts, being oh-so-much-more laddy now that he has an audience. "Well, suit yourself, lady."

"Oh, I will! Don't worry," I huff.

"Oh, and say hello to my friend Fleur for me, will you?" he shouts.

"She misses you desperately too!" I snap, picking up my bag and turning on my heel sharply.

"Er . . . okay then!" shouts Jimi back. "Well, I'll see you around then!"

"Don't be so sure!" I yell over my shoulder, storming off.

"Huh . . . *pghhhh* . . . ," splutters Jimi, slightly pathetically. "And you can give me my Final Warning CD back too!"

"Oh, *whatever!* Your stuff's all in a trash bag. Come and get it before I give it to a thrift shop." I grunt, storming toward the dining hall to tell Fleur the whole highly irritating saga.

Fleur says Jimi Steele's a pig.

She says I should just forget all about him and date Miles Boon in the lower sixth, as she's *sure* that he likes me.

"And he's not at all like Jimi," says Fleur. "He does charity fun runs for Third World famine relief! So he's like totally sensitive as well as hot."

I groan, stuffing another lump of Millionaire Shortbread into my face. The last thing I need is another boyfriend.

"And anyway, Ronnie," continues Fleur seriously, "Miles has

got a VW Golf with tinted windows. He's, like, so totally streets ahead of Jimi."

poor life choices

Just after final break, which was livened up by the traditional end-of-term hoax fire alarm and an appearance by four gorgeous firefighters who took their tops off and grappled with a hose (phew), I grab my bag and head for life studies. In case you're not familiar with Blackwell School's curriculum, life studies is that weird compulsory class every pupil has to take weekly at some point where teachers are paid to dissuade you from "making poor life choices." Y'know, stuff like having babies too early with Royston Potter, sniffing aerosol cans, auditioning for the Peppermint Palace All-Nude Dancing Bar or even growing your shoulder hair into tufts and parading about in a T-shirt.

Okay, I made that last one up.

Weirdly enough, I rather enjoy life studies. Especially when we have rollicking class debates about the stuff we're studying. It seems that I, Veronica Ripperton, have emerged this term as the number one class debating maestro! Okay, I do get told off for being sarcastic to my opponents quite a lot, but when it comes down to the vote, I'm always winning.

Praise be! I do have a skill, after all.

Claude, on the other hand, loathes life studies. She simply cannot get her head around why people would even *consider* making any of these retarded life choices in the first place. She spends every double period with the countenance of a girl being heavily patronized. It's actually pretty funny to watch. Especially last week when the class debated, "Is passing your GCSE exams important in the outside world?"

Ha ha ha! She went properly loopy at anyone who dared to say no! That was really great.

Today, as a final treat, we're being allowed to watch a DVD. The girls' choice won the vote, so *Notting Hill* with Hugh Grant is screening on the telly and everyone's making a huge screaming fuss every time there's a slushy-kissy scene, as if they've never seen anything so rude before. Me, I'm just finding it all a bit painful to watch.

"You're a right misery this week," whispers Liam Gelding kindly as I shuffle in my chair. "I'm glad I've got six weeks away from you. Quite frankly, you make me want to hang myself."

At some level, this is Liam Gelding asking me how I'm feeling.

"Thanks. The feeling's mutual, rat boy," I whisper back, propping my long face up on the desk and sighing.

"Oh, flipping cheer up, Ronnie," Liam says. "Look, I'm smiling and I have to sit beside Claudette and she smells of wee."

That makes me giggle a bit.

"I do not smell of wee! You disgusting boy!" squeals Claudette, punching Liam's arm. Liam must go home each night black and blue, Claude gives him so many dead arms. "And at least I do bathe! Not just in cheap rancid body splash like you do! Yuk! And anyway, leave Veronica alone. She's not feeling herself at the moment."

I nod pathetically in agreement.

"Why?" asks Liam. Liam's second ear piercing looks a bit infected to me. It's oozing pus.

"She's got . . . er, *personal problems,*" whispers Claude.

"Personal *private* problems, poo-face," I say, aware that the next two rows are earwigging furiously. "So keep your schneck out and turn the volume down on your big pie-plate-shaped head."

Picking on Liam is making me feel a lot better.

"Oh, right," says Liam, furrowing his brow, a mischievous smile growing across his face. "So, this got anything to do with Jimi Steele dumping you last Friday?" he says loudly.

"Huh! What?! *He has not,*" I gasp. "I've dumped him! Well, I've not dumped him but . . . well, it's . . . *gnngnnnnn!* Nothing to do with you! Look, why don't you bog off and grow the rest of that mustache you've been threatening to since the spring?"

I can't believe I've just played straight into Liam's hands.

"Hoo-hoo! Gossip! I got the gossip!" he shouts. "Heard the latest Jimi/Ronnie news, everyone? I know the full details!"

"Shut. Up. Now," says Claude firmly. "Or. Else."

Liam does immediately.

Of course Liam has hit the nail on the head. Jimi Steele has officially done my head right in.

I just don't think I can do this "snub him for a month" thing. Jeez, I only managed to blank him for twenty-four hours when he forgot my fifteenth birthday and went with the lads to see *Combat Zombie Explosion II* instead. I caved in like a bad soufflé when he brought me those flowers and took me to Paramount Pizza.

Seeing him at lunchtime hasn't helped my plight at all. My head's totally mixed up. It wasn't Jimi's first attempt to speak face-to-face to me, either, so it's not like I can say he doesn't care about the whole thing.

Last Tuesday, he appeared at the Fantastic Voyage on the off chance I'd be in. Sadly, I was over at Fleur's house, plotting our route to Astlebury as well as dissuading her from strangling her big sister Daphne, who's just home from a year in Nepal. Tempers were fairly frazzled at the Swan house, but that was cool, as it quite distracted me from my own angst. It's a difficult time for Fleur, not being the number one center of attention in the Swan household. I mean, Daphne Swan is a totally cool person, I want to be just like her when I'm twenty, but jeez, does she like talking about her traveling adventures!? I only popped down to the kitchen for a glass of water and had to sit through a forty-five-minute yarn about her "awesome experiences" at the Nepalese Festival of Panchak Yamar (which she says making a weird clicking noise with her tongue and spitting all over you, just like the natives). Of course, while I was brushing up on advanced Nepalese anthropology, the beautiful Jimi Steele was at the Fantastic Voyage, throwing stones up at my window.

"He had a face like a bag of wet greyhounds," Dad said.

"Ooh, yeah, Ronnie!" scoffed Mum. "He was laying it on thick. He even had me feeling sorry for him. I told him to buzz off. He wanted an Oscar for that performance."

"Cheers, Mum," I said, pretending to be grateful.

But if deep down Jimi's as upset as I am, does that mean I should let him get away with sometimes being a thoughtless, hurtful berk? Am I making a mistake?

Oh, please God, pleeeease let the LBD be allowed to go to Astlebury! Please let there be tickets left. I need to get out of this town before I go mad.

"Don't worry, Ronnie," whispers Liam Gelding quite sincerely as Hugh Grant and Julia Roberts lick each other's ears. "It'll be okay . . . I'll have a word with him."

"Don't you flipping dare!" I squeal.

"Liam! Don't make me have to enforce a grave medieval-style punishment upon you," warns Claude.

"*Pggh* . . . I'm only trying to help!" moans Liam, looking a bit confused.

"Well, I don't need your help, Liam, I'm doing *just fine*," I say.

And then the final bell of the summer rings loud and clear. It sounds absolutely wonderful.

It sounds just like freedom.

no destination

"What do you mean, *all over,* Fleur? What's all over?" shouts Claudette, trying to catch up with the blonde bombshell as she clip-clops rather briskly along Lacey Avenue, school bag swinging in the breeze. After the bell, we'd found our chum in the I.T. lab, frantically typing an e-mail to an address I didn't recognize with red-rimmed eyes and a mascara river trickling down her cheek.

"Look, calm down a second, petal," says Claude, cupping an ebony arm around Fleur's willowy waist. "Tell Auntie Claudette and Uncle Ron what the matter is."

I draw along beside them and pull out a packet of pocket tissues, passing one to Claude, who begins dabbing Fleur's face as if she were three.

"Fleur Swan . . . ," I begin patiently, "please tell me you've not been posting your photo on that 'Am I a Hottie or Not?' website again."

"Oh, surely not!" groans Claude.

Last time Fleur played this game, posting one fairly flattering snapshot of herself on the information superhighway, some anonymous cybergeek in Michigan USA kindly pointed out she was "gawky," "wore too much lip gloss" and "was probably a total airhead." We didn't hear the end of it for a week. Of course the eighty-five other voters who gave Fleur the 9/10 "Total Babelicious Minx" rating were totally forgotten in a cybersecond. Sometimes I don't envy Fleur's beauty. She sets herself some fairly high standards.

"No, of course I've not been on that site," mumbles Fleur. "It's a stupid site anyhow."

"So what's up?" I ask.

"Hmmm . . . It's pretty bad," sniffs Fleur. "Well . . . very bad."

"Hit us with it," I say. I prefer my bad news in one quick "punch to the stomach" bulletin. I can't stand waiting about.

"Oh, poo," sighs Claude, shutting her eyes. "I know what you're going to say. It *is* all over, isn't it?"

"Yup," says Fleur. They both stand still, staring at each other. "They're all gone. The Astlebury tickets are completely one hundred percent sold out."

"Wah! How?" I cry. "What? Like, sold out from the official ticket office?"

Fleur turns to me, wiping her eyes on her school shirt.

"No, like sold out *absolutely everywhere*. It was posted officially on the website at three-thirty P.M. I logged on in I.T. I've been ringing around other box offices ever since, but even then, tickets were vanishing as quickly as I could find them."

"There has to be another way!" Claude says vehemently, putting her hands on her shapely hips.

"Well, I can't see one, Claudey," says Fleur. "I mean, I even went on eBay and found this guy called Dave in London who had tickets he wanted to get rid of . . . but then loads of other eBay bods began bidding too, and it all got really out of control."

"How much were they?" I ask gingerly.

Fleur looks at me, and her eyes well up again. "Five hundred and twenty pounds each by the end of school. Oh, and he's got only two." She sighs. "Well, he *did* have two. Someone bought them."

After a period of staring blankly at one another, we carry on meandering along the street. No one knows what to say.

Suddenly, I've got this horrible, panicky feeling that I've no direction in my world anymore.

I've got no school to go to tomorrow.

I've got no Jimi Steele as my boyfriend.

I've got no fantabulous rock 'n' roll LBD adventure to chuck myself wholeheartedly into.

I've got no clue what I'm going to do with the rest of my summer.

Ditto my entire life.

In fact, all I have right now is the LBD . . . and neither of them are the feisty, foxy, fighting force that I know so well. They look like wounded soldiers staggering home from battle.

Aaaaaaaagh, I'm free-falling!

And right that instant, a horridly familiar plummy voice, as soothing as nails scratching a blackboard, splats me back to Earth. "What?" the girl's voice is squealing into her mobile phone. "Her skirt? Oh my God! I know! Did you see that hideous creation she had on in the dining hall today? How cheap and nasty? Jeez, the only label Stacey Hislop wears is 'non–flame retardant.' Ha ha! What a complete pauper, eh?"

"Uggggh," I groan.

Fleur jumps slightly, steadying herself quickly and pulling her shoulders back to greet the delightful vision of Panama Bogwash, sashaying home to Goodyear Mansions. Panama hasn't spotted us yet; she's far too engrossed slagging off poor Stacey, a really meek lower sixth girl who always eats by herself, reading a book at lunch. Eventually she sees us all standing in a row, staring at her, and visibly blanches. It's almost as if Panama is terrified that some of the LBD's grubbiness may leap the gap and infect her.

"Afternoon, Panama," nods Claude bravely.

"Oh, hello, er, Maud . . . and er, Ronnie," says Panama, totally ignoring Fleur as she clips by. Today Panama is wearing an indigo Japanese silk kimono-style blouse, black leggings and pristine white pumps; her trademark auburn bob glistens in the late afternoon sun. Much as I loathe Panama, she probably possesses the most perfect slim figure I've ever seen in real life.

(I told my dad about this once, around the time that Panama

snogged Jimi. *Gnnngnnn,* I can't even think about that time now. Anyway, Dad said I was talking utter pig swill. He said men like women "with a bit of meat on their bones" and not ones like Panama who look like they'd have to run around in the shower to get wet. He also pointed out that Panama has slightly too many teeth for her mouth. "Well, I wouldn't give her a bite of my apple, that's all I'm saying," Dad shuddered. "It'd be like sharing it with a racehorse." My dad's totally brilliant sometimes.)

"So anyway," Panama continues to bark into her phone, snub nose aloft, "if you want to swing by later, Leeza, please do. My mother's manicurist is calling between six and eight, and I'm having the full French works and tips . . . Actually, now that I think about it, you definitely should too. You've got hands like a Russian dockworker at the moment. Abigail and I were laughing about it earlier."

Panama seems to raise her voice slightly at this point, as if she really wants us all to hear her as she walks away.

"Oh, and best of all, if you round up the gang, I can give out the Astlebury tickets too! Daddy says they arrived today!"

Claude, Fleur and I all gaze at one another glumly. In an instant Panama Goodyear vanishes, leaving a sickening waft of Coco Chanel eau de parfum in her wake, as well as a macabre silence.

"Well, all this really messes up my chances of meeting Spike Saunders again and marrying him," mutters Fleur eventually, with a forced smile.

She's only half joking here.

"I think I'm the most gutted about missing the Kings of Kong," I say to no one in particular. "They confirmed they're playing this week. They're totally amazing."

I suppose I'll just be listening to them in my bedroom now.

"It's not just missing the bands that I'm upset about," says Claude. "And if Panama wants to go, well, good bleeding luck to her . . . I'm narked about not going away to Astlebury with you two. This was just going to be like the most fabulous LBD fandango ever . . . wasn't it?"

"Yup," I say.

"Yeah," whispers Fleur. "Look, don't, Claude, you'll make me cry again."

Sometimes Fleur's a bit like one of those fey female characters in a Victorian period drama; once she's tearful, the slightest maudlin word can open the floodgates.

"Okay, let's try to snap out of this," says Claude, clapping her hands as if to signify the end of feeling sorry for ourselves.

And failing miserably.

"So . . . anyone fancy coming to mine for coffee and cake? My mum made a Victoria sponge yesterday that's about as big as a castle."

Fleur and I look a bit shell-shocked. That's the power of Panama.

"Oh, c'mon," says Claude. "Mum would love to see you. Hey, and Mika bought that new Carmella Dupris remix album on Saturday. You've got to hear track two—it's excellent!"

I shake my head, "No ta, Claude. Gonna go home."

"Nah, thanks," says Fleur grumpily, walking off. "Gotta get

home and do my chores, haven't I? Oh, and of course, I've got to listen to Daphne yaddering on about her wonderful fun-filled existence. I mean, why do I need a life when I can hear all about hers?"

"Oh . . . okay then," says Claude disappointedly. "Well . . . see ya both, er, soon, eh?"

"Yeah, see you, er . . . later," I say, turning the corner alone to the Fantastic Voyage and commencing my trudge toward . . . well, now I come to think about it . . . toward absolutely nothing.

comedy night

It was just my luck, Chuckles and Co. were upstairs in the kitchen when I got home. Both Mum and Dad were taking a breather, Dad bouncing Seth on top of his denim-clad knee, while Mum leafed through a *Brewers Trade* magazine, making uncharitable remarks about other local bartenders.

"She's got a face like a ferret peering through jelly, that woman at the King's Head, hasn't she, Loz?" says Mum, pointing at a woman with a huge pair of bazonkas, clad in a skintight, low-cut top.

"Ha ha! You're not wrong, love. But who looks at her face?" laughs Dad.

"True, Lawrence," agrees Mum, slurping her tea.

"Oooh, who's this? I think this might be our number one daughter home to see us!" announces Dad, noticing me standing glumly in the doorway.

"Aha! It is!" He laughs. "And look, she's full of the joys of summer already!"

I gaze at them, then sigh deeply.

"Well, Loz," laughs Mum, looking at her watch. "She's been on her summer break for over half an hour now. She'll no doubt be bored."

"Bored and broke," adds Dad, checking his back pocket for his wallet.

"Every time I see her at the moment, I feel like I've been mugged."

Believe me, they really can be this funny all day long. I don't know how I get anything done.

"Oh, pumpkin," Mum says to me, rearranging the neckline on her very trendy off-the-shoulder vertical print top, "how is my little ray of sunshine? How was your last day?"

"Hmmm, okay-ish. 'T'sovernowanyhow," I mumble.

"Huh. I bet that McGraw's got a big clean-up job to do," chuckles Dad. "I saw loads of egg-splattered kids running down high street."

"Hmmm. S'pose so," I say.

Dad's dress sense is much more predictable. Mottled jeans, old T-shirts, smelly sneakers, sandy hair sticking up in flyaway points—he's actually genetically incapable of looking smart. Even when Dad wears a suit and tie, he just looks like a tramp making an effort for a court appearance.

"So, any big plans for the summer?" asks Dad.

"*Gnngn,* mmm . . . not now," I huff, opening food cupboards and staring into them. I do this every night. Mum calls it "the cupboard ritual."

"Ooh, brace yourself, Loz," says Mum. "Looks like we're in the midst of a word shortage. She's playing that teenager game again. The longer our sentences are, the shorter hers become!"

"Oh, I like this one!" chuckles Dad, warming to the theme. "Sooooo, Ronnie . . . any word from that boyfriend of yours?"

"Pghhhgh," I grunt, opening the fridge and staring at a yogurt.

"That wasn't even a word!" says Dad. "She's good at this, isn't she, love?"

"She's the best," says Mum quite genuinely. "A real chip off the old block."

Eventually, the will to speak is too strong. "Y'know, you two really get on my nerves!" I tell them. "I mean, has it ever occurred to you that I can't get a word in edgewise for your incessant wittering?"

"Hurray, Magda! She spoke! We rule!!" cheers Dad, high-fiving Mum.

"Fogies one, teenager zero!"

I can't help laughing at them now.

Mum looks at me, realizing I'm genuinely upset tonight. "Awww . . . what's up, my little precious?" she says soppily. "Tell us what's troubling you."

"I'm okay, really," I tell them. "Just a bit, er, melancholy."

"Cool word," says Dad, spooning mushed banana into Seth's gob. "What's that mean?"

"I don't know exactly," I confess. "I think it means sort of thoughtful, but in a kind of sad way. It was in a poem I learned at school. By Keats."

"Didn't he kill himself?" says Mum, drawing fangs on the King's Head bartender's photograph.

"Mmm, no, he died of . . ."

"Oooh, they all kill themselves, those artistic sorts," Mum says. "I can't be doing with sensitive types."

"No, I don't think he . . ."

"Anyway, enough about suicide," says Dad, picking up a copy of the *Local Daily Mercury* newspaper and opening it theatrically at the local sports pages at the back. "Now you're here, you can point out to your mum and me where you're standing in this group photo!"

"Eh?" I say.

"The Blackwell End-of-Year Sporting Achievements Round-up!" smirks Dad, reading the caption beneath a nauseating group shot of jocks and glossy-haired girls holding balls and bats.

"Ugggghh," I sigh, tossing my hair moodily.

"Yeah! Where are you, love?" giggles Mum. "We've looked and looked! Which prize did you get?"

"Prize for invisibility!" guffaws Dad, holding the page up really close to his face. My mother's laughing so heartily by this point, she has to hold on to the kitchen table to steady herself.

"Shuttttup," I groan.

"Special commendation for sulking!" Mum finally catches her breath to say, before collapsing in fits again.

"Right! That's it! I'm going to my boudoir," I snap. "And I don't want to be disturbed."

"Oh, well, nice chatting," says Dad, wiping his eyes. "See ya when you next surface."

"Oh, and no writing poetry while you're in there," shouts Mum after me. "It's the slippery slope!"

"I won't, don't worry," I assure her, flouncing away.

"Ooh, and Ronnie, before I forget," says Dad, sticking his head around the kitchen door as I head for my room, "you got a letter today. Dunno who it's from."

"Ooh, we never got that one steamed open, did we?" mutters Mum in the other room.

Dad winks, then begins searching about on the telephone table, passing me a package.

"Eh?" I say, looking at the bright red thick envelope with its glamorous London postmark.

"Oooh, come on then," says Dad. "Open it!"

I grab the envelope and scurry into my lair.

there's nothing as queer as Polk.

After putting on my new Kings of Kong CD, I sit down on the bed and begin opening the letter. This is very irregular. Nobody writes to me, ever. As I tear open the outer package, I notice that inside the first large red envelope is a smaller, pale yellow envelope. Upon the yellow envelope, in ink, is written:

Ronnie Ripperton + 3

Weird. The yellow envelope feels as though it may have something chunky inside it. I put it to one side and concentrate on the piece of white paper. A letter! As I begin reading, my breathing becomes unsteady and my heart begins to beat a big hole through my chest. It says.

Hi there, Ronnie! Kari from Funky Monkey Management here!

Er . . . what? Who!? I carry on . . .

Sorry these are so late. We're all mad busy over here at the moment and shamefully behind with the passes. Hope these are still of use? I've just been going through guest lists with Spike for the August date and he told me about you having hassle getting to his gig last summer. Spike says he had a great time with the BDL and hopes these make up for it. Also—thank Fleur for tipping him off about PRIZE being hosted illegally.

He's got his lawyers on the case. Any problems with the passes, just give me a call. See ya soon.

Kari xxx

Errrrrrr, eh? What on earth is going on?

Kari who?! And Spike who?

Spike?

SPPPPPPIKE!!

OH MY GOD! SPIKE SAUNDERS!

Nooooooo, she can't possibly mean *the* Spike Saunders!?

I read the letter again, then another time looking for any evidence that this might be a hoax from Liam Gelding or some other satanic being.

But the letter looks very, very genuine.

I grab the yellow envelope and carefully rip it open, reaching inside, suddenly feeling a strong urge to go to the toilet.

Is it possibly possible, even in a parallel wonky universe, that Spike "so beautiful it actually hurts, multimillionaire, Duke of Pop" Saunders actually remembers meeting the LBD (or the BDL, as he puts it) last year, and has got his personal assistant to send us something?

Surely not.

From the yellow envelope, I pull out four, thick, shiny gilt-edged pieces of paper with a silver hologram of a tent perched upon a hill glittering on each one. And then I gaze at them, totally spellbound by their majestic beauty.

Four Astlebury Festival tickets!

In my hands!

Four "with compliments of Spike Saunders" Astlebury Festival tickets!!!

I look at them and begin to laugh.

And then I begin to really roar.

And then I lie back on my bed and laugh so flipping much, I actually begin to cry.

Chapter 3
Pull house

"I knew it! I knnnnnnew it!" squeals Fleur Swan, clapping her hands and jumping around her bedroom, causing her *Mega Beats and Breaks* CD to skip and legions of teddies to rain down from the top of her bulging wardrobes. "I knew it!"

"So . . . they're . . . for . . . us?" says Claudette Cassiera slowly, with a look of total dumbfoundment, clutching the four tickets. "They're, like, really for us?"

"Yes!" I say. "They're for us. Reeee-ally, really all for us! Spike Saunders remembered meeting us! He sent us some tickets!"

"No . . . they can't be for us," says Claude, wrestling with the nonlogic of the situation. "It's probably a mail mix-up and . . . it's probably . . ."

"No, Claude. Believe me," I say. "I called the number and spoke to a girl called Jo in the Funky Monkey offices. The tickets are totally, nonnegotiably for us! We were put on the guest list."

"I knew it!" squeaks Fleur for the twenty-eighth time, her voice especially triumphant this time. "I knew Spike Saunders fancied me!"

Fleur pirouettes past us with a euphoric smile, then leaps up onto her bed and begins to bounce, shouting in time with each jump: "Spike . . . Saunders . . . fancies . . . me!"

And then, in a posher, more hoity-toity accent: "Well, helllloooooo there, Ronnie and Claude! I'm Mrs. Fleur Saunders! Soooooo terribly pleased to meet you!"

And then, eventually: "Ha, back atcha Jimi Steeeeeele! Stick that up your trouser leg and smoke it, flobberlips! The LBD are going to Astlebury!"

I shake my head, suppressing a giggle. Fleur is not making this situation any less surreal.

"So, they're really for us!?" says Claude yet again, her hazel eyes as wide as dinner plates. "It doesn't seem possible! This is just like the part of a totally scrummy dream when it gets so good that you wake up and realize you're just in bed all along." Claude looks at the tickets again, the silver holograms transforming slightly as she moves them. "It's just . . ."

"Amazing?!" I laugh.

"It's just . . . ," says Claude breathily, "the best thing that has ever happened to us in the whole history of the world ever! I mean, Spike Saunders must meet a zillion people every year! And those tickets are worth hundreds of pounds! It's just incrrrrredible!"

"I knooooooow!" I laugh, and we throw our arms around each other and jump up and down. (We'd have included Fleur in this LBD hug, but she seemed just as content bouncing and squawking on her bed.)

I'll give Fleur Swan her due here: She may be as mad as a hat stand, but she did predict that something amazing would happen if we asked our parents about Astlebury. I do love her sometimes.

"I'm going to mail Spike's message board tomorrow and tell him we're coming!" yells the squeaky blonde. "And go on the Astlebury website to find out where all the coolest people camp! Oh God, and I totally need my hair cut before we go, don't I? Ooh, have I got time? Claude, pass the calendar! Hey, and we'll have to travel down on the Friday morning, won't we? Because that's when the gates open! I mean, the bands aren't beginning till Saturday, but all the cool boutiques and small stages open on Friday! And the campfire parties all start on Friday night! And . . ." Fleur is just gabbling now. "Oh my Lord! I don't fancy those festival porta-toilets, do you?! I'm not going to wee for the whole weekend! Or go to sleep! Oh my God, this is sooo great!"

I'm beginning to feel quite dizzy just watching her. There is so much to plan! When I look back at Claude, she's slumped on Fleur's futon, looking quite perplexed.

"What's up, Claude?" I say. "Are you okay?"

"Yeah, I'm more than okay, Ronnie, I'm wonderful," says Claude. "I'm just, er, thinking . . . look, Fleur, get down, I think we need to talk."

"But I'm bouncing!" says Fleur, bouncing.

"We've still got a glitch to sort out," Claude says.

"Pah! Spoilsport," chuckles Fleur, climbing down. "This is sooooo excellent, though, isn't it?!"

"Yep!" I say. "Majorly excellent!"

You can tell that Claude would like to enjoy this moment, but I also know that two minutes' frivolity is all her brain allows before getting logical.

"Okay, so this is all totally fantastic," says Claude. I can hear the "but" coming here. "But we've still got a teensy-weensy problem that needs to be ironed out."

"Noooo . . . Our problems are over! We have tickets!" says Fleur, grinning from ear to ear.

"Well, *nearly* over," says Claude. "Look, I'm not trying to wee on the LBD bonfire here by being negative, but let's recap. None of our parents knows about these freebie tickets yet, do they?"

"Nah. Only us," I say.

"So, despite the fact that Spike Saunders has officially invited us to a festival, we still need to get permission to go, don't we?"

"Yeah. I suppose so," I say.

I've been quietly blocking this from my mind for the past few hours. You see, the free ticket/Spike Saunders hoopla was so fabulous, I suppose I was also hoping that magic dust might make the parents vanish.

"Oh, permission, permission!" scoffs Fleur, wrinkling her tiny freckled nose. "Look, let's ask the mumbly-grumblies, and if they all say no again, well, let's just go anyway! Come on! We only live once, don't we? Spike would be offended if we didn't go!"

Claude rolls her eyes. Sometimes it's almost like Fleur has just met Claude that very second.

"Yes, Fleur," says Claude, "because leaving Astlebury Festival under police escort because our school pictures have been plastered all over Sky News as missing children would be totally noncringeworthy, wouldn't it?"

Fleur stops in her tracks and goes quite, quite pale. That is *exactly* the sort of humiliating stunt that Paddy Swan would pull. No question about it.

"Oh, bum cracks to them all!" says Fleur. "Well, I'm not letting anything get in the way of this one. We'll *have* to get the go-ahead. Somehow. Won't we, girls?"

"Yeah. Somehow," I say rather weakly.

Claude says nothing. But then we all know that Gloria Cassiera is the candidate most likely to balls this up with a divine decline.

"Look, if you two can go and I can't, you'll just have to go without me," says Claude genuinely. "I'll be okay. I'll just watch the highlights on MTV and . . ."

"No way, Claudette!" says Fleur. "We all go together or not at all. That's the rule, isn't it?"

"Yep, together or not at all," I repeat. "That was the point of Astlebury, wasn't it? An LBD adventure?" I grab Claudette's tiny brown hand and squeeze it. "We're not leaving you, C. That's the law."

"Cheers, birds," says Claudette softly. A tiny little tear appears behind her spectacles, which she quickly bats away. "It's always me, isn't it?"

"Nah, Claude, we're all in the same boat here," corrects Fleur. "We've all got parents who think serial killers lurk behind every road corner. Paranoid androids, the lot of 'em."

This is all heavily ironic. I cast my mind back to that time we met Spike, standing in the marquee at Blackwell Live with his perfect teeth and beautiful blue eyes. There we were, trying so hard to act cool and mature that Spike must have totally forgotten that underneath the lip gloss and the itsy-bitsy thong underwear, we were actually only fourteen years old and still under the brutal regime of parental dictators. (Okay, that's slightly untrue. Claude and I acted cool with Spike; Fleur tried to nibble his shoulder at one point.)

"So what d'you reckon, Claude?" I say.

Claude mulls over the question a bit before speaking. "Hmmm . . . well, I can't help thinking there must be room for some sort of compromise here," she begins. "Now, bear with me, as you might not like what I'm saying here . . . but, I mean, we have got a spare ticket, haven't we?"

We certainly have. I don't know why Spike sent us four tickets. Maybe he just deals in even numbers. Or maybe he thought the "BDL" had another mystery member.

"Yeah, and we're selling that extra ticket," says Fleur. "Five hundred pounds! A hundred and sixty-six pounds each! With my cut I'm buying a leather jacket." Fleur begins counting off fantasy purchases on her fingers. "And I can get some new modeling shots done and . . ."

"Not so fast, Fleur, we might need to keep the ticket . . ."

"Why?" asks Fleur.

". . . and give it to someone else. Someone who can, er, escort us."

"Escort us?" says Fleur, almost spluttering out the offending word.

"Escort us?" I repeat. I don't like the sound of this.

"If we want to go, it might be our only option," continues Claude.

"You mean like a *grown-up*?" I say nervously.

"Well, some sort of, er, 'responsible' person, anyhow," says Claude.

At that moment, in my mind's eye, I'm visualizing Magda Ripperton, in a paisley cheesecloth caftan and sandals, letting wild and loose with free-form frugging, right in front of the Hexagon Main Stage area and a 120,000-strong cheering crowd. "That's Ronnie Ripperton's mother!" People are jeering and pointing at me. "That girl with the brown hair over there! She's here with her mum! Ha ha! What a dweeb!"

Gnngnngngn!!

"I feel a bit sick," I groan, standing up and pacing about the room, finally slumping on Fleur's wide window ledge, which looks over Disraeli Road.

"Er . . . your dad's dead into music, er, isn't he, Ronnie?" mentions Claude ever so casually. "And he can be, sort of, quite a decent laugh . . . er sometimes, can't he?"

I know her game. "Don't even think of it! What are you trying to do to me?" I shriek. "Stop it now! Not another word!"

Suddenly Fleur sits up straight on her bed, as if she's got the answer. I find this rather difficult to believe, but I'm up for a surprise.

"Right. I see what you're saying," says Fleur. "What we're looking for is . . . and this is strictly if we have to take someone with us . . . an individual who is responsible. Well, at least considered responsible by the powers that be, but also someone who can be trusted not to crucify the LBD with embarrassment in a public place and stay out of our faces when we're having a good time?"

"Yes," Claude and I both chorus. "Any ideas?"

"Errrrrr . . ." Fleur scrunches up her face, applying every single one of her brain cells to the equation. Claude and I wait with bated breath . . .

"No," Fleur says.

"Great," I sigh.

"Back to the drawing board," says Claudette glumly.

At that moment, we're provided welcome distraction by the familiar rumblings of a Swan family argument springing to life in the hallway outside Fleur's room. The Swans love nothing better than a good argument with each other. I'm surprised any of the doors in the house are still on their hinges. However, this time it sounds like Paddy is embroiled in a furious disagreement with only himself. This is pretty good going, even for him.

"How? How?! How?" Paddy is shouting. "Please tell me *how* you can get halfway round the bloody world on a rickshaw, dodging killer crocodiles and flash floods, but you still can't turn a light off when you walk out of a room! How?"

Silence.

"Oh, yes, of course, I know!" continues Paddy. "It's because it's my money paying the bills, isn't it? My money that I slave blood and sweat in the coal mines every day for."

"Isn't your dad an investment banker?" whispers Claude.

"Yes," affirms Fleur. "His office is down a mine shaft, apparently."

"Because it doesn't matter if it's Paddy paying the bills, does it? Yes, you can survive in the Nepalese Khumbu region on two rupees a day, can't you? But once you're under my roof, you're as spendthrift as your mother! Why don't we just all go out in the garden and burn my money! Burn it all! We could call it Paddy's Summer Money Barbecue!"

"He's really making some headway with his anger management course, isn't he?" I whisper to Fleur.

"He's the star pupil," says Fleur witheringly.

"Of course, who would care if I went bankrupt? You'd all soon find another poor cretin to sponge off of," continues Paddy. "I'm just a walking ATM to all of you. I should have a keypad fitted to my chest!"

The voice begins to feel louder and closer.

"And where's that other daughter of mine? Is she in or out?"

"She's in. Her bedroom light is on," snaps Daphne "Nepal" Swan, finally squeezing an angry word in.

"Pah. That means nothing! I mean, sure, her bedroom light's on. I can hear the jungle drums. But does that really mean anything? She probably went out hours ago. You're all the same!"

"Blah, blah, blah," says Fleur, yawning widely and miming a big mouth opening and closing with her right hand.

Finally, Daphne begins letting rip: "Oooooh, you make me sooo cross sometimes, you infuriating man!" she screams. "Listen to yourself. Going on and on about lightbulbs. You are so boring! And also totally wrong on every count. I'll have you know that I'm a very resourceful and sensible person . . ."

"Cuh, well . . . ," snortles Paddy.

". . . I'm still talking! Yes, where was I? That's it, I'm a very resourceful young, er, adult. And it's time you began treating me like that! It's not my fault if I occasionally forget things like light switches! I'm a free spirit! But I'll remind you that I managed to trek from Khari Khola right through to Gorak Shep without

74

your constant nagging, thank you very much, Dad, and I can do without it now!"

Slam, crash, thump. It sounds like all areas of the Swan household are involved in the battle.

"Oh, well, congratulations!" scoffs Paddy. "I'm over the moon about your Nepalese shindig! Meanwhile, back in the real world, I was having panic attacks imagining you leaving a curling iron plugged in, draining the Nepalese national power grid and me getting invoiced for the outbreak of civil war!"

I have to smirk at that bit, but Daphne is certainly taking this to heart. "Ooooooooh, *gnnngngnn!* Right, that's it! I'm leaving!" bellows Daphne, sounding almost choked. "I can't wait to get out of this house. And this time I'm going to go even farther away and stay away for even longer! In fact, *forever!* Just you wait and see!"

"Hoo-hoo! Don't get me excited!" guffaws Paddy. "What time does your banana boat leave? I'll help you with your rucksack!"

We don't call him Evil Paddy for nothing.

"Excellent," mutters Fleur, filing her nails. "If she's going for good, I'm definitely getting her room this time."

"Awww, Fleur!" mutters Claude. "She sounds dead upset."

"Ooh, you'll regret saying that when I'm gone," Daphne warns Paddy.

"No, I won't," he says. "I'm not in the slightest alarmed. The more I try to get rid of you bloody people, the more you come back! That brother of yours is the same! Oh, yes, he keeps *threatening* to leave but oh, no, from the stench of feet and cigarette smoke billowing from under that door, he's very much still in residence too. Oh, how I long for you all to leave me alone! How I dream of a quiet house where I can sit in peace without you bloody children!"

"You *will* regret being so mean to me! You huge pig!" Daphne rants. "I'm calling Mother at her Pilates workshop *right now* to tell her how you've chased me away. I'll tell her I'm going to live in a hostel for vagrants and work in a massage parlor until I can save up for my ticket to remotest Tibet!"

Long silence.

"Seems a bit extreme," mutters Paddy.

"I feel extreme!" shouts Daphne. "Stop telling me off like a little girl! I'm a twenty-year-old woman. I'm a responsible adult! Why can't you just admit it!"

"Well . . . hmmm . . . that's as may be," grunts Paddy.

"Go on, then, say it!" warbles Daphne.

Another long silence.

In Fleur's bedroom, all three sets of LBD eyes are fixed upon the bedroom door. This is better than *Eastenders*!

"Okay! Okay!" grumbles Paddy. "*You're a responsible young adult.* Now can I go, you annoying woman? I want to watch *Robot Wars*!"

As Paddy crashes down the stairs into the den, Claudette sits up on the bed with a start, wearing that bright-eyed, bushy-tailed look that so often scares the pants off me.

"Noooo!" says Fleur, catching Claude's drift immediately and springing to life.

"But this could be our only solution!" argues Claude, waving the final ticket at Fleur like a matador.

"Well, he did say she was *responsible*," I say.

"Nooooooo!" shrieks Fleur again. "Nooooooo!"

It was a crazy plan, but it might just work.

And just at that instant, something I can't really explain made me turn my head and look down upon Disraeli Road. Below, in the distance, my heart lurched as I spotted a familiar blond figure, skateboard under his arm, slowly walking away. Baggy jeans, red hoodie, shoulders slumped in a defeated manner. I'd know that silhouette anywhere, although somehow today he seemed different. The cocky swagger had all but gone.

thicker than water

Of course, Fleur kicked up a right fuss about the suggestion of inviting Daphne to Astlebury. She went totally ballistic, ranting that Daphne was a total dweeb (not really true: Daphne's pretty cool, really, she's into good music and is never short of a date) and an evil tyrant (also not true: she's one of the knit-your-own-yogurt hippie-dippie brigade). Fleur also screeched that Daphne was a "proper little Princess Tippytoes," "totally spoiled" and "always has to get her big schneck into everything." Claude and I had to try really hard not to smirk at this point because . . . oh, well, you know.

At one time, I thought having a big sister would be ace. Just like a best friend who lived with you all the time. And you could spend all your free time either gossiping about snogging or facedown in her vast makeup box or even braiding each other's hair. Plus you'd have double the supercool wardrobe because you could steal all her hottest clothes.

Yes, I was a real dweeb when I was younger. I got more real

after witnessing a row between Daphne and Fleur escalate into the sisters actually rolling around on the carpet, pulling each other's hair and screeching.

It was over a pair of tweezers worth fifty-nine pence.

"It was the principle of the matter," Fleur fumed as she was being grounded until just after 2012. "They were my tweezers!"

So anyway, suffice to say Fleur didn't want Daphne cramping her style when she was on a mission to marry Spike Saunders.

But over Sunday and Monday when the LBD told our parents the stupendous news about the free tickets, it became the final card up our sleeve. Because *of course* our folks were ecstatic about Spike Saunders sending us tickets. And *of course* they all knew what a totally fantabulous once-in-a-lifetime happening this was. *Of course* they didn't want to stop us having fun. No, no sirree. And *of course* Magda wanted me to "stop moping around over Prince Retard and enjoy being young." And of course, Gloria Cassiera wanted to reward Claude for those eight straight A's she got in her Year 10 exams. And extra specially, of course, Paddy wanted Fleur to stop stalking him around his own home asking him if she could go again and again like a stuck record.

But the bottom line was they just couldn't let us.

Because we were just too young to go alone.

"We *must* come clean about that final ticket and invite Daphne," Claude finally warned me and Fleur that Wednesday night. "Time's running out. We've only got one week left now."

Fleur fumed for a while, staring at her "Wall of Spike" poster montage, featuring several pictures of Spike Saunders's naked bum, tattooed intricately with the sun rising from his bum crack. Eventually she turned to us with a pained yet stoic tone: "Okay, let's just flipping do it then, shall we?"

Daphne and Paddy were summoned into LBD HQ, where we confessed exactly how many tickets Spike had given us. That wasn't fun: I've been telling a lot of lies recently, but it never gets any easier.

Of course, all hell immediately broke loose. Daphne went absolutely wild with excitement. She even offered to drive the LBD the 600 miles round-trip to Marmaduke Orchards, where the festival is held, in her silver Mini Cooper.

"That would be like a proper road trip! Woweeee!" I grinned.

"Oh my God, that would be sooooo great, Daphne!" hooted Claude.

Fleur said nothing.

"Er, excuse me, has someone thrown my invisibility cloak over me again?" shouted Paddy, looking more than a little weary. "Can anyone actually see me here?"

"Oh, sorry, Dad," said Daphne respectfully. "Of course, I know you've still got final say on this. I mean, you're the head of the house, after all."

"You total ass kisser," whispered Fleur.

"Oh, why don't you just shut your trap, knock knees," retorted Daphne.

"I'd rather have knock knees than a wonky eye," said Fleur, crossing her eyes cruelly.

"Shh, Fleur. Daphne's doing us a favor here!" shouted Claude.

"Oh, go on, take her side!" huffed Fleur, crossing her arms.

And at this point I was just about to get in with my tuppence worth, when I noticed that Paddy's eyes looked about ready to explode.

"*Enoooooooough!*" shouted Paddy, clutching his stubbly head. "*Enough bickering! You're all driving me insane!*"

Now we'd really blown it. Not only had we lied to Mr. Swan in a bid to go to Astlebury alone, but we'd then added insult to injury by squabbling like kids in front of him. Paddy was staring at the four of us with a look of utter bamboozlement, his eyes had narrowed and his mind seemed to be racing with thoughts.

"Right. I'm going to act swiftly on these new developments," he announced officiously, slamming the door to Fleur's bed-room as he left. Paddy did act swiftly. He vanished into his study, plundered his Rolodex and within that very hour tele-phoned Loz, Magda, and Gloria, inviting them to a meeting at the Swan house the following evening.

"Oh, this will really be a night to remember, believe me!" I heard Paddy ranting down the phone line as I tiptoed to the bathroom. "I'm really ready to let off some steam."

Back in Fleur's bedroom, the girls let out a groan when I told them.

You should never make Paddy Swan angry. You wouldn't like him when he's angry.

"Oi *bleugh*," grunts Joshua, stuffing his face with an enormous tortilla chip and mayo sandwich. "If you were a proper sister, you'd give those tickets to me."

"Oh, go and die, Joshua," says Fleur crossly as the LBD

80

slump miserably around the Swans' kitchen table, gathering our nerves to face Parent Inc., who are gathered in the den. "I'd rather drop them down the drain."

"Oh, well, that's charming," says Josh. "That's the last time I give you lot a lift anywhere."

"You don't give us lifts anywhere," says Fleur.

"Well, that's because you're all about ten and you don't go anywhere," says Joshua smugly.

Fleur scowls at Josh, clearly wanting to strangle him.

"And from what I gather from Paddy," Josh smirks, "you *especially* aren't going to Astlebury Festival!"

Josh picks bread out of his back teeth, examines it, then eats it.

Yuk. How can he be so vile and still have so many women hanging about him?

"Right, anyway, girlies, can't waste time gossiping," Josh says. "I'm off to Wazzle's house. We're building a laser. See you later, eh?"

As he reaches the door, he turns and grins. "Oh, and by the way, I won't be requiring those tickets anyway . . . kind of you to offer though."

"Why's that?" sighs Fleur.

" 'Cos I'm off to Amsterdam next weekend with the lads, remember? For Fordy's eighteenth birthday? We're taking him to a strip joint. It's gonna be a total riot!"

We all stare at him in varying stages of annoyance or disgust.

"Hey, but before I go," he smiles, "Ronnie, pull my finger, will you?"

Josh holds out his hand with the little pinkie stuck out.

"Why?" I ask.

"Just pull it," he says.

I pull the slightly nicotine-stained finger as Fleur looks on in total disbelief.

"Ronnie! Don't!" she squeals, but it's too late. *Paaaaaaaaaaaaaarp* goes the unmistakable sound of Joshua's bum letting rip. A tremendous unholy stench fills the air.

"*Gahhhhhh!* Jossssssssh! You're vile!" screams Fleur, running for the window.

"See ya!" says Josh, with a huge satisfied grin, exiting stage left.

"Ladies, we're ready for you now," announces Mr. Patrick Swan, sticking his head around the door. "Could you all make your way orderly into the interrogation chamber, er . . . pardon me, I mean, the den."

"We're on our way," says Fleur in defeated tones.

Paddy looks around the kitchen, wrinkling his nose. "I take it I've just missed my son?" he says, flapping his hand around to disperse the acrid bum fumes.

Fleur says nothing. She just scowls.

the crunch

"It was a farce, Patrick, a total farce," mutters my mother, perched on the Swans' pale leather sofa. "The police should never have been involved. What a waste of time!"

"Thank you, Magda! Yes, the whole fandango was a diabolical miscarriage of justice," Paddy fumes from his leather La-Z-Boy chair.

"*Everyone* at my golf club agrees with me too."

"Not *everyone,* darling," says Saskia Swan, clad in flawless cream silk trousers and an elegant cream cotton blouse. "The judge who cautioned you plays a round or two down at Greenford Drive? He certainly thought you were guilty."

Paddy's silvery-grayish crew cut seems to bristle with fury. "Pah! That mad old goat? Well, he clearly hasn't got teenage daughters, or he'd have sympathized with my plight! I should've got a medal, not a police caution!"

Poor Mr. Swan. He's still getting over catching Fleur's ex-boyfriend, Tarrick, climbing through her bedroom window at 3 A.M. last January.

Ouch! Fleur's little Romeo and Juliet fantasy hadn't included ear-shattering burglar alarms, swarms of police cars, all the neighbors out in their gardens in their pajamas and Paddy Swan being cautioned for threatening a fifteen-year-old boy with a golf club. He was in the *Local Daily Mercury* and everything.

POLICE TAKE DIM VIEW OF LOCAL VIGILANTE

As Paddy rants on and on, my father stares at him, trying to find noncommittal words that won't get him into trouble with anybody. Dad's probably feeling very much like I do when I'm summoned into the Swans' lounge with its cream carpet, fawn curtains and masses of sandy leather furniture and luxurious *objets d'art* scattered precariously—that is, scared to exhale in case he leaves a grubby smear somewhere. How do they live like this? Our house has got clutter everywhere. No wonder they try to keep Josh quarantined in his bedroom.

"Cuh. Britain today, eh?" Loz eventually remarks while Paddy rambles on, ignoring him.

"I mean, for crying out loud," splutters Paddy. "Me? Patrick Swan? Leaping around a community center with a dozen other stressed executives learning anger management!?"

Paddy shakes his rather purple face crossly. "Tell them, Saskia! I'm not an angry person, am I?"

"Of course you're not, darling," Saskia agrees serenely. Saskia's the kind of woman who can wear cream trousers like that all day long without getting a blob of marmalade down the front of them. In the far corner sits Gloria Cassiera, clad in one of her scary business outfits: smart navy suit and shiny black court shoes. Claude's mum is secretary to the best solicitor in town, so she always looks really smart. She's one of those people who really loves her job, y'know, really embraces the whole idea of loafing about, slurping tea and hiding from their accountant. "Isn't anyone eating the nibbles?" asks Saskia, pointing at the table of expensive-looking stuffed olives and vegetable tempura before her.

"I will in a moment," says Gloria. Gloria's keeping a serene silence over the whole Tarrick incident, although she knows the story better than all of us, having been the main peace negotiator in the days after the spat. Not only did she let Fleur sleep over at the Cassiera house while the dust settled, but she even swung by the Swans' house with a bottle of rum and homemade banana bread, somehow sweet talking Paddy out of putting Fleur up for adoption. Apparently Paddy became much more affable after several cocktails. Fleur was home in time for supper.

Over by the drinks cabinet, Daphne Swan is fixing Paddy a shaken-not-stirred martini in a fancy glass with a sliver of lemon peel.

"I thought he was a bloody burglar!" Paddy says again.

Claude and I step gingerly into the room, perching on the three dining room chairs that Paddy has arranged in the middle of the den.

Fleur flounces in after us, not acting in the least humble and coy like we'd expressly requested.

"A burglar? *Really,* Father?" Fleur announces. "You know, that's the first time I've heard that story. Ooh, please! Again, again!" she says, clapping her hands.

"Fleur, try not to rile Daddy," husks Saskia rather pointlessly.

"Button it, Fleur!" hushes Claude.

"Yeah, big mouth, shut your trap!" tuts Daphne.

"No, you shut up, Daphne duck eyes!" squeals Fleur.

Paddy stares momentarily at his warring daughters with an irate look. Then his face seems to soften. He looks almost happy . . . as if he's just envisioned himself in a quieter, idyllic place.

Weird.

"Let's get down to business, shall we?" says Paddy, putting down his drink. "And I'll chair this meeting, if there are no objections."

Paddy loosens his tie and looks to the parents. "Oh, and don't worry, I'll be keeping this as short as possible, as we're all busy people. I know the Rippertons have a pub to run . . . and Gloria, you have choir practice, don't you?"

"I'm singing the lead," says Gloria, looking at her watch with a little concern.

"Well, let's get this one nailed quickly then," says Paddy.

The LBD shuffle in our seats uncomfortably. This doesn't sound good.

"So, as we all know," begins Paddy, "our delightful daughters have come into possession of tickets for a two-day pop festival, taking place next Friday over three hundred miles away."

"I've heard about nothing else," says Magda, rolling her eyes.

"Amen to that," says Gloria with a firm gaze.

"Now, I don't know about you, but over the last few days I've formed some very strong opinions on this," says Paddy, beginning to wag his finger.

"Here we go," whispers Claude, so quietly only I hear.

"I'm on the edge of my seat," says Fleur crossly.

Everyone stares at Paddy, waiting for him to begin ranting.

"I believe," he says, "I believe that this could be a marvelous character-building opportunity for our daughters."

Errrr what?

"In fact, under controlled circumstances, it could be a valuable life lesson that these young women will always refer to in later years," Paddy enthuses, waving his hands.

The LBD look at one another in bewilderment. Are we hearing things?

"*However,* I also strongly believe," continues Paddy, flourishing his hands like a stewardess pointing out emergency doors, "that Daphne, my eldest daughter, should accompany the girls for the four-day trip."

Daphne bristles with pride. She begins waving her hands

too. "I've traveled a lot, you see," she smiles. "In fact, I've just got back from Nepal."

Fleur opens her mouth, then shuts it again quickly.

"That's right, Daphne's just got back from Nepal," says Paddy, nodding enthusiastically. "And she's proven herself to be a very, er, mature and responsible young woman."

Daphne's head is inflating by the second.

"I feel she'd be the ideal chaperone," continues Paddy. "With her at the helm my worries would be more than assuaged . . . So, in conclusion, I'm saying yes to the girls attending this festival."

What?

Either Paddy's even more evil twin, who seeks to destroy him, has finally shown up at Disraeli Road, or Paddy Swan is actually fighting in the LBD's corner. What the bejesus is going on?

The remaining parents all pause to mull over the news. Gloria Cassiera doesn't look exactly overjoyed.

"Well . . . *pgghh* . . . that's *your* opinion, Paddy," huffs my mother. "And what do you think, Saskia?"

Saskia Swan looks rather vacantly at my mother, then pauses as though it's the first real time she's thought about the question.

"Mmm . . . ," she begins. "Well, I suppose I'd be happier if Fleur and Daphne were together in Holland," Saskia pouts through cosmetically enhanced lips.

"It's *Joshua* who's going to Holland, darling," Paddy corrects her. "The girls want to go to Astlebury."

"Oh, right . . . well, it's not as if I'll be here anyway," says Saskia, patting her washboard stomach. "I'm at a yoga retreat on Friday and Saturday anyway. I've got to tone myself up for my trip to Antigua."

My mother stares crossly at Saskia, clearly resisting the urge to tell her that she's a rubbish mother who has already yoga-contorted herself into something that resembles a bag of bones, and that she should be concentrating a lot more on her wayward youngest daughter.

"Right," Mum finally says through gritted teeth. "So you're a yes, then, Saskia?"

Saskia looks around the room at her daughters and then at Paddy.

"Well, if they're all at peace, then so am I," she says in an eerily calm manner.

"And believe me, I will be *extremely* peaceful," mutters Paddy, beginning to rub his hands. Then he thinks better of it and clamps them down by his side.

My mother doesn't look too pleased at all. "Whoa! Hang on a minute here, Paddy!" she splutters. "I'm not so sure. I mean, even if Daphne chaperones the girls, they're still flipping fifteen years old. They're kids! There would still have to be some pretty stiff ground rules if Ronnie's going to be out of my sight for four days."

Mum turns to Dad. "Wouldn't there, Loz?"

"Er, yeah! Certainly, love, *ground rules,*" repeats Dad, then whispers, "like what, though?"

"Like the girls have to call home every single day," says Mum. "And they always stick together and never lose Daphne. And they don't talk to any weirdos. And no canoodling with boys . . ."

Claude, Fleur and I gaze at her angelically as if these social ills had never crossed our snow-white minds.

Mum pauses for breath, her brain whirring through a whole myriad of naughty stuff we could get up to.

"And no smoking!" she adds. "And certainly no drinking . . . and no going near anyone who even looks like they've taken any kind of drug, and by that I mean any sort of pill, herb, powder, fungus or any other drug invented nowadays that your dad and I haven't heard of yet."

"Ground rules would be compulsory, Magda," assures Paddy, sounding a lot more like his old self now. "In fact, I could draw up an official contract and the girls could sign it."

"I'll sign it!" beams Claude. Claude looooves contracts.

"I'm not signing any . . . ," begins Fleur as I poke her sharply in the ribs.

"We'll sign it!" Fleur and I both say.

My mother pauses for a second. She hadn't bargained on the LBD's total nonquibbling compliance.

"So, Mrs. Ripperton, if all this happened," begins Claude extra carefully, "in theory, you could say yes?"

"*Hmmmph*, well," says my mother, sitting back on the sofa and taking a deep breath, "I never thought I'd hear myself say that, but . . . okay, I suppose so, yes."

"Just don't make us eat these words, Ronnie," says Dad, winking at me.

Oh my God. I don't believe this. The Rippertons have caved in!

I emit what can only be described as a squeak.

"Yesssss!" hisses Fleur, leaping over and kissing Paddy smack on his stubbly head. "Thank you! You're the best dad in the whole world ever!"

I give her one of my looks.

We promised Claude it was one for all and all for one. Didn't we?

"Gloria?" says Paddy respectfully. "What about you?"

"Come on, Mum, let's have it," says Claude quietly.

Gloria Cassiera looks silently at the entire room. Everyone draws forward to hear. "Well, Claude," she begins, her posh-British tones smattered with a Ghanaian lilt, "when you told me Daphne was willing to escort you to the festival, I did reconsider the matter. Really. I've thought long and hard about it, but it doesn't change the facts: Astlebury is an adult environment."

Claude's face stiffens, ready for disappointment.

"Don't look at me so crossly, Claude," says Gloria firmly. "Look, this is a big deal for me. I don't want to stop you having a good time, but you're my responsibility. How would I feel if anything happened? I couldn't . . . couldn't live with that."

Claude stares at her mum, her eyes beginning to fill up.

"So anyway," continues Gloria, "I brought up the matter with my prayer group."

Claude rolls her eyes. She's always grumbling about her mum discussing household problems with that lot.

"I told them about the great exodus of young people coming together to listen to music," says Gloria, getting a little more animated. "We talked about the banging of drums and the all-night dancing, and we even talked about the devil and his clever ways of enticing young people . . . It was a really rewarding discussion, actually."

Gloria's manner of speech can be very intoxicating. However, Claude's clearly not in the mood for a sermon right now.

"Okay! Okay, Mother!" Claude cuts in with slightly exasperated tones. "And which Bible passage did you all decide was the answer to the moral dilemma *this* time?"

Gloria stares back at her daughter with a small twinkle in her eye. "Job," she says.

"Job?" I mouth at my dad.

"Haven't the foggiest," mouths back Loz, shrugging.

Claude pauses, then begins casting her mind back through her biblical knowledge. Her nostrils begin to flare.

"Ooooh, *gnnngn, Mother!*" she splutters. "If that's flipping Job twenty, verse eleven, 'Our bones are full of the sins of our youth' excuse again, I'm going to get really, really annoyed!"

This is definitely the most surly I have ever seen Claude be with Gloria in entire recorded LBD history.

"No, cupcake. Wrong verse, actually," protests Gloria. "We actually found a wealth of wisdom in Job thirty-eight, verse seven."

Claude, for once, is stumped. "Well, I don't know that one," she fumes.

" 'And music filled the courts of heaven'?" says Gloria, jogging her daughter's memory. " 'As heavenly beings praised our Lord and Creator'?"

Claude looks at her mum, and a small grin seems to cross her face.

" 'And when God created the world,' " continues Gloria, getting a little more flamboyant, " 'the morning stars sang together and all the angels shouted for joy'!"

Gloria finished her quotation, giving her daughter a small sheepish smile.

Claudette deciphers the code immediately, and a huge grin

sweeps over her face as she catapults across the room, throwing her arms around Gloria for a massive cuddle.

"Okay. What's happening now?" says Paddy, shaking his head.

"Oh, I'm sorry, Paddy," apologizes Gloria, spitting out mouthfuls of Claude's hair. "I've decided to say yes. I'm going to place my trust in the girls to be sensible and to stay out of trouble. Claude should go to Astlebury . . . I think there's certainly a place in her life for praising the Holy Father through the power of music and dance."

"Oh, hallelujah!" squeals Fleur, leaping up and pirouetting about the living room.

"Praise be," mutters Paddy, shaking his head.

"Thank you, God!" I babble, coming over all religious momentarily.

We've only gone and done it!

As all the parents and Daphne dissolve into a furious hoo-hah about rules and restrictionzzzzzz (snore), the LBD spill out onto Fleur's driveway, whooping and a-hollering and jumping up and down on the spot, chattering furiously.

"This is soooooo excellent, isn't it?!" I scream, so loudly that curtains all along Disraeli Road begin twitching.

Claude is dancing about with a rather shocked expression. "That . . . just really . . . happened, er, right?!" she says to me.

"Huh! I knew we'd convince them! I just knew it!" remarks Fleur, grinning mischievously, then taking her voice much quieter. "Ha ha! I mean, imagine us signing a contract to say we'll be good! *Pgghh*, have they never heard the old saying 'rules are there only to be broken'?"

Claude looks so shocked, I don't think she's really taking in what's been said.

"And as for that boring big sister of mine," Fleur whispers directly to me under her breath as Claude twirls around and around, giggling into the distance, "well, let's not worry about her, Ronnie. We'll lose her, no bother at all, won't we?"

ASTLEBURY BEHAVIORAL CONTRACT

SUBJECTS: Fleur Marina Swan,
Claudette Joy Cassiera,
Veronica Iris Ripperton

We, the undersigned, agree to adhere fully and
without deviation to the following specified rules.
This contract applies to the entire duration of
our time outside of normal parental supervision:

1. We agree to stay within proximity of Daphne
    Swan as much as feasibly possible.
2. We agree to call home once a day.
3. We agree not to talk to weirdos.
4. We agree not to indulge in any form of
    canoodling with the opposite sex.
5. We agree not to imbibe alcoholic beverages.
6. We agree not to even so much as go near
    anyone who looks as if they might be under the
    influence of illegal substances.
7. We agree not to bring the Swan, Ripperton, or
    Cassiera families under newspaper or television
    scrutiny because of any manner of irregular activity.

Signed   *Ronnie Ripperton*
Claudette Cassiera
~~Minnie Mouse~~ Ms. Fleur Swan xxx

Chapter 4

packing light

Of course, once the euphoric, so-psyched-I-could-spew stage subsided, I quickly began stage two: the nail-biting worry phase. I suppose I've a tendency to overthink certain situations, especially monumentally ginormous ones like this. My parents can never understand why I get so antsy about stuff like discos and parties. They say stuff like, "You're only happy when you've got something to worry about" and even, "You could find the winning lottery ticket and still have a face like a bulldog eating wasps."

But what do parents know, anyway? They have no grasp whatsoever how stressful being fifteen really is. I mean, for crying out loud, I'm on my way to a forty-eight-hour rock 'n' pop, living-in-a-field, partying-all-night LBD extravaganza . . . and I have to be prepared! It's an absolute minefield of problems. I mean, do I pack all my coolest clothes? Or will they all get stolen from my tent by marauding hooligans? And do I need my full makeup bag? (Executive decision: Yes. I look so hideous when I first wake up, I practically have to draw my face on with a variety of pencils.) And are there proper bathrooms or just yucky porta-toilets? And will the weather be rainy or sunny? Or rainy *and* sunny? It's Britain in August, it could do *anything.* And how is it possible to look cool in a rain suit if a flash flood begins? And should I re-dye my hair deep auburn before we set off, risking a repeat of events on the geography field trip when it leaked down my face during light rain, making me look like an ax attack? And why does every *practical* item of clothing I own make me resemble a frumpy troll en route to ensnare the Billy Goats Gruff? Sigh.

I've seen those paparazzi pictures of gorgeous supermodels and actresses hanging around backstage at pop festivals looking skinny and fabulous. They always wear stuff like skintight white Gucci dresses with Prada heels. How do they look so fabulous when they're camping!?

"Pah!" remarked my mother cattily as I pored over the "Backstage Bites" photo section of *JukeBox* magazine trying to glean some "festival chic" tips. "Because they get dressed in their Winnebagos and live on fresh air and Marlboro Lights the rest of the year."

"Oh, dear," I sighed.

"You're beautiful as you are, Ronnie," Mum said. "And don't you dare go changing into one of those vacant doe-eyed clothes racks or I'll have you adopted. *And I mean that.*"

I should be so lucky, I thought, *on both counts.*

But in times of confusion, such as last Monday night, when this cruel, confused world conjures up a plethora of questions and not a great deal of answers, when my troubles are weighing me down like a wet duffel coat, I always follow the same ritual. I mooch over to Flat 26, Lister House, to ask Claudette "Clipboard" Cassiera what she reckons.

Claude always knows the score.

"Well, Ron, this is what I'm taking," said Claudette, rustling in her Astlebury file, pulling out a list written neatly on crisp white paper. "And I took the liberty of photocopying it for you, 'cos I know how you're a bit, er . . ." Claude stopped herself.

"A bit what?!"

"A bit, er . . . right, never mind, here it is anyhow."

I would have pressed the little madam further. However, I was far too busy beholding Claude's wonderful, majestic, all-consuming list.

It went like this:

CLAUDETTE CASSIERA'S ASTLEBURY CHECKLIST

VERY IMPORTANT: Borrow rucksack from Mika (Approx. 5 kilos when empty. Remember to weigh full rucksack, as we may have to walk a long way from designated car park area to campsite.)

ABSO-FLIPPING-LUTELY DO NOT FORGET:

* 4 X Astlebury tickets
* Outdoors Venturer 4-man tent (important—check poles and water-proof roof are in bag)
* Sleeping bag
* Small inflatable pillow
* Camping air mattress
* Mini bike pump
* Camping mallet
* Flashlight
* Batteries (approx 5-hour life span)

* Emergency flashlight batteries (being in a dark tent would be poo)
* Tiny rucksack
* Chocolate (for sugar-level maintenance/or in case we need to assist festival-going diabetics)
* Museli bars (fiber to keep us "regular")
* Vitamin tablets (not sure about nutritional value of veggie burger)

* Nuts (or other high-protein food)
* Band-Aid (note—try to dissuade Fleur from bringing stiletto boots)
* Emergency Tampax
* Emergency pads
* Emergency Feminax period pain pills
* 5 fresh thongs—all colors
* 2 more emergency fresh thongs

* 5 fresh pairs of white mini socks
* 2 bras—1 black, 1 white
* Safety pins
* Sewing kit
* 3 pairs combat trousers (khaki/camouflage/navy blue)
* 4 T-shirts ("Sleep when I'm dead." Black tight-fitting "Spike Saunders on tour." Hot pink Gap crop top. White tight low cut.)
* 1 black bikini
* 1 sun hat
* 7 hair bands
* 1 hairbrush
* Factor 25 sunblock
* Sunglasses
* Reading glasses

* 2 large packets of all-purpose wet wipes
* Moisturizer
* Bug repellent spray
* Money (festival ATM might be far away and dangerous to use late at night)
* Notebook and pencil (just in case we need to give addresses to lush lads)
* Toothpaste / toothbrush
* Mints (in case of horse breath between tooth-brush stops)
* Headache tablets
* Hay fever tablets
* Toilet paper X 3
* Jersey
* Spare sweater

* Waterproof Jacket
* Small pack-away umbrella
* Nail clippers
* Disposable razor for legs
* Shave gel
* Shampoo /conditioner
* Deodorant
* Mini towel
* Emergency mobile phone battery
* Tweezers
* Earplugs
* Water bottle
* Print out directions to Astlebury—there and back—from MapFinder.com
* CDs for Daphne's car
* Flag

"Wow," I gasped. I hadn't thought of any of this stuff.

"Oh, I just chucked anything in, really," said Claude, trying to sound breezy.

"Yeah, so I see," I say, stifling a giggle. "I didn't realize Daphne was driving us there in a monster truck."

"*Hmpgh,*" spluttered Claude. "I think you'll find that the whole kit and caboodle weighs precisely twenty-one and a half kilograms. I could carry that by myself easily." she flexed her beautifully toned ebony right arm. "Well, actually, when I say twenty-one kilograms it might be more like twenty-two . . . but hey, who's counting?"

"Right," I smiled, folding the list and shoving it in my bag.

"Anyway, while we're on the subject, do we know if Fleur has even thought about packing yet?" Claude asked, rolling her eyes and placing one hand on her hip. "Or are we going to end up doing that for her?"

"Oooh . . . dunno," I chuckled.

" 'Cos that would be classic Miss Swan behavior," continued Claude, straightening her bunches in the mirror. "I mean, I love her and all that, but at the best of times she's as much flipping use as a one-legged man at a bum-kicking party, isn't she?"

I tried to remain neutral on the matter, but sometimes Claude makes me laugh so much when she takes the mickey out of Fleur, I almost pee my pants.

Out of sheer nosiness, I left Claude's and wandered up high street, past the Fantastic Voyage and over to Disraeli Road to see how Fleur's Astlebury countdown was really shaping. Happily, the platinum-haired diva was in residence, sprawled out in a star-shaped position upon her king-sized divan, plastered in avocado face mask, downloading a new ring tone onto her mobile while leafing through *Vogue*.

For all Claude says, Fleur sure can multitask.

"It's the Kings of Kong! Listen!" Fleur said, passing me the flashy handset, which was emitting polyphonic screeches not dissimilar to a fire in a petting zoo. "Only two quid a minute to download too! The numbers are in the back of *Seventeen* magazine."

"Bargain," I said, passing Claudette's list over to Fleur for a quick gander. Fleur gave it a cursory look before promptly rolling about on her bed, kicking her legs in the air, laughing.

"Eh? What? Where is Field Marshal Cassiera taking us?" scoffed Fleur. "Are we fighting our way down the Congo or something? She's bonkers, that woman. Hello! Paging scary organization woman!"

"Mmm, well, she likes to be on top of things," I said tactfully, trying not to chuckle.

"Cuh, she won't need half this stuff," said Fleur, chucking me her own Astlebury list, scrawled on the back of an old envelope. It made interesting reading:

Astlebury Stuff I Need

*Mirror

*Emery board/ cuticle stick

*Azure Dream nail polish

*Cuticle softener

* Nail varnish remover

*Leave-in hair conditioner

*Supermodel Eau de Parfum

*Nail-strengthening vitamin pills

*Cleansing wipes with vitamin E

* Sensitive-skin toner

*2 pairs of earrings (1 dangly and 1 hooped)

*Underarm wax strips

*Lemon juice hair-lightening spray

*Ultrarich moisturizer

*Lip gloss with gold tint

*Cerise sun visor

*Huge sun shades

*Smaller tinted sunglasses

*Denim mini hot pants

*Cut-off combat pants

*Black mini kilt

*Black halter neck

* Silver bikini
* Four crop tops (pale pink, cool turquoise, lemon and black)
* Small muslin cardigan
* Helena's Boudoir bra and thong set X 3

* Stiletto boots
* Black stack-heeled sandals
* Hair ribbons
* Mobile phone
* Whistle
* Angels' wings
* Water pistol

* Sparkly deeley-boppers
* Klaxon horn

"No sleeping bag, Fleur?" I asked, scanning the list again.

"Oooh, er, yeah, might be useful," Fleur said, chucking me a pen, then picking up *Vogue* again. "Write it down for me, will you?"

Oh, dear.

～～～～～

eleventh hour

So here I am, it's Thursday night and I'm in my thoroughly ransacked boudoir, counting down the nine remaining hours till Daphne and the girls collect me. Amelia Annanova and the Dropouts are blaring a succession of angst-ridden tracks out of my stereo system (Amelia totally rrrrrocks, by the way) as I'm stuffing my rucksack nervously with bras, mascara and sunscreen.

I pull open the top drawer of my dressing table, searching for my favorite hot pink thong, only to let out a deep sigh at what I find hidden within.

There, underneath my old 32AA starter bras, lies a framed picture of Jimi and me, the one I hid from myself after Blackwell Disco.

Sometimes I have to play games with myself to get through crappy times.

This photograph was taken late last August when the LBD, Aaron, Naz and Jimi hung out down by the banks of the River Caldwell till long after dusk.

Sigh.

Jimi has his top off. His face is sun burnished from a summer spent skating, and he's wearing a navy trucker's cap. I'm crouching under his arm, wearing his outsized checkered Quiksilver shirt. I borrowed it after the boys decided it would be sooooo hilarious to chuck me in the water.

My eyes look really alive.

We both look really happy.

Better remember a spare sweater, I think. *There's nothing worse than waking up cold in a tent. I'll take the big blue one, it goes with my jeans. Sneakers? Hair clips? Where are my sunglasses? Got to keep myself busy.*

When it got totally dark, we recamped en masse at the Red Recreational Park behind Sainsburys. Fleur was flirting with Aaron. (She didn't really like him, Fleur just does that sort of thing.) Claude was holding court doing daft impressions of Mr. McGraw, making everyone howl. I was sitting on Jimi's knee on the old vandalized bench. He kept kissing the back of my head. That was a brilliant day.

I slam shut the drawer on the dresser, hiding the evidence of my sort of, nearly almost, ex-boyfriend. It's making me feel sick.

I slump down on the bed, wrapping my arms around my giant teddy. Not a gift from Jimi, I hasten to add. Dad just thinks it's hilarious to buy his little girl big tacky gifts on Valentine's Day.

I stare at my mobile phone, feeling rather agitated all of a sudden.

Uggggggh! This stupid, messed-up situation is all your fault, Jimi Steele!

Not mine.

Yours!

And yes, okay, maybe I should have called you back by now and discussed our problems, and yes, it's a bit rubbish of me going off to Astlebury without saying good-bye, but the LBD are right, Jimi, you do need to be taught a lesson. I mean, whooopity-do, last summer may have been the most wonderful time of my life. I'd managed to ensnare you, *yes, beautiful, gorgeous you* as my real live boyfriend, and unbelievably you were utterly besotted with me . . . but by late winter it had all started to go a bit . . . well, *weird.* Hadn't it?

First, I started noticing your two very different faces; on one hand the "mushy-slushy can't get enough of you" side, which made me feel like the luckiest bird at Blackwell . . .

. . . and then on the other, that annoying "Yeah, see you around whenever" side that you put on whenever your mates were within earshot.

Oooooh, that really got my goat.

Just because neither Naz nor Aaron can stay with one girl longer than a party! Has it occurred to you, Jimi, that your friends are shallow losers? And there was tons of other stuff too. Like that time I wasn't allowed to go to Suzette Law's eighteenth birthday party 'cos I had a 10 P.M. curfew so you went with the lads anyhow and were spotted dancing with Suzette.

Okay, I know it was her birthday and you were just being friendly, but I was absolutely livid.

And I was annoyed when you canceled dates at the last minute. And you used to get narky when you wanted to be "spontaneous" and take me out when I'd prearranged slumber parties and movie nights with the LBD. And okay, the fact that Fleur began to hate your guts didn't help. I could never choose between you both. *Gnnnnnnngn.*

So, all told, it's more than a pain in the ass that I'm completely, madly in love with you.

Especially as you don't feel the same way.

"All set?" says Mum, poking her head, without knocking, around my bedroom door, disturbing me from my woes.

"Oooooooh, Mum! Why does nobody ever knock?!" I snap. "I could have been naked or anything!"

Mum doesn't even turn a hair at my tantrum. "Oh, dang! Because seeing your bare ass would be such a novelty for me, wouldn't it?" Mum says dryly. "Jeez, until you were four we couldn't keep clothes on you. You were always tearing about in the nude."

"Mother, I thought we saved anecdotes like that for when my friends were in?" I mutter.

"Oooh, I've got far bleaker ones than that," smiles Mum, looking around my room. "So . . . you're still going then? Not changed your mind and staying home with your old, decrepit mum who loves you?"

Mum says this jokingly, but I know she's sort of not. She's really edgy about this whole trip.

"Nah, sorry, Mum." I smile.

Suddenly it hits me that I should forget about all of this Jimi stuff.

There's a whole new chapter of LBD history waiting to be written tomorrow. That's more than a bit neat.

"I'll give you a shout at seven A.M. then, okay?" says Mum. "Gotta go and sort the cash registers out now while Seth's asleep. Enjoy your last night in a proper bed, cupcake."

"Night, Mum."

I prop my rucksack against the wall, then change into my pink cotton pajamas. Slipping under the duvet, I reach across and press "repeat play" on my Amelia Annanova CD. The first rather feisty song, "Escape," cranks up as I examine the CD box where Amelia sits smoldering on the back of a Harley-Davidson, wearing a skintight white vest and indigo snakeskin trousers. Her long brown locks are ironed straight with blunt-cut ends dyed gold, a bright red streak falls down the right-hand side of her face, and her deep green eyes are breathtakingly beautiful.

"Sometimes you gotta . . . You really gotta be on your own
Sometimes you don't need a man buggin' you on the phone!
I'm gonna run this kingdom on my own!
Get out my face, boy, 'cos I'm fine alone."

The packing has exhausted me. Quickly I'm drifting into a peaceful state. And just as I'm nearing the threshold of the Land of Nod, my phone beeps loudly on my bedside table. A text message:

29 JULY 23:47
FROM: CLAUDE
SO EXCITED NEARLY SPEWING.

I'm just about to reply when I notice that the memory on my phone is almost full and needs texts erased. I go into the in-box, scanning the list of previous texts, lingering sadly on one from almost two weeks ago.

13 JULY 18.06
FROM: JIMI
MURRRRRRRRRRR!

I glare at the message for ages, really, really wanting with every fiber of my being to type back:

MURRRRRRRRRRRR! MURRRRRRRRRRRRRR!

However, I don't.
I switch off my bedside lamp. And after what seems like an eternity, I fall asleep.

hit the road, (jack)

If the incessant honking of Daphne's car horn hadn't dragged me to my window, then Fleur and Claude giggling and squabbling as they rearrange rucksacks in the jam-packed, newly

106

waxed, silver Mini Cooper certainly would have. Daphne's fabulous car, a present from Paddy and Saskia for her eighteenth birthday, is parked up in the Fantastic Voyage's delivery area.

"Claude, dah-link? You've forgotten the emergency anvil!" shouts Fleur, clad in a saucy black halter neck and denim mini shorts. "And what about the kitchen sink? Were they not on your list?"

"Shut it, Swan," Claude says primly. "There won't be all this lip service when you're begging to borrow my stuff."

I open my bedroom window and yell down from the first floor. "Errrr . . . am I going on the roof? It looks a bit cozy down there."

"Hey, Ronnnnnnnie!" shouts Daphne, looking extremely pretty in army combats and faded antique silk shirt. "Hurry up, I need somebody sane to talk to!"

"I'm in the front, though!" butts in Fleur. "I've got the longest legs!"

"*No, Fleur,* Claudette is sitting in the front," Daphne argues. "She's good at map reading."

"Precisely," beams Claude. "I was top of my pack in Brownies. Anyway, Fleur, you can sit in the trunk with the other cumbersome objects."

"Ha, and indeed, ha," groans Fleur.

I lug my fourteen-cubic-ton (or so it feels) rucksack downstairs. Loz and Magda follow me through the back doors to bid me adieu.

"My little girl! Off by herself for the first time," rasps Mum, pretending to sniffle. "I can't bear to watch! Just go! Go quickly!"

"Hey, look after yourself, ladies," Dad says sagely through the car window as I cram myself in beside Big Bird Swan and her endless miles of thighs. "And remember those rules we all agreed on, eh?" Dad says, tapping the side of his head. "Keep them up there, will you?"

"Of course we will," chorus Daphne and Claude.

"You can count on us, Mr. Ripperton!" winks Fleur.

Daphne zaps the switch on the electric windows and we begin negotiating the Mini down the narrow cobbled back lane. The LBD are waving and grinning like mad. I almost feel tearful. We're off! I can't believe this is actually happening, I've imagined this so many times before. My heart is really thumping! Then suddenly, before we've even reached the corner to the main road, a male figure seems to appear from nowhere, literally chucking himself in front of the car, thrusting his hands on the hood as if to stop it.

We all jump and scream.

"Stop!" shouts Claude.

"Ronnnnnnnie!" shouts an agitated voice. "Sttttttttop, Ronnnnie!"

"Oh, no," groans Claude, spying who it is immediately.

"Uggggggghggh, *this guy again*?" announces Fleur, turning up her nose. "Just drive over him, Daphne!"

Instead, Daphne pulls up the emergency brake.

"Oh my God! Is that my Jimi?!" I shout, grabbing frantically for the window buttons. "Jimi, what are you doing here!?"

"Aside from ruining our day?" grumbles Fleur.

Jimi gazes at Fleur, but doesn't retaliate. He looks about ten pounds thinner than usual, sort of more little-boyish. Tired. Bess, his prized skateboard, is sitting in the gutter looking similarly disheveled.

"Where are you going!?" he says.

"Away," I say. "We're off to Astlebury Festival."

"What!?" he says. "How?! When did all this happen?"

"It's a long story," I say.

"Er, but . . . but." Jimi looks dumbfounded. "You . . . you can't go! You've got to stay. Stay and talk to me, Ronnie!"

"Oooooh, I've heard it all now!" butts in another familiar voice. Oh, no, it's only my mother, who's spotted the commotion and decided to wade in.

"Look, what do you want exactly?" Mum shouts at Jimi.

I look at Jimi and then Mum quite hopelessly, not knowing quite what to do.

"I'm trying to tell your daughter, Mrs. Ripperton, that . . . that she has to stay here and sort out whether she's my girlfriend anymore!" Jimi garbles, sounding totally exasperated.

"Ronnie doesn't *have* to do anything! She's her own free agent now!" yells back my mother.

God, this is soooooo embarrassing.

"And she's off now to have the time of her life, hundreds of miles away, without you driving her crazy with your stupid antics!"

That sounds kind of cool, actually.

"Exactly!" Fleur says, putting her arm around my shoulder, shouting ahead to Daphne, "Drive on, driver!"

"Come on, let's get going before we have to pitch the tent in the dark?" says Claude tactfully. "We'll see you sometime, Jimi, eh?"

"Bye," I mouth, feeling totally choked.

Daphne puts her foot down and we turn into high street, picking up some speed. Claude unfolds her map, slamming Amelia Annanova into the CD player to break the awful silence. In the backseat, I wipe away a tiny tear, then crane my neck to grab a final glimpse of the Fantastic Voyage. Very quickly Mum and Jimi have become such small dots on the horizon, I've no idea whether she's let him out of that headlock.

Famous people Part too

"Oh my Gaaaaaawd, I can't believe this," gossips Fleur, avidly reading her *Red Hot Celebs* magazine. "Amelia and Giovanni are actually flying into Astlebury on Saturday night from their yacht harbored in Salinas Beach in Ibiza! They're on their European vacation! And they've got a helicopter pad on their yacht! And a recording studio so they can lay down tracks as they travel! How megarich must they be!?"

Outside the car, miles and miles of beautiful English countryside hurtles past as Fleur reads on. "Ooh, and the Kings of Kong have had special Astlebury stage outfits made by Hazel Valenski, the prestigious New York designer! Huh! Everyone listen to this!

"*'Apparently, Curtis, lead singer with Detroit rock gods the Kings, has been spotted enjoying intimate dinners with A-list fashion stylist Hazel in the Tribeca area of Manhattan, kindling further rumors of a split with longtime companion Canadian supermodel Tabitha Lovelace.'*

"He's soooooo bonkers, splitting up with Tabitha!" says

Fleur, as if they're all old friends. "She is absolutely the most beautiful thing in the entire world. She's so tall and blonde!"

Fleur loooooves *Red Hot Celebs.* In fact she loves it so much, she's actually barred herself from reading it on the bus after going straight past her stop once without realizing it and ending up in an adjacent county. Magazines like these just seem to transport Fleur to another cosmiverse, one that pleases her more greatly than her own. Saying that, after that run-in with Jimi, I could do with some escapism too.

"Fleur, who are all of these people?" giggles Daphne, carefully changing lanes. "Who's Giovanni?"

Fleur sighs as if this is the most idiotic question in the world history of speaking. "*Giovanni Baston*, Daphne dearest, is Amelia Annanova's Italian actor boyfriend. They've been together, like, forever, although apparently she wants to get married but he's still not sure. They argue and split up a lot."

"How do you know that?" laughs Daphne, shaking her head.

"She just knows," chortles Claudette. "Believe me."

"Now, Curtis Leith is lead singer in the Kings of Kong," continues Fleur.

"He's totally hot, albeit obviously insane if he's letting that Hazel Valenski woman get her schneck in at him."

"Hang on," I blurt out. "Wasn't Hazel Valenski snogging Pharrell Mars at the MTV Awards last month? She's a fast mover, isn't she?"

"See, Daphne?" laughs Fleur. "Ronnie Ripperton knows the score!"

Damn, busted.

I always profess I'm not that bothered about celebrities . . . but deep down I really am. Saying that, I'm different from Fleur. It's not the glammy pics of people "Beyond the Velvet Rope" that I love . . . ooh, no, I crave those sneaky paparazzi shots of stars buying their washing detergent or wearing baggy sweatpants and walking their dogs. I find them totally fascinating. It makes me realize that famous folk are really just as boring as me. Or that I'm just as exciting as them. One of the two.

"Anything about Spike Saunders this week?" asks Claude, handing around a bag of candies.

"Mmm, don't think so," says Fleur, examining her hand. "Hang on, these are licorice! You know I don't like the licorice ones!"

Claude tuts, then begins picking Fleur's favorite, blackcurrant candies, out of the bag for Miss Pickyknickers in the rear seat.

"Ooh, I tell a lie," Fleur corrects herself. "Apparently Spike's bought a new hot tub with a twenty-four-karat-gold faucet and a turbo-bubble button."

"Ha ha! Why are you all so interested in this stuff?" hoots Daphne.

"Why *aren't* you?" retorts Fleur. "You're totally weird!"

"I'm not weird!" argues Daphne. "I mean, is it so weird that I find my normal everyday *real life* friends much more interesting than complete strangers I only see on MTV?"

Fleur yawns dramatically behind her big sister's head.

"You know, when I was in Nepal," Daphne continues, "we were totally cut off from the whole media celebrity thing. And you know what? The local inhabitants were so much more spiritually happy within themselves as human beings and . . ."

"I've heard this one before," Fleur says sarcastically, nudging me. "It's grrrreat."

Daphne stops talking abruptly.

"*I'm* listening to you, Daphne," Claude tells her, not wanting the LBD kicked out 200 miles from Astlebury on the hard shoulder of the road.

"I just find it odd," continues Daphne to Claude, "that people are obsessed with people they'll never meet, but bored by the world underneath their noses!"

"Ahhh, well, that's where you're soooo wrong, Daphne," butts in Fleur. "Because all of these people will be at Astlebury! So we will be meeting them! That's why I need to bone up on *Red Hot Celebs* magazine. Cuh! Everyone knows how uncool it is to talk to celebs about their latest album or film!"

"Mmm, Fleur, dear?" Daphne patronizes back. "Don't you realize that the beautiful people will all be hiding away in their little VIP enclosure? We won't be seeing them unless we hang about the Main Stage with binoculars with the rest of the hundred and twenty thousand fans!"

Daphne gives a smug little smile. Fleur flares her nostrils.

"Not that it bothers me anyway," Daphne continues. "I'm only coming for the Healing Fields and the Ethnic Drumming Zone."

"Good," replies Fleur dryly. "Well, I hope you'll feel healed of the need to cramp my style for the entire bloody weekend."

"Believe me," says Daphne under her breath, "the feeling is entirely mutual."

Claude turns to pass me another candy, arching an eyebrow in a "Did you hear that?!" sort of way.

Daphne's mobile phone bleeps, signaling a text message. She picks it up and quickly glances at the message, giving a small grin before changing tack a little.

"Anyway, you know what really riles me about those stupid magazines?" Daphne lets out a little snort. "Those ridiculous celebrity beauty sections! 'Give up dairy products and you can marry a rock star too!' and 'Drink six liters of water a day and get a body like a Brazilian lingerie model!' It's all total rubbish! Who believes this pig swill?!"

In the backseat, Fleur, ignorant of her sister's ranting, is devouring a "stars looking fat in their bikinis!" special pull-out section, slurping her way through two liters of Evian water.

"Errrr . . . how far have we gone now?" Fleur asks, shuffling uncomfortably.

"Ninety-eight miles," says Daphne, examining the mile counter.

"Errrrrrr . . . any chance of a bathroom stop?"

karma

This wee stop suited me fine.

No, not because, like Fleur, my back teeth were floating, but because I was hoping for a text message too. I wanted to check my phone, but the LBD seemed so convinced that I was rock solid about teaching Jimi a lesson, I wasn't going to ruin my reputation by openly pining for his phone call. However, as Fleur and Claude caused mayhem in the Sunny Vale Heath M6 Service

Station (Fleur faffing about getting swanky business cards printed, Claude indulging her clandestine pinball addiction), I realized something quite alarming:

I'd forgotten my phone. Ugggggggghhhhh!

It wasn't in my handbag. Or in my rucksack. Or in any of my jacket pockets. In fact I could almost swear I'd left it on my bedside table. Durrrrrrbrain! Suddenly I felt exceedingly cold and alone. Ronnie Ripperton, away from home and without her mobile phone! I felt like I was on my way to a handstand competition without my underpants on.

"Ooh, never mind, Ronnie," said Fleur when I finally blurted out my trauma thirty miles or so out of the rest stop. "Time you got a new one anyway. Your old one's, like, totally sad. Hey! You could even get one with a camera, like mine!"

Fleur flourishes her silver phone at me, which is displaying a picture of a hairy lad she was chatting up twenty minutes ago in the café at the rest stop. He looks slightly bemused, shoveling a burger into his stubbly face.

"There was soooooo much talent in that service station, wasn't there, Claude?!" giggles Fleur. "And they were all going to Astlebury! Did you see those hotties in the yellow van with all the graffiti on the side who were just pulling in as we were leaving?"

"Lads? Yellow van?" mutters Claudette, pretending to examine the map. "Never noticed them."

"But I feel guilty about the phone," I warble. "That was Rule Two: I had to ring my mum every day, didn't I? I've been away two hours and I've broken a rule already!"

"Hey, I've been talking to a weirdo, if that makes you feel

better," offers Fleur, showing me the picture again. "That contravenes Subsection Three."

"You can use my phone, Ronnie," laughs Claude. "Stop worrying about stuff!"

"Ooh, let's ring *Red Hot Celebs* magazine! 'Ronnie Ripperton in Unnecessary Worry Shocker!' " giggles Fleur.

"Button it, Fleur," says Claude. "Ronnie can't help it."

"Errrr . . . Does anyone else hear something weird?" Daphne butts in, turning down "Too Much Love" on the Kings of Kong CD.

"Only Ronnie moaning," laughs Fleur. "That's hardly weird."

"Shh," shushes Claude.

We drive along in silence for about half a mile. Daphne looks quite anxious.

"Yep, I can hear that, Daphne," says Claude edgily. "Something sounds a bit, well, *clunky.*"

"And the steering's gone all shaky too," gasps Daphne, gripping onto the wheel and frowning.

"What's that mean?!" I ask, getting worried all over again. There's a definite grinding sound coming from the right side of the Mini Cooper.

"Well, something's certainly wrong," says Daphne, her lip wobbling slightly. "But I don't know what."

"Daphne, did you not have this car serviced last week?" Fleur asks unhelpfully.

"Yes, Fleur," snaps Daphne.

"Look, let's not argue," suggests Claude. "Should we stop and see if we can suss out what's wrong?"

"As soon as we can. This is getting really tough to drive

now," says Daphne, slowing her speed as juggernauts scream past us at 80 mph. "Everyone keep an eye out for a good place."

"Sounds like a flat tire to me," remarks Fleur, but everyone ignores her.

A motorbike flies past, the rider jabbing his horn and waving at us furiously.

My heart's in my mouth now. As Daphne struggles to keep the Mini in one traffic lane, a bus passes by, with the driver beeping its horn and pointing at us to get off the road. Oh my God, is this what it feels like to die?

Fleur reaches over and grabs my hand tightly.

"There!" points Claude. "Turn now!"

Daphne turns left, wrestling the poor car, extremely shakily, to a resting place.

We all sit quietly, breathing deeply, before piling outside to gather bleakly around the Mini's hood. Umpteen cars and vans scream past, people craning their necks at us damsels in distress. I feel like crying, but I'm not going to be first.

"See, told you so," says Fleur, pointing at the offending right front wheel.

"It's a flat tire."

"Oh, no!" sniffles Daphne. "Oh, no, no, no! I don't believe it! This is total bad karma! I knew I shouldn't have begun eating meat again!"

Claude steps up and puts an arm around Daphne. "Er, Daphne, mmm . . . surely it's not that bad," she says gingerly. "Could we not, er, call someone?"

Daphne stares at the LBD, thinking deeply, then begins to root about in her patchwork bag for her phone. "Okay," she says, biting her lip, looking at Fleur. "I'm going to have to phone the only person I can think of."

"Oh, hang on a minute, no, you don't," explodes Fleur, catching her drift. "We are not ringing Dad! No way! We'll never hear the end of it from that pompous, grinning goon! Are you berserk, Daphne? He'd love to hear us begging for help!"

"I'd rather beg for help, Fleur, and be en route to Astlebury than spend the weekend sitting on the side of the road!" argues Daphne.

Right at that moment a vehicle speeds by at about 97 mph, honking its horn joyously. We all look up, praying for a passing Good Samaritan; instead we catch a flash of green Land Rover, the sun bouncing off its gleaming metallic rhino repellent. Inside the vehicle, Abigail, Panama Goodyear's brain-dead sidekick, sits in the front passenger seat smirking while Derren and Leeza in the backseats wave and whoop. In the front seat, their vile leader Panama tries to keep one snooty eye on the road as she savors the LBD's misery.

I can't see Zane. Here's hoping they stuck him on the roof rack and his orange head was decapitated by an oak tree.

"Ha ha! No luck! Better get hitchhiking!" shouts Abigail, giving us a saucy thumbs-up.

In a flash they're gone, hurtling toward Astlebury without a care in the world. We all stand staring silently at the broken-down Mini.

"Oh, look, Fleur, let's just ring Paddy, shall we? It's our best option," I say nervously, suddenly feeling like we're just four very silly girls absolutely out of their depths who need a grown-up to hold our hands. I'm actually slightly shocked that Panama would just drive past us. I mean, she's a bitch, fair enough, but we're really in trouble here. We wouldn't have done that to her.

"Oh, bum cracks to calling Paddy," shouts Fleur at the now long-gone Land Rover as she walks over and peers at the saggy front wheel. "And bum cracks to them! I'll change the tire."

We all stare at Fleur with our mouths agog, almost as if she'd said, "Don't worry, girls, I'll just spin us all a new golden car from straw!"

"What?" splutters Claude.

"I'll change the tire," Fleur says again matter-of-factly. "I've done it before. It's not flipping rocket science."

"Errrr . . . I'm not sure, Fleur," I say.

"Oh, well, that's just wonderful," says Fleur sniffily. "Is that because you think I'm a dizzy blonde who can't possibly do it?"

"No, it's just . . . ," Daphne butts in, but Fleur's got the bit between her teeth now.

"Just what, precisely?" she snaps. "Just that I've changed tires with Dad twice before when we've been on road trips together? Just that Dad made me pay flipping attention because, in his words, he couldn't bear having three useless women in his family who can't change a tire?!"

Daphne blushes and looks away.

"Or just that I'll have to batter you all to a bloody pulp with my Louis Vuitton vanity case if I miss this ruddy festival?!"

"Well, when you put it like that," mutters Claudette.

"Right. Daphne," snaps Fleur, clapping her hands, "please tell me you've got a jack, a wrench and a spare tire?"

"Obviously," says Daphne huffily.

"Good, well, let's roll then, girls," Fleur says. "Claude, you can give me a hand with the heavy stuff, 'cos you've got the biggest muscles."

Fleur holds out one dainty sugar-pink-tipped hand. "And besides, I've just had these false nails stuck on and they were *très* kar-ching. I'll be devastated if I break one."

Claude and I stare at each other apprehensively.

Fleur ignores us, snatching the car keys from Daphne's hand and opening the trunk. Then she turns to us, getting quite exasperated.

"Oh, c'mon, you wet farts! We wanted an adventure, didn't we?" she scoffs. "Right. Daphne, stop being rubbish and stick the car into gear with the handbrake on, *s'il te plait?* Claude, take this wrench and help me get this hubcap thingie off."

"What do you want me to do?" I say, feeling quite surreal.

"You hold this jack. I'll tell you where and when to stick it in," Fleur tells me, winking.

"Hey, we're just like a proper Formula One team!" smiles Claude.

"We're a lot hotter than your typical pit stop crew," says Fleur, taking a pink scrunchie off her wrist and thrusting her blonde locks on top of her head in a pineapple style.

"Right, Claude, first we're going to loosen these wheel nut thingies, but don't go postal and take them right off. Then once the jack's in, you'll be in charge of pumping it up."

"Okay," says Claude.

"I'm a bit scared," I say. My lip feels a bit wobbly.

"Don't be daft, Ronnie. It's all going to be coolio," smiles Fleur. "Anyway, what's the point of being dangerous bambinos if we never do anything dangerous?!"

Daphne is staring at the LBD in utter disbelief at what she's allowing. This Mini is her pride and joy.

"Now, important, girls, everyone keep your schnecks well out when we're jacking the Mini up, as we don't wanna get any bits of us under the car. No one get squished, right? That's totally the opposite of what we're trying to achieve."

"No problem," says Claude, beginning to loosen the nuts.

It sounds so weird hearing Fleur taking charge. I can't help but admire her, even if she does make an unlikely mechanic in minuscule hot pants and a sequined disco top.

"Ronnie, you're on!" shouts Fleur. As Claude finishes the last silver nut, I maneuver the heavy, clumsy jack into position and screw it into place securely.

Fleur pauses for a second, staring at my handiwork, furrowing her brow. "Right, Claude, that's gotta be right. Start jacking!" shouts Fleur, Claude begins to pump the lever, using her toned biceps. At first nothing happens, but then something miraculous occurs.

"Ooh my God, look! It's rising! It's rising!" squeals Fleur, sounding much more like herself as just over a ton of metal and engine begins to ascend an inch at a time.

"I don't believe it!" says Daphne.

"Oh my God, we're doing it!" I shout, putting my hand to my mouth in surprise.

"This is so ace!" laughs Fleur, rolling the spare wheel closer to the jacked car. "Now, that is proper bird power, eh?"

"Ooooh, hang on a minute," says Daphne nervously. "It looks like we've got some company."

Daphne's right. A scruffy yellow van covered in spray-painted graffiti has pulled in behind us, honking its horn. This is largely caused by Fleur bending over, showing more peachy butt cheek than common decency allows.

Honk! Honk!

Claude stops pumping and stands up straight, hands on her hips.

"*Bonjour-o,* chickadees!" leers a voice from the van's passenger seat.

"*Phwoaaar,* you girls can check my oil gauge any day!" squawks another voice, which seems to come from the back of the van.

"It's those lads from the service station!" squeaks Fleur, immediately pivoting round on one heel and frantically pulling her blonde locks out of the scrunchie. "Hello, boys!" she purrs, twinkling her hand.

"Having problems, ladies?" asks the van's dark-haired, rather tanned driver.

"We're fine, thank you," assures Claude primly. "Almost finished, actually."

Fleur pokes Claude in the stomach.

"Oooooh, well, we're not sure, reeeeeally," contradicts Fleur, employing a suddenly baby-dollish voice. "You see, we think we may have got one of those silly puncture things in our wheel, but we're not sure? You know what we girls are like! We don't have a clue!"

Claude rolls her eyes. I stifle a titter.

"Hey, do you want me to have a look?" suggests the dark-haired guy. "I mean, we can't just leave you girls stranded, now, can we?"

"Oooooh, hee hee!" titters Fleur. "That would be sooooo fantastically kind of you! Thank you very much, er, sorry, I didn't catch your name."

"Oh, good grief," mutters Claude.

"Joel," says the driver, switching off the engine and getting out. Joel must be about eighteen years old, with close-cropped brown hair and sort of tufty brown sideburns. He has deep hazel eyes and a smattering of stubble. Okay, dagnamit, he's actually rather lush. He probably knows it though—his type always does.

"And you are?" Joel asks, smiling and holding out his hand.

"Fleur Marina Swan, enchanted to meet you, Joel," purrs the blonde vixen.

"Daphne," waves Fleur's big sister slightly coldly.

Then Joel spots me trying to mop oil off my forehead with a wet wipe.

"Oooh, I'm Veronica . . . ," I tell him, beginning to babble. "Er, I mean Ronnie, well, people call me Ronnie anyhow, or sometimes just Ron . . . You can call me Ronnie."

"Okay, Ronnie," laughs Joel as I flush an uncool shade of cerise.

"I'm Claude," announces Claudette, shaking Joel's hand firmly. "So anyway, are we changing this tire correctly or what?"

Joel crouches down by the front tire as the rest of his motley crew tumble out of the van.

"Gawwwwd, don't ask Joel, he can't even change his underpants without an instruction sheet!" remarks a blond shaven-head lad in baggy pale blue jeans and a white vest, his left arm a mesh of Celtic tattoos.

"Shut it, Damon!" retorts Joel, looking at the perfectly jacked wheel, then turning to the LBD with a curious expression. "You've changed tires before, right?"

"Ooooh, well, not really, just a lucky guess," simpers Fleur.

"Er, well, you lucky-guessed right," Joel says. "You just need to finish the job now."

"Oooh my God! That is such a cool tattoo!" squeals Fleur, pointing at a sun rising from the nape of Damon's neck. Trust Fleur to become distracted from her job by the merest sniff of testosterone. "Spike Saunders has got one like that on his bum crack!" she squeaks. "Hey, who's got any more they want to show us?"

Within seconds, Fleur has totally led second mechanic Claudette astray, making her examine Damon's rather broad, heavily tattooed back, while two other lads, Nico with black curly hair and Franny with longer blond hair, are throwing off their T-shirts and swapping tall tales about eight-inch needles and fainting in tattoo parlors.

"Don't worry, Ronnie, I'll give you a hand," the more introverted Joel says to me. "Well, unless you want to be here all day."

"Ooh, no, we've got to get to Astlebury tonight," I say. "We need to erect our tent before nightfall."

Noooo! Isn't that the most un–rock 'n' roll thing you have ever heard? I have never used the word "nightfall" before in my entire history of being. Why have I gone all Shakespearean? Shut up, Ronnie, shut up now!

Sadly I don't.

"We want to get a good camping spot, y'see? Y'know, not too close but not too far away from the toilets?"

Gnnnggngngnn!

"Has someone got a weak bladder?" Joel chuckles, batting his long brown eyelashes as he wrestles with the wrench.

"Ooh, not me!" I laugh, letting out an inadvertent snort. "Got a bladder like an elephant! I can plod for ages!"

I stop wittering. Joel is staring at me.

"You can plod for ages?" he repeats.

"Without, er, weeing," I say shamefully, feeling utterly defeated.

I wish Daphne had just driven that damn Mini into a tree.

"Now, that's quite a party trick," laughs Joel as we begin fitting the new tire together. This gives me cause to come very close to Joel's chest, which, I might add, smells rather sumptuously of expensive aftershave and a hint of washing detergent. This differs slightly from my beloved Jimi, who very often smells of clothes retrieved from the laundry basket and WD-40 oil.

"Saying that," laughs Joel, "it's not as impressive as our Franny. He can regurgitate beer into a pint glass, then re-drink it!"

"*Euuuuughhh,* groooooossss!" I moan.

"Tell me about it," says Joel. How someone as sensible as him ended up kicking about with such a raggle-taggle bunch is quite a mystery.

Joel hands me back the jack, which I place into Daphne's trunk, spying her chattering quietly on her mobile phone. Daphne takes her voice down lower when she spots me.

"So, anyway, we're on our way to Astlebury too," Joel says, wiping his hands.

"Oh, really?!" I say.

"You didn't think we were an amateur breakdown service, did you?" he chuckles.

I look around. While Claudette is comparing lat muscles with Damon, Nico appears to be doing press-ups on the tarmac in a bid to impress Fleur.

"Er, not really," I smile.

"Hey, they're done!" shouts Fleur. "Let's hit the road! Thanks, Joel!"

"Maybe see you down around the Hexagon Stage?" says Joel, obviously just being kind.

"Er, yeah. Maybe!" I begin, suddenly feeling very disloyal.

"Ronnie, in the car now," yells Claude, interrupting us. "We're well behind time, gotta push on now."

Joel smiles at me, shoving his gang into the yellow van, which is packed with guitars and rucksacks.

"See ya, weird bird," shouts Damon, winking at Claude.

"Bye-bye, Damon!" says Claude pretend-primly. "Hey, and try not to get any more tattoos. You look like a freak."

Damon crosses his eyes, jumping into the van.

"Bye! Thank you!" we all chorus, and then Britain's best-looking breakdown team disappears in a cloud of dust.

"Are we nearly there yet?" sing-songs Fleur as we rejoin the motorway.

"We're about one hundred and fifty miles away," says Daphne, checking her mirrors. "But we quit the motorway in about an hour and hit some narrow, winding country roads up to Marmaduke Orchards, so we'll slow right down then. That's when I need your map skills, Claude."

"No worries," beams Claude, who seems to be curiously extra chipper since the flat tire incident.

Quickly, Fleur is facedown in *Red Hot Celebs,* while Daphne witters to Claude about the Nepalese transport system. I'm resting my face against the warm back window, zoning out to the sounds of the traffic.

"Get out of the way, you old dinosaur!" mutters Daphne as we trundle along behind a midnight blue Volkswagen Beetle, going more slowly than I can run. "I want past you!" says Daphne mock-crossly. "You're in the fast lane!"

"Awww! Check out the picnic baskets and the tartan rugs," chuckles Claude. "He's just an old guy on a day out, bless him!"

As Beetle bloke takes the hint and switches lanes, Claude and Daphne carry on blathering. I rest my head again, catching a millisecond glimpse of the Beetle's passengers as we pass them; the driver is an ancient man with a tweed bonnet and a white twirly mustache. He looks like Sherlock Holmes. Sitting beside him is a far younger man with sandy blond hair wearing a red hoodie. In a flash we're past the Beetle, hurtling way ahead.

Gnnnngn, *that's it! I've officially gone bonkers!* I think to myself. *I've actually begun seeing things!*

I take a deep breath and shut my eyes. Rapidly I'm drifting soundly off to sleep, where my fuddled mind is replete with stuffing golden rucksacks and sandy hair and splattered eggshell. And yellow vans full of mushed banana and giant chess pieces.

127

And filling Fleur's stiletto boots with tea. And Job banging his drum in the kingdom of heaven and eventually being thrown into the Caldwell River and borrowing Jimi's shirt. And catching tiny pieces of rolled-up magazine in my open mouth.

Hang on.

I'm not dreaming that last bit.

"Stop it, Fleur. She might choke," Claude nags Fleur.

"I'm trying to wake her up!" says Fleur, throwing another ball of ripped-up magazine at my open gob. "She's been asleep like that for hours, she looks like a flipping Venus flytrap."

"Come on, Ronnie. It's time to wake up now," Claude says quietly.

I open one sleep-jammed eye. Outside of the Mini, the sun is beginning to set. We're traveling at a snail's pace now. A convoy of vehicles reaches out before and behind us as far as the eye can see.

"Ronnie, are you with us?" Claude says, poking me ever so gently in the shoulder.

"Ronnie! We're here," says Fleur.

Chapter 5

Fruit, Freaks and Fairy wings

Maybe I'm still dreaming.

As the Mini Cooper wends its way upward on the twisty, rather steep dirt track, right, then left, then right again, the pungent smell of ripe fruit floods into our car. On either side lie the most breathtaking orchards, boasting row upon row of laden apple trees. Luscious red fruits crowd every leafy branch, scattering down messily over the grass and soil below, squishing under the tires of the festival traffic. Enough apples to keep Nana in crumble, pies and turnovers for a hundred more lifetimes.

And just as apples become vaguely passé, we move on to acres and acres of large juicy pears. Apparently I snored like a gurgling drain all the way through the plums.

"Marmaduke Orchards!" I gasp. "I just totally didn't expect there to be . . ."

"Aha! You're alive!" laughs Claude. "No, we didn't expect actual orchards either."

"Baron Marmaduke owns the land," chips in Daphne, nudging her brake as a lady with flapping flamboyant pink angel wings on the back of her rucksack cuts in front of our car.

"He's one of those eccentric millionaire types, isn't he?" laughs Claude. "And I mean, he'd have to be eccentric to let a hundred and twenty thousand strangers have a party in his back garden."

Fleur is looking all around her impatiently, craning her head to see over the hill. All this fresh air and fauna is clearly giving her the heebie-jeebies. "We're miles from civilization!" she mutters. "I mean, where's the flipping festival? We're in the middle of a fruit farm!"

Daphne tuts nervously as just ahead of us an ancient multi-colored double-decker bus struggles with its brakes. "Pleeeease don't roll back!" she whispers. "We'll be toast!"

Nervously, Fleur checks behind us to see if we've got any room to maneuver, letting out a sharp yelp as she spies something in the queue. "Errrrr, don't all look at once," Fleur gasps, staring straight ahead again, pretending to be calm, "but I think there's a Land Rover about three cars behind us!"

"What? Noooo!" sighs Claude, dying to look but restraining herself. "Not *Panama's* Land Rover? It can't be! They passed us hours ago!"

"Yeah, well, it certainly looks like them," says Fleur.

I sneak a peek. It's difficult to see, but I'm almost certain I can see Abigail's white-blonde straight hair.

Euuuugh!

"Pah, let's face it," Fleur tuts. "They possess only five collective brain cells between them. They're bound to be behind us; they probably got lost."

Just that instant, a deafening burst of bad pop music with a loud female vocal blares from the Land Rover's powerful speaker system.

"I'm runnnnning to your love!
Wah wah hooooo!
I'm runnning to your love!!
Wibble bibble boooo!"

"Oh my God! That's a Catwalk song, isn't it?" shudders Fleur, recalling the breathtakingly terrible all-singing and all-dancing pop group Panama and the gang used to torture us all with. Catwalk even brought out a lame CD single, "Running to Your Love," which was played three times on the local radio station Wicked FM, well, before Panama sacked Derren, Zane and the whole gang to pursue a solo singing/modeling/acting career.

"Yeee-hah! My love is in the sky! Like a big love pie," squeal the profound lyrics, accompanied by a Casio keyboard bossa nova drumbeat.

Inside the Mini, there's a collective LBD slapping of foreheads and dropping of jaws.

It's definitely Panama and the gang. And they're listening to their own terrible music!

"Ahhhhh, jeez! I remember Panama!" sighs Daphne. "Wasn't she that stuck-up brat a couple of years below me who was suspended for bullying?"

"Nah, they didn't suspend her," sighs Fleur. "Lack of evidence. The girl who complained about Panama ended up seeing the school shrink. McGraw reckoned she was paranoid."

We all sigh.

"Right," huffs Claude. "Don't even acknowledge them. That's what they want."

We all feign indifference, staring instead at the hundreds of hairy kids flocking all around us, armed with rucksacks, tents and sleeping bags, making their way up the hill on foot. Other pierced, dyed and braided kids are slumped down on rucksacks, taking a breather, swigging from bottles and munching newly swiped fruit.

Claude gathers her composure, retrieving the Astlebury tickets from her bag for the twenty-sixth time this journey, just to ensure they've not evaporated into thin air.

"Sorry to hassle you, Daph," says Claude. "But, just to check, we are heading for Gate A, aren't we?"

"Yes, Claude, for the ninth time, we certainly are," smiles Daphne.

"Sorry," chuckles Claude. "We're just so close now, it'd be a bummer if we were in the wrong queue."

"Don't fret," says Daphne. "We're totally, one-hundred-percent-certainly on the Gate A route. I made sure back at the bottom of the hill."

"Why is there more than one gate?" I ask. I'd not even noticed we'd taken a specific route.

"Well, they have to divide tickets into different entrances so there's not a stampede of people," says Daphne. "Gates B, C, D and E are dotted all around the perimeter fence."

"There're more people scheduled to come this weekend than live in our entire town!" replies Claude, holding the tickets to her heart.

"But where's everyone going to fit?!" Fleur asks as we eventually reach the very steepest point of the hill, pausing on the brow to behold the fabulous view on the other side.

"Well, how about down there?" Daphne laughs, turning to us with saucer-like eyes. We all emit a succession of gasps, cheers and whimpers . . .

Astlebury Festival!

Wowwwwwwweeeeee!

In the green valley before us, literally thousands and thousands of tents are pitched already! Hosanna! Tents, tents and more tents as far as the eye can see! Orange tents, blue tents, green tents, red tents, yellow tents, plus a zillion other hues and tones, crowd the two square miles of festival site. Teensy-weensy one-man bivouacs, massive hulking ten-man "field hotels," swanky Winnebagos with blacked-out windows, battered camper vans covered in spray paint, sprawling makeshift hippie communes fashioned from wood and tarpaulin, as well as, dotted throughout the site, smoky bonfires, yellow twinkling nightlights and occasional exploding fireworks. In the middle of the settlement, we can just about recognize the legendary main Hexagon Stage, where Spike Saunders and Amelia Annanova will be performing this weekend; its angular framework is still being hammered together by a swarm of technicians and roadies.

"It looks just like a proper city!" squeaks Fleur.

"Or a magical kingdom!" gasps Claude, although we can barely hear one another now, as all the various vehicles' sound systems are battling for airspace. The Kings of Kong are blaring out from a large battered mini bus ahead of us. Behind us, a man in a motorcycle sidecar is letting rip with some African bongos, totally drowning out Panama and Co.'s hideous atonal screeching.

"It all just looks so amazing," I say, feeling a bit choked.

the great outdoors

As we trundle up to Astlebury's Gate A, the track divides into five sections, where five different, yet curiously similar, big, burly security guards are examining tickets. In the lane adjacent to us, Panama's Land Rover glides into view, its electric windows winding down, displaying the gruesome gang in their full glory.

"Wonderful," Claude smiles, quickly putting on her best polite face to greet our security guard.

Every morsel of space in Panama's Land Rover is full of bags and cases; in the back trunk area, the place usually reserved for dogs, I spot Zane's fake-tanned face, squashed and gasping for air.

"Best place for him," Claude mutters.

"Abigail, speak to the man," Panama commands, chucking the tickets at her friend as a fierce security guard with a jet black ponytail and a name badge that seems to read "Boris" approaches their vehicle. At the same time, we're being faced with our own rather scary security guard dressed in the uniform black shirt, black combat trousers and a pair of twenty-holed Doc Marten boots. Hagar, for that's his name, is a formidable presence with fire red hair, huge hands like clusters of bananas and a nose reminiscent of the Blackwell School caretaker's prizewinning strawberries. After snatching our tickets and holding them up to the floodlights, Hagar peers at us all suspiciously, raising the right-hand section of his fluffy ginger monobrow.

"Everything okay?" smiles Claude. "This is Gate A, isn't it?"

Hagar looks at Claude, sighs, then points at the huge ten-foot, neon orange Gate A sign glowing behind him.

"Oh. Okay!" giggles Claude nervously. "So we're fine then?"

"Hmmm . . . well . . . s'pose," grumps Hagar, whipping a clipboard from under one beefy arm and flicking through the pages crossly before scratching his head a bit, then smiling in a rather sinister way.

"Right . . . okay . . . take these," he huffs, eventually producing four elegant golden wristbands from a drawstring bag. We fasten them tightly to our wrists.

"And don't you be taking these off before you leave on Sunday, right, ladies?" Hagar snarls. "Under pain of death. Or worse fates."

Gulp.

"Er . . . but what if I, y'know, accidentally lose mine?" ventures Fleur foolishly.

The atmosphere inside the Mini turns distinctly chilly.

Hagar sighs again even more deeply, causing the curly red hairs pouring from his nostrils to flutter; then he pushes his face slightly through Claude's window, so close that we can practically smell on his breath the small children he's just gobbled up for supper.

"Oh, well, then, in that case, you just come and find your uncle Hagar," snaps Hagar the-turning-out-to-be-really-quite-Horrible, swiveling around and winking at Boris. "I'll just be sitting here on the edge of my portacabin, waiting to give you another one."

"Don't worry, Mr. Hagar, sir. We won't lose our wristbands," interrupts Claude, trying to make merry of Hagar's sociopathic tendencies. "We won't be any trouble. And can I just say, by the way, what a great job you're doing checking all these tickets? I mean, wow!"

Claude sure can kiss ass when she has to.

Hagar looks at us all, allowing a small proud smile to cross his lips before wandering off to spook out the car behind us.

"Let the Silver Mini through!" he shouts at the gatekeeper.

"What a simply lovely man," says Fleur dryly. "I hope we meet him again soon."

Meanwhile, over in the other lane, events don't seem to be going as smoothly for Panama.

"What do you mean, we're in the wrong lane?" squeals the unmistakable Panama Goodyear in full hissy-fit mode.

"Panama, pipe down," Derren says, thrusting their tickets again under Boris's nose. "I think you'll find you've made a mistake. Nobody informed us we had to go to a specific gate."

"It's written all over the tickets," growls Boris, folding his tattooed arms.

"Is it?" squeaks Derren, examining the pieces of paper again.

"And all over the website," continues the guard.

"Well, we didn't see any of that! And we're here now!" flaps Panama.

"And I think you'll find that those tickets are perfectly legitimate. So if you'll be so good as to stand aside and let us in, I won't report you to your boss."

136

"I'm not saying the tickets aren't legitimate," says the guard firmly. "I'm saying you should be at Gate D."

"But, but surely . . . surely you can turn a blind eye to it?" simpers Derren. "I mean, no one needs to know. Do they, er, ahem, sir?"

This is the most polite I've ever heard Derren being, ever.

"Look, that's more than my job's worth," Boris huffs, obviously having had this conversation eighty-five times already today. "We have these rules for a reason. If everybody came through the same Astlebury gate, there would be a safety threat."

"You should have known about this, Abigail!" Panama fumes wildly, poking her cohort's chest. "You were in charge of travel plans!"

"*Pggghhh* . . . God help them then," hoots Claude, loving this unfolding drama.

"Shh . . . they haven't even noticed us yet!" laughs Fleur, putting her finger to her lips.

"If I make an exception for you, then I'll have to for everyone," says Boris firmly, although clearly feeling a little guilty.

"Okay, okay!" flaps Derren, fiddling about in his wallet and pulling out a large note. "But are you *sure* there's *no way* we can dissuade you?"

Derren looks at Boris arching one smug eyebrow and waves the money closer to him. It looks like a £100 note to me. You can see Boris is quite tempted; it's probably more than he's earning in the entire day. But then a deciding factor presents itself noisily.

"Oooh, that's right! Go on! Take our money!" sneers Panama, throwing her head back to snort. "Take the bribe! Pah! You should just let us through anyway, you pumped-up gibbon!"

Panama begins leaning across Abigail, pointing at Boris and shouting, "Did you know that my father is the CEO of the entire European wing of Farquar, Lime and Young Pharmaceuticals? He could buy this whole piddling security firm, fire the lot of you and reemploy gibbons in less time than it would take you to pocket that hundred-pound note!"

"Precisely, Panama!" pipes up Leeza in the backseat dumbly.

"Shut up, both of you!" snaps Derren, praying Boris hasn't heard that bit.

No chance.

"Oh, is that right?" snarls the guard, turning and signaling to his colleagues.

"She didn't mean that!" shouts Derren hopelessly. "Errr, she has Tourette's syndrome! She hasn't had her special brain medicine today yet! Honestly!"

"Land Rover leaving for Gate D!" shouts the guard, signaling to the other guards. "This one's going to the back of the queue over in Hayward's Pasture."

"Hayward's where!?" squeaks Derren.

"Hayward's Pasture," says the guard with an evil smile. "Right back where you joined the queue for Gate A, but approximately a mile to the left. Just follow the signs."

Derren and Abigail stare at each other in horror as Panama grumpily slams the Land Rover into gear and speeds off, shouting something unrepeatable about Boris's mother.

"Oh, and one thing, kiddiewinks," shouts Boris, now standing shoulder to shoulder with Hagar, who is waving them farewell with a murky handkerchief. "When you get there, make sure that the letter on the gate matches up with the letter on your ticket. 'Cos we wouldn't want all this to happen again, would we now? Bye!"

"Awwwww, bye-bye!" laughs Fleur, waving at the trail of dust in Panama's wake.

"Come on, Daphne! Onward!" laughs Claude, signaling at the wide-open Astlebury gates in front of us. "Let's get going before they change their minds about us too!"

"No worries!" laughs Daphne, slamming the Mini into first gear and speeding away.

We're in!

~~~~~~~~~~~~~~~~

the magical glade

"So what's with the change of plan, Claude?" I yell, wrestling a rucksack, a huge cardboard box and two sleeping bags the half mile from the car park to the Magical Glade Quadrant where we're setting up camp.

"Yeah, Claude. What gives? I thought we were camping near the Hare Krishna fields where it's apparently more chilled out," shouts Fleur, carrying a monogrammed vanity case and rolling a black Samsonite suitcase through the long dry grass. Numerous pieces of woodland glade and wildlife are becoming trapped in Fleur's wheels as she sashays through. However, the shirtless boys hammering tents up are distracting her too much to care.

"Noooo, you must have misheard me," says Claude, who is lugging the most stuff of all. "The Magical Glade has *wonderful* facilities! And it's close to all of the different stages too. And look! They've decorated the forest with pieces of muslin and fairy lights! It's so pretty! We should definitely camp here."

"Suits me, Claude, as long as we can stop walking," shouts Daphne from behind a pile of bags and boxes. Her silver one-man tent is in a bag over her shoulder.

"Okay, then . . . well, what about here!?" yells Claude, pausing momentarily to survey the setting. "This is the perfect spot! Here by this oak tree! Everyone agree?"

"Yeah!" we all puff and pant.

"So Fleur," says Claude, holding up the tent instructions, which appear to be in Cantonese, "you could change a tire, fair enough, but can you put up tents? I mean, I'd ask Ronnie, but as we all remember, she was chucked out of Brownie Guides after two weeks for sarcasm."

I sigh in agreement. I hated that pack leader with a passion.

Fleur lets out a little incredulous chuckle, chucking down the pegs and poles of our four-man midnight blue tent.

"Huh! Does the pope have a balcony, Claudette?" she laughs. "Of course I can put up tents!"

The thing you have to remember about Fleur Swan is, she tells lies.

After ten attempts to erect the impossible tarpaulin puzzle, during which time Fleur proves extremely useful at messing about, doing handstands, flirting with some lads from the nearby camper van and eating the emergency M&Ms, but no use whatsoever with tents, Claude appears to be brandishing a camping mallet at Fleur, who in turn threatens to hitchhike home, taking her spare sleeping bag with her.

Me? I stay well clear, sussing out a nice tree to sleep underneath, possibly in another field away from the pair of them. Thankfully, after a lot of loud arguing, a guardian angel appears in the form of a nice Welsh hippie called Gavin with long flowing dreadlocks. Gavin points out that our outer tarpaulin is in fact, inside out, our main supporting tent poles are through the incorrect slots and, more shameful still, we're using our tent's roof as a ground sheet.

"So close, yet so far," mutters Fleur.

"Let us never speak of this again," announces Claude once our Good Samaritan has wandered off in search of cider.

Minutes later, with a few vital alterations . . . we have a home!

"Now all there is to do is put this up!" says Claude, unveiling her *pièce de resistance:* a huge bright red flag standing at just over 1.5 meters high, reading in huge black paint letters:

LBD

"Wow!" gasps Fleur. "We're like our own republic now or something!"

"Yeah, and there's no excuse for getting lost," announces Claude, attaching it to the tent's roof, where it flutters majestically in the evening breeze.

We all pause a second to survey our handiwork.

Agggh! It feels so marvelous to be here!

As Claude and I start to become a touch sentimental, Fleur disappears into the tent to begin commandeering space for herself.

"Ooh my God! It's actually quite dark in here!" she shrills. "Did anyone bring a flashlight? And I feel a bit hay-fevery too. Has anyone packed tablets?"

Claudette rolls her eyes, then looks at me and winks. We both crack up giggling.

"Right, girls," says Daphne, crawling out of her tiny silver tent. "How's it all going?"

"We're good!" I say, smiling.

"You must be tired by now, eh? It's nearly ten o'clock. Sheesh, I know I am," she announces, rubbing her eyes dramatically, not sounding the slightest bit sleepy.

"Er, not really," I mumble.

"Me neither," says Claude.

"Oh," says Daphne disappointedly, looking at her watch.

Then her mobile phone bleeps again. Another text message?

Fleur lets out a little muffled grunt from inside the tent, sounding very much like she may have chanced upon Claude's stash of muffins.

"Daphne Swan!" she shouts. "You're not trying to get us to go to bed, are you?"

"No, er . . . nooooo!" mumbles Daphne. "Well, not really."

"What do you mean *not really*?" shrills Fleur, poking her head out of the tent, with chocolate chips around her mouth.

"Mmm . . . well . . . ," says Daphne, looking a little put on the spot, "it's just that . . . er, I was going to pop along to another field and sort of . . . ahem . . . meet someone."

Daphne mumbled that last part. I didn't quite catch it.

"You're going to what?" squeaks Fleur. "Meet someone? Meet who?"

"Nobody you know, Fleur. It's just someone I met when I was in Nepal," stammers Daphne, "who, er, happens to be at Astlebury too."

"Oh, right! Now, that is convenient, isn't it?" scoffs Fleur.

"Did they come all the way from Nepal especially? That's a long bus ride!" Fleur is clearly loving this piece of gossip.

"No, he's British," huffs Daphne. "And he's called Rex, actually."

"*Rex!*" hoots Fleur.

"My aunty had a dog called that," says Claude seriously, before deciding to stay well out of this conversation.

"Rex!" repeats Fleur. "Well, that's just great, isn't it? There you were, groveling up to Dad saying you want to *chaperone* us! And all the time you've got a boyfriend up your sleeve that you want to hook up with!"

"*Pgghh!* He's not my boyfriend, actually," fumes Daphne. "And I offered to escort you out of the goodness of my heart."

"Goodness of your heart, *my ass*!" shouts Fleur.

Claude looks at me and sighs.

"Fancy a can of Coke?" she says, rooting about in her rucksack.

"Ooh, go on then," I say, sitting down on the camping rug.

"You're just a troublemaker, Fleur. Always have been!" sniffs Daphne.

"Pah, takes one to know one!" splutters Fleur. "Dad would never have known Tarrick was climbing through my window if you'd not reset the burglar alarm!"

"Oh, pur-lease, that was your own stupid fault!" shouts Daphne. "Who in their right mind asks their boyfriend to climb up the front of their house?"

"Oh, shut up, Daphne!" hisses Fleur.

"You're the one who should be shutting up, Fleur!" snaps Daphne.

"Oh, for the love of Moses, both of you shut up!" shouts Claudette. "You're beginning to drive me loopy!"

Both the sisters stop bickering and turn around, folding their arms.

"Thank you!" Claude says, standing up and looking like she's about to knock the girls' heads together.

"Right," she says, turning to Fleur. "So, as far as I can gather, you, Fleur, want rid of Daphne, is that right?"

"Hmmph," says Fleur.

"And you, Daphne, want to go and meet your pal Rover?"

"It's Rex, actually," says Daphne meekly. "But yes, I do."

"So why, oh why, Daphne, don't you go and see him and the rest of us can entertain ourselves?" suggests Claude.

"Suits me just fine," says Fleur. Then she realizes what Claude's suggesting and gives a small mischievous smile.

Daphne looks at us apprehensively.

She knows this wasn't strictly what was on that contract.

"Well . . . er, are you sure you'll be okay? I mean, I won't be long, and . . ."

"We'll be fine," assures Claude. "I promise you, Daphne."

Claudette Cassiera possesses these weird Jedi mind trick powers, which makes people do things they wouldn't normally dream of.

It's really quite remarkable.

And in this case, faster than you could say, "I'll be two hours, max. Don't get into any trouble. Call me if you need anything," Daphne Swan has scooched herself with a cloud of Body Shop White Musk perfume and vanished to the Ethnic Drumming Zone, leaving the LBD alone and totally free at Astlebury Festival!

I've not seen Fleur look so happy since Jimi last sprained his wrist skating.

"Right, let's go exploring!" shouts Fleur as her hippie-dippie sister becomes a patchwork dot in the distance.

"Coolio!" agrees Claudette.

"Let's go now!" I shout.

We burst through the Magical Glade's gates and scamper down the tiny dust track separating us from the main body of the festival, bouncing with excitement as we join the growing nighttime chaos. It feels like we've been transported to a different faraway galaxy. The Magical Glade is now utterly jam packed with tents, and new arrivals are spilling into the neighboring area, called the Karma Quadrant, which is also home to numerous Sioux-style teepees and a squadron of noisy folk improvising Cajun tunes on screeching banjos and tom-tom drums.

Everywhere we turn, boys, girls, young and some not-so-young folk are walking with piles of camping gear, knocking up tents, gathering bonfire kindling, or simply standing about in gangs, chattering and laughing. Lots of people, like the LBD, are out wandering, sussing out where all the zillion fantabulous, weird and wonderful Astlebury attractions will be.

The atmosphere is totally zingy!

My stomach keeps doing somersaults!

It feels like everyone has made monumental journeys to reach this place today, and now we're all determined to let our hair down for forty-eight hours.

"Wow, what's that?" coos Claude as we spy a humungous rhubarb-and-custard-striped big top on the horizon, with sparkly flags and streamers pouring from a spike on the top. The loud 130-bpm dance music pouring from its doors gives us a clue to the location.

"Oh my God! It's the candy-stripe twenty-four-hour dance tent!" cheeps Fleur as we hurry past the hordes of smiling people hanging about outside. "MTV is broadcasting live from here this weekend! Let's see if we can get on *Big Beat Dance Party*!"

We dance into the big top, straight into the middle of a hot, sweaty full-swing party crowd of about 1,000 people, all going totally doolally, blowing whistles, waving their arms and shaking their tushies to a storming booty-quaking track. Up in the booth, a stunning Asian female DJ dressed in a silver lamé dress and diamanté tiara is cueing up her next record on a space-age telephone.

"It's DJ Mai Tai!" shouts Claude, pointing upward with her mouth agog. In the middle of the floor, a flurry of MTV cameramen and sound crew are filming people frugging wildly. Of course Fleur can't resist shimmying into the viewfinder for a flagrant bout of bumping and grinding.

"Oh, dear, I hope Paddy is watching James Bond and not MTV!" smiles Claude as Paddy's daughter displays her bottom-juddering to most of Europe.

Elsewhere on the dance floor, guys in sweat suits and neon headbands have chucked down a big square of kitchen linoleum on the floor where kids are break-dancing and spinning on their heads.

"This is all too bonkers!" I say after we've frugged and grooved wildly for more than half an hour.

"I know," says Claude, catching her breath. "Let's move on and see what else is here!"

146

We duck out of the candy-stripe tent, dragging Fleur with us, passing a delicious-smelling Vietnamese noodles stall, and then an even more yummy-smelling Olde Cornish Pasty Shoppe that lies beside the Marmaduke Orchard Cider stall, staffed by cotton-wool-haired ladies in pink aprons selling mugs of frothing sweet cider. Here, random puddles of merry folk are lying around on increasingly dewy grass, enjoying apple beverages, while other folk peruse the adjacent Wonderland Fruit Smoothie Emporium and the Back to the Old Skool Kandy Grotto, which sells all the cool candies that we remember from when we were tiny, like Cola Cubes, Sherbet Spaceships and Crackling Space Dust.

"Thank God there are shops!" hoots Fleur, jamming a blackcurrant penny candy in her mouth. She leads us over to the Fabulous Faraway Farm Survival Shop, an incredible stall run by a man called Jet with long red dreadlocks, selling every single, itty-bitty thing you'd ever need for camping, except, of course, far groovier versions such as sequined silver sleeping bags or fabulous tents embossed with fractal patterns that make your eyes go goggly if you stare too long. Beside the Faraway Farm lies the "I Don't Quite Feel Myself Today" Fancy Dress Boutique, hiring out and selling bonkers outfits like Spider-Man costumes, spaceman outfits and cheerleader garb, plus all lengths and styles of wigs from long spooky gothic to fluffy towering Afros. The boutique also sells goofy teeth, oversized glasses and false Spock ears if you really want to go unrecognized. Here, the LBD try on daft hats and fake stick-on face boils until we nearly pee our pants giggling at one another. My head is really spinning now!

But there's still more to see. We carry on through the

crowds, almost losing each other in the mess of bodies spilling in every direction. Fleur's wearing her newly purchased red devil's horns, which pulsate and sparkle, while Claude looks resplendent in a golden cardboard crown. It really rather becomes her. It's impossible not to be intoxicated by the Astlebury atmosphere. It feels like all the sensible rules of society have vanished only to be replaced by high-quality silliness. Like all the dull, gray, snoresome bods in Britain have vamoosed and all the party animals from every town and city have converged in one place for one weekend. It's just *fantastique!*

"Okay, where to now?" asks Fleur as we reach a fork in the paths.

"Well, we could go to church," says Claude.

"What?" we say. "How?"

"Over there!" laughs Claude, pointing at probably the weirdest apparition of the festival so far . . . a grand inflatable cathedral.

"Oh. My. God!" I yell.

The LBD gasp as this huge, holy, bouncing entity, with its inflatable spire and ornate stained-plastic windows, jiggles and wobbles merrily in the midnight air, tugging at the ground ropes preventing it from floating heavenward. As we draw closer, we notice the spongy spire nodding in time to some loud, joyous gospel music blaring from a righteous sound system. I run up, pressing my nose against the windows. "There're kids inside dressed as monks and nuns! It's a disco!" I shout.

"Let's go inside!"

Okay, I think they're just dressed as monks and nuns—by this point I'm not 100 percent sure.

"And you can get married here too!" shrieks Fleur, pointing at a sign informing loved-up festivalgoers how to arrange emergency wedding licenses. "Do you think I could get a wedding dress from the fancy dress stall?"

"Oh, dear," laughs Claude as we drag her through the inflatable gates.

"Poor Spike Saunders, he doesn't stand a chance."

Bumph! Bumph! Bumph! Bumph! thumps the beat.

"*Agggghh!* I really feel like dancing now!" shouts Fleur, heading for the center of the congregation and immediately beginning to shimmy with a handsome vicar.

"So do I!" shouts Claude, jumping up on a wooden bench and waving her hands in the air, her tiny black T-shirt riding up to reveal her flat brown stomach and slightly outy belly button. "Hallelujah!"

Ahhhh, her mother would be so proud, I think to myself as a rather good-looking fake priest with gorgeous green eyes and a cassock over his jeans and T-shirt grabs me by the waist and begins swinging me around and around until I collapse on a fake plastic pulpit in a fit of snot and giggles.

It feels like something has changed for me and the LBD tonight.

It feels like life will never be the same, ever again.

meet the neighbors

"So, is that what Gloria's church is like, Claude?" I ask as the LBD dawdle our way exhaustedly through the Magical Glade and its numerous campfire parties, home to our tent. There are fields and fields left to explore, but we've decided to make an early start tomorrow when our brains can process more madness. I'm feeling particularly splendiferous on this warm summer's evening, wearing my orange sparkly deely-boppers, a steal at only £1 a pair from a stall near the Karma Quadrant.

"Yeah, Mum's church is exactly like that!" says Claude dryly, her golden crown perched wonkily on her head atop raggedy hair bunches.

"Sheesh, those Ghanaian Methodists sure can party hearty once they get going."

We all dissolve into giggles, envisioning Gloria Cassiera and her holy pals having it large at the annual chicken cookout.

I don't think I've ever laughed as much as I did tonight. My face is aching.

"Uggghh, okay, now I'll admit I'm lost," sighs Fleur, stumbling over her fiftieth guide rope. "Where did we leave that tent again?"

"Easy, it's a big blue one, beside a ginormous oak tree, isn't it?" I say, with a creeping realization that there are twelve equally impressive oaks within spitting distance of us, not to mention twenty midnight blue four-man tents that could have fallen off the same factory conveyor belt as our own.

"Don't panic," says Claude. "There's the LBD flag! We're over there."

"Good one, Claude!" I sigh.

As we reach our tent, a huge cheer erupts from the nearby candy-stripe dance tent, accompanied by someone appearing to go buck wild with a Klaxon horn.

"Do you think the twenty-four-hour dance tent ever shuts up?" groans Fleur. "A girl like me needs her beauty sleep!"

"I think the clue is in the title," I laugh. However, by this point I'm talking to her tangerine-sized posterior as it wriggles through our tent's entrance.

"No Daphne yet?" asks Claude, tapping the side of Daphne's tiny silver house. No one is home.

"Oooh, I hope she's okay," I say.

"Me too," says Fleur quite genuinely from inside the tent. "That Rex better be a decent bloke, or he'll have me to answer to!"

When you catch Fleur off guard, she's actually quite a sweetie.

I'm just about to suggest that we call her, when suddenly, in the distance behind some camper vans, an acoustic guitar springs to life and a male voice begins belting out.

" *'I'm lost . . . lost at the heart of you-hoo hoo hoo,'* " a lad is singing. " *'I don't know what I can do-hoo hoo to get through to you-hoo.'* "

He's quite talented, whoever he is—not that he's getting much encouragement from his pals.

"Ooooo hoooo owwwww-ooooo bleughhh!" mimics one loud-mouth, breaking off to belch ungraciously. Soon the whole gang is howling and jeering the cabaret as Claude and I earwig furiously.

" *''Cos, I'm lossssssssst, at the heaart of yoo-hooo,'* " the lad continues, ignoring the slander.

"Oh, kum-by-yah, my Lordy," mutters Fleur, poking her head out of the tent. "Claudette, go and have a word, will you?"

"Aw! I think he's good!" I say, suddenly realizing why the

song sounds familiar. "Hang on, isn't that the song 'Lost' from the new Spike Saunders CD? You know, the new CD that you burned for me, Fleur?"

The LBD all stand very still, straining our ears.

" ''Cos I'm loooooooost,' " croons the lad.

"Oooh my God, now you come to mention it . . . yes, it is!" gasps Fleur, her eyes lighting up. "Ronnie! Claude! You don't think that it's . . ."

Fleur starts flapping her hands about excitedly, starting to hyperventilate.

"No, Fleur, I don't think that's Spike Saunders singing, you silly mare!" I say, shaking my head.

Fleur looks very disappointed.

"But he's quite good anyhow, isn't he?" I add.

As our neighbor struggles with the difficult key change in the third chorus, he's drowned out completely by the growing roar of his friends.

"Regurgitate! Regurgitate! Regurgitate the beer!" the boys are yelling.

And then after an ominous silence, we hear a squishy splatter.

"Uggggggghhhh! You're disgusting, Franny, you minger!" yells one lad.

"Stop encouraging him then, Nico," shouts another.

"But he hasn't re-drunk it yet, Damon!" the lad replies. "He's not getting the five quid unless he re-drinks the vomit!"

Before I can say another word, Claude Cassiera has sprung to life and vamoosed through the maze of tents toward our neighbors.

What's she up to? She's not going to tell them off, is she?!

I want to follow her, but something's holding me back. They seem a bit wild to me. What if things get nasty?

"Could you pur-lease keep the noise down!" I hear my hard-hitting bambino buddy snarl. "Some of us are trying to go to bed!"

Fleur and I wince, waiting for a tirade of abuse and beer cans. Instead there's a stunned silence . . .

. . . and then a huge joyous cheer!

"Wah-hayyyyyyyy! Claudette!" erupts the bunch. "How you doing!?"

"Hellllooooooo, boys!" hoots Claude back. "Sorry, did I give you a shock?"

Eh?

I bound toward the racket, not quite believing my own ears. These guys can't possibly be who I think they are, can they?

Surely not? Oh my God, it is!

It's Joel, Damon, Nico and Franny! Our knights in shining armor from this afternoon, slumped around a hearty bonfire, less than twenty meters from LBD HQ, strumming guitars and regurgitating lager beer for kicks!

"Ronnie!" shouts Joel, putting down his guitar and grinning broadly. "You made it!"

"Oh, my word, Ronnie, isn't this an incredible coincidence?" announces Claude. "I had no idea this lot were camping in the Magical Glade! Isn't that freaky?"

Claude should never get a job in the theater.

Damon jumps up, hugging Claude warmly. For some reason he is wearing a girlie blonde bobbed wig, perched all crooked on his head.

They must have been at the fancy dress stall too.

At this point, faced by a wall of testosterone, it strikes me that not only am I covered in grass and mud stains, but I'm wearing sparkly deely-boppers and . . . *gnngnnnng* . . . a stick-on comedy fake boil on my chin! I pull off the deely-boppers and ker-ping the boil somewhere past the Hexagon Stage.

"Take a seat, Ronnie! Everyone shift up a bit!" says Joel, patting a space beside him on the camping blanket he's perched on. "So the tire held out then?"

"Yeah! We're all here in one piece," I smile, vaguely mesmerized by Joel's long brown eyelashes and hazel eyes. Joel's eyelashes are, dare I say, even longer than Jimi's, which I'd never have thought possible.

"Hey, thanks again for helping us out before," I say, trying to smooth down my fringe, which has gone a bit woo-hah because of the deely-boppers.

"No problem at all." Joel smiles, picking up his guitar, and strums a perfect G chord. "So, are you ready for a sing-along?"

"Ooh, I'm not much of a singer," I blush. "I play a bit of bass guitar . . . Hey, but you can fairly belt it out, eh? Was that one of the new Spike Saunders CD tracks?"

"Yeah!" Joel says, grinning. "I mean, it's not released for weeks, but . . ."

"You downloaded it off the Internet, didn't you?" I grin. "So did we!"

"Ugghhh! Not another Spike Saunders fan!" groans Damon, glugging a can of lager. "What a total moron that guy is! Total popified girlie rubbish. Joel must be the only geezer in Britain that likes 'im. I reckon it's just a ruse to woo ladies. Y'know, show off his sensitive side? Not that any of you girls would be as daft as to fall for that."

Joel blushes now.

So do I, for that matter.

"Actually, I just think he's a brilliant songwriter," Joel says to me. "I know all his stuff off by heart. That new album *Prize* is his best yet!"

"What?" I smile. "You can play all the tracks off *Prize* already?"

"Er . . . yeah, sad but true," Joel blushes again. "You think I'm a total dweeb now, don't you?"

"No, that's totally cool!" I begin to tell him, only I'm interrupted by a loud familiar voice and a fragrant waft of Supermodel Eau de Parfum.

"You guys again!" squawks Fleur Swan, who has made a swift costume change into delicate pink cotton pajama bottoms, a cream cashmere sweater and fluffy kitten-heel slippers. "What are you lot doing in our field? Ronnie, call security! Have them release the hounds!"

All the boys cheer as La Swan makes her entrance.

"Eh? What do you mean, your field?" laughs Franny, clearly in an advanced state of beer-induced relaxation. "We were always going to camp here. In fact, we told Claude . . ."

"Hey! How about another song?" interrupts Claude "Dark Horse" Cassiera. "Let's have something off Spike's last album, eh, Joel?"

Fleur finds a pew and everyone cheers as Joel strums the

opening bars of "Merry-Go-Round," Spike's most famous, multimillion-selling, award-winning hit.

Ah, up close he sounds even more excellent! He can do all those twiddly bits and complicated chord changes, just like Spike's guitarist Twiggy Starr, and he can do the swooping high and low notes straight after each other too! When I first met Jimi, he used to play his guitar loads; his band Lost Messiah were always playing little gigs. I was so proud of him. That all went down the drain when the town council built that new skate park. Now his guitar just gets used as a door stop.

" *'Life's just a merry-go-round,'* " sings Joel, giving me a sweet smile. " *'It makes you dizzy. It makes you feel down.'* "

Pggh, I think, *at least Joel has a hobby that's sociable. Not one that involves having his limbs bandaged up and antiseptic cream applied to gammy wounds at the end of the day. And I bet Joel wouldn't stand me up on Blackwell Disco night. No, he'd probably arrive super early with a one-man band strapped to his back, crashing cymbals between his butt cheeks, serenading me with love ditties.*

Sigh. He's sooooo totally lush.

Would anyone notice if I licked his face?

Oh, pull yourself together, you great soppy gorgon.

"Help yourself to beer, girlsh!" slurs Franny, signaling to a pile of cheap beer cans beside the van. It's so high it may well have a snowy summit.

"Nah, I'm all right for now," says Claude, who seems, curiously enough, to be high on life at the moment.

"Ooh, okay, I'll have one!" says Fleur, eyeing up the pile of cans before noticing Franny's vomit-splattered chin and diced-carroty-smelling clothes.

She shudders a little.

"Y'know what, Franny, I think I'll pass," she whispers. "I only really drink chilled champagne anyway. Have you got any Cristal?"

"Er . . . no, not really," says Franny, scratching his head. "We've just got two hundred cans of Tesco's store-brand lager. It's a cheeky little number though."

"Then I'm good," says Fleur, wrinkling her nose a touch.

What a peach of a day this has turned out to be!

By 2 A.M., a dozen Spike Saunders songs and daft conversations later, Franny has passed out among the ashes of the dead bonfire while Nico is adding a mustache to his friend's face with a neon marker pen. The lovely Joel and I are gossiping about great bass guitarists, while Claude and Damon are lying on their backs pointing out star formations in the exceptionally clear night sky. I feel like I could talk to Joel all night.

He's one of those lads who really listens when you speak and chooses his responses really carefully. I want to stay up till dawn, putting the world to rights, even though I can also hear my eyelids pleading with me for some sleep.

"Right, people, I'm going to love you and leave you," yawns Fleur, blowing us all a kiss and making her way back to the tent.

I have to admit I'm shattered too. I feel like curling up here on this blanket and snoozing while Joel plays guitar. That would be perfect.

"I suppose we should head off too, Claude?" I whisper to Claude. "It's pretty late."

Claude mouths "five minutes" at me, then carries on chattering to Damon.

"Okay, just me then." I smile, standing up.

"Oh, you're off too?" says Josh, putting his guitar down, then picking it up again, then placing it down again. Then wiping his hands on his jeans.

He seems a bit awkward. "So, do you want me to er, y'know, walk you back to your tent?" he suggests.

I stare at him, almost wanting to say yes . . . but sort of also understanding the hidden code of this illicit scenario. Walking places with lads? After dark? Just you and him, away from all your mates? Well, it sort of means a lead-up to snogging, doesn't it? It sort of says, "Something naughty's going to kick off." Something involving tongues and lips and possibly hands. Something your mother wouldn't like. Not, I hasten to add, that I'm adverse to a bit of canoodling, especially with a hottie like Joel . . . It just feels sort of weird after what happened with Jimi this morning.

Of course, I could just be being presumptuous here. Maybe Joel's just being gentlemanly.

(I can almost hear Magda snorting raucously at that last thought.)

"It's okay, Joel," I say quietly. "I'll walk by myself. We're only just camped over there."

"Okay then," smiles Joel matter-of-factly. "I was just trying to be, y'know, gentlemanly. 'Night, Ronnie."

" 'Night then, Joel," I say, walking away, slapping my forehead.

Gah! He was just being a gentleman, I think. *What a total numpty I am!*

"Ah, what an incredible night!" whispers Claude as she crawls into the tent just after me, trying to find a space around star-shaped Fleur. "That was indisputably the best night of my entire life ever! If I died now, I'd be content. But we're here for two more days! It's unreal!"

"Claudette Joy Cassiera!" I whisper back, feigning shock. "You mischievous, scheming madam! What is going on between you and that . . . that boy?"

I poke her as she wriggles into her sleeping bag.

"Stopppit!" Claude giggles.

I go in with a two-handed tickle. Claude hates being tickled. "Stoppit! Stooooopppppit. Hee hee! Or I won't tell you about the totally amazing, fantabulous tongue-snog we've just had!"

"About the what!?" I shriek as Fleur rolls over, letting out a snore like an asthmatic warthog. "You naughty girl! I'm utterly appalled!"

"I know!" beams Claude.

"Tell me everything now!" I squeak.

As we dissolve into a gargantuan gossip and giggle session, discussing the whys and wherefores of Joel's and Damon's butt cheeks and pecs, we barely notice footsteps and heavy breathing drawing closer to our tent.

"And then he said I had the best eyes he'd ever seen on a real-life girl!" coos Claude. "That's quite good, isn't it?"

A twig cracks loudly right beside the front of our tent. I hear someone stumble a little.

"Shh, Claude, hang on, there's someone out there!" I shudder.

"Oh my God, you're right!" whispers Claude, grabbing my hand nervously.

"Play dead!"

We both lie dead still. I open one eye very slightly.

A ghostly face is pushed up against the gap in the tent's zipper, peering in at us.

I daren't breathe!

"It'sh okay, Rexshhh," whispers the mystery presence slightly tipsily into her mobile phone. "They're all totally fast asleep," she coos. "They must have gone straight to bed when I left. I know! Straight to bed, can you believe it? What absolute little angels!"

I have to put my hand over Claude's mouth at this point to stop her howling with laughter.

Chapter 6

morning has broken

"Well, that's just flipping charming!" huffs Fleur Swan, sticking her head through the tent doors.

Fleur appears to be wearing a baby-pink turban over her blonde locks and a pair of large, glamorous dark glasses.

"Wah . . . *gnnngn* . . . wha'timeisit?" I grunt, sitting up in my sleeping bag, realizing I've been sleeping with my face precariously close to Claudette Cassiera's exposed brown rump.

Bleeeeeee!

Claude's a good pal and all that, but this level of intimacy is beyond the call of friendship.

It's Saturday morning, our official first day at Astlebury . . . and I feel like absolute poo! My back is stiff and aching. Claude and I were far too idle to blow up the air mattress and then drag Fleur on top of it, so we've kipped on the cold, hard ground. I also seem to have Cheesy Footballs, the remnants of last night's midnight feast, embedded in my forehead and a mouth like a pilgrim's flip-flop. To make matters worse, our neighbors at the twenty-four-hour dance tent are still thumping away, accompanied by an emcee with verbal diarrhea who's yelling, "Wakey, wakey, party people! Oi! Oi! Oi! Big shout going out to the Astlebury Massive! In da areeeeeee-a!!!" again and again and again.

It's only 8:15 A.M.!

I am sorely tempted to storm over in just my grunderwear and cut the plug off his microphone.

I am not a morning person.

"So, I've just walked over to the Karma Quadrant to begin my beautification progress," huffs Fleur, "and I asked the security oompa-loompas where the shower block was . . . and they just laughed at me! I mean, how incredibly rude!?"

I shuffle out of our tent in my sleeping bag like a giant slug, blinking in the bright morning sun. Fleur, dressed in a pristine white fluffy terrycloth dressing gown, kitten-heel slippers, and holding a luxurious lemon-colored bath towel over her arm, is glowering back at me.

"You went looking like that?" I ask, suppressing a smirk.

"Of course I went like this," says Fleur, gazing at me like I'm an imbecile. "And yes, obviously it raised a few eyebrows with the great unwashed out there, but I just told anyone who commented that it was *style, darling,* and nothing they needed to worry about . . . Oh, and Ronnie, suffice to say, that Karma Quadrant shower block doesn't exist. It was just an Astlebury myth. What am I going to do now?!"

"Er . . . rough it for a few days?" I say.

Fleur gives me *that look* again.

"Time to hit the wet wipes?!" I venture, chucking her Claude's bumper-sized pack of antiseptic wipes. All around us Astlebury folk are crawling out of tents and vans, clutching their heads, making unpleasant remarks about DJ Retinal Migraine over at the dance tent and begging for ibuprofen. Near to us, three guys with shaven heads and goatees who have been crammed into what appears to be little more than a child's playhouse are glugging down bottles of water and staggering toward the porta-loos. Last night, it seems, was a big night for everyone.

It's like a scene from *Zombie Hell IV*.

"Morning, campers!" zings Claude's smiley face, poking out of the tent.

"Ahhhh! What a beautiful day! What a great day for seeing some bands, eh?" she cheeps.

"*Morgen*, Frauline Cassiera," flounces Fleur, turning to me again to continue her rant. "Oh, and don't even *start* me about those disgusting portable toilet cubicle thingies! They're absolutely covered in . . . in . . . well, I can't even say it . . . they smell really, really gross! And some bloke was asleep in the first one I went in! And there are no mirrors anywhere . . . or any toilet paper! And nowhere to wash your hands afterward except the occasional primitive water outlet pipe with a queue of about fifty hippies beside it. There was a woman in the nude soaping her bits when I walked past too! It's just . . . just . . ."

"Exactly like we warned you it would be!" smiles Claude.

"It's worse! It's like I envision Earth after an all-out nuclear attack!" gasps Fleur. "There's nowhere for me to plug my straighteners in! My hair's going to be like a static badger by the end of the day!"

Fleur pauses for a second, then gasps as the most hideous thought of all crosses her mind.

"Oh my God! If my hair does that mad woo-hah thing at the front again, well, I'm simply going to kill myself!"

"Oh, shut up, you insane old goat," chuckles Claude, standing up and strrrrrretching with a small satisfied groan.

"Ooooh, that's right, just insult me! Everyone pick on me as usual!" says Fleur, pretending to be offended. "It won't be like this when I meet Spike Saunders and he says, 'Yes, Fleur, I did used to fancy you! Yes, I was going to marry you and let the LBD have an annex in my Mayfair mansion for you all to live in, and let you have a splishy-splashy in my Jacuzzi with the gold turbo-bubble buttons . . . but now that I've seen you looking like a Sasquatch that's been run over by a tractor, I think I'll pass, thank you!' *Pghhh* . . . That'll serve you all right!"

Claude and I stare at Fleur; then we all burst into fits of snottery giggles.

Fleur crawls into the tent, dragging her makeup behind her.

"Now both of you shut up and leave me alone!" she huffs. "I have to unleash the magic."

When Fleur's in good form, she can make you pee your pants laughing. But then suddenly, as I'm reaching for some toilet paper to blow my nose, I notice something strange about Daphne's tent. It appears to be emitting two sets of loud snores! One little girlie one and another big boomy one. On further inspection something highly irregular is poking out from underneath the door.

"Claudette! Look!" I shout, pointing at two rather large size 14 black boots. "There're extra legs in Daphne's tent!"

Whoever is in Daphne's tent must be absolutely enormous; he can't lie in her one-man tent without spilling out onto the grass.

"Wow!" laughs Claude. "When did he arrive? We were still awake at five!"

"Is that *Rover*?" gasps Fleur, sticking her head out. "Has he infiltrated LBD HQ?"

"It's Rex!" Claude says, her eyes wide with delight. "Ooh, I wonder what he looks like. I can't wait to see! Shall we throw sticks at his feet until he sits up?"

"He's not an evil giant, Claude," I say.

"Oh Gawwd, he'll be some stinky new-age type with egg in his beard and a 'Free Tibet' T-shirt, no doubt," smirks Fleur. "I bet he plays didgeridoo too."

"Shh, he'll hear you!" I shush as Daphne's tent reverberates with a particularly hearty snore.

"*Hmmmph* . . . don't care," says Fleur. "What's he going to do? Garrote me with his friendship bangles?"

"It's nice to be nice, Fleur," says Claude, pretend-primly.

"Oh, whatever," says Fleur, brandishing a large blusher brush covered in pink powder. "So anyway, ladies, evil giants aside, what's the sketch for today? Claude, have you got an itinerary worked out?"

"Who, me?" says Claude unconvincingly. "Nah . . . I just thought we could, y'know, go with the flow? Just see what happens?"

"Really?!" I say, feeling disoriented.

"Er, well, sort of . . . I mean, sure, I took the liberty of printing off the Astlebury timetable from the website and making a few markers of stuff we might like to see."

Claude grabs her Astlebury file, producing three charts, all marked in a variety of felt tips with squiggles and arrows.

"Now, I've put a gold star beside bands, et cetera, that we love, and added a point system to bands when there's a timetable clash." Claude puts her plan down on the grass. "For example, Brassneck Ruffians are on at noon on the Hexagon Stage, but we're not that keen on them so I've given them a low rating. I thought we could go and hang out at the Astlebury Fun Fair then. I've rated that as choice two . . . or we could go to the new-band area, as long as we get more central for Final Warning at four P.M. We all love them so they've got a gold star. And then the Losers are on after that."

"The Losers?! Wow!" I say. "I'd forgotten about them! They're ace!"

"It's Carmella Dupris that I absolutely have to see!" says Claude excitedly. "That's a must. I can't miss that."

"Oh, and then it's Color Me Wonderful," says Fleur, taking her schedule and looking at it. "They're meant to be so amazing live!"

"Er, but Claude, you haven't scheduled bathroom stops," I say dryly, looking at the plan.

"Of course not," smiles Claude. "I'm not that bad now, am I?"

"*Pgghh,* well, that suits me fine, girls!" sniffs Fleur. "After seeing those poo-traps, I'm not drinking or eating another morsel until I get home. I'm just going to wear lipstick and look pretty instead."

Fleur smears on some plum-colored lipstick and blows us both a kiss.

I don't think she's joking.

"But anyway, girls," coos Claude, "basically, we can do whatever we want! That's the bestest part!"

"Oh, really?" I say, delving into my rucksack, trying to work out which creased items I can throw together to create "festival chic." "So we're not hooking up with any lads later on then? Any tattoo-covered, shaven-headed guys? Guys called *Damon,* by any chance?"

"Ooooh, shut up!" blushes Claude.

"Eh . . . what? What's going on here?" says Fleur, sitting up on her haunches, waving a mascara wand. Fleur Swan can sniff out hot gossip at 500 meters with a clothes peg on her schneck. "Have I missed something?"

"Nooooo!" says Claude.

"No, not really, Fleur. Claude only snogged Damon last night!" I blurt out.

Ahhh, isn't it great to be the first to tell someone gossip?

"Whahhhh? When!?" squeals Fleur. "And how . . . how do I not know this?!"

"You were zonked out!" I laugh. "It was when they were walking back to the tent. They ended up playing face invaders over there by that tree. And she felt his bum. She said it was so firm, you could take the top off a pickle jar with it."

"Noooooooooo!" squeals Fleur. "That is soooo contravening Rule Four of the Parent/LBD Behavioral Contract! For shame, Claude! For shame!"

"Gnnnngnnnn," groans Claude, covering her face.

"And Damon said she had a better bod than his favorite *Sports Illustrated* model!"

"Ooooh my God!" hoots Fleur. "Then what happened?!"

"Then she floated into the tent and waffled endlessly about him till her throat nearly packed in," I smile.

"Hee hee!" hoots Fleur. "Was she being all mushy?"

"Totally!" I say. "She sounded like one of those padded valentine's cards you get in Clintons Cards. She is sooooo in love!" I conclude, opting for my favorite ripped denims, a little black vest top with lacy straps and a pale blue patterned headscarf.

"I am soooo not in love!" protests Claude, burying her head in her hands. "Stoppit! You're giving me a headache!"

"Ahhh! See? The headache . . . ," says Fleur authoritatively. "A classic sign of being in love! Love hurts, y'know, Claude?"

"*Phhhhgh,* tell me about it," I groan, suddenly recalling Jimi's contorted face as we pulled away in the car twenty-four hours ago.

Right. Forget about that, I tell myself.

"Okay, everyone shut up about me and get dressed!" says Claude, changing the subject. "Now, chickadees, my itinerary denotes that the Beyond Las Vegas Casino opens in half an hour. I quite fancy a few hands of blackjack . . . you can win amazing stuff like the entire top one hundred CDs or your body weight in chocolate. Actually, this map says there's a stall next door where some folk are giving out free breakfasts from seven to eleven A.M. . . . well, it's free as long as you promise to listen patiently while they talk about their religious beliefs. No, on second thought, that'll be just like being at home," Claude says, rolling her eyes. "Let's just buy breakfast instead!"

"Mmm, breakfast!" I say, imagining a big greasy sausage sandwich smothered in tomato ketchup.

"Exactly! Come on, let's get a shift on," says Claude. "If it's escaped your attention, ladies, we have to have another fabulous fandango today. One even more fabulous than yesterday!"

pleasing paddy

Half an hour later, after ten Fleur Swan costume changes and an LBD decision to tape a note to Rex the Evil Giant's boot telling him and Daphne that we've gone for breakfast, we're ready to rrrrrock.

"Do I look like a dog's dinner?" asks Fleur, looking utterly stunning in a pale turquoise cropped vest top and black mini kilt. Fleur's hair is concocted effortlessly into that "messed-up San Fran beach babe look" that I tried so hard to do before Blackwell Disco. It's knotted at the top with lots of tousled strands spilling out and a deep red silk flower placed in the middle.

"You look great," I assure her.

"You too, Ron! Hey, fab T-shirt, Claude!" says Fleur, admiring Claude's striking magenta Lycra number, which shows off her smooth brown skin and voluptuous curves.

We tumble down the lane, this time taking a left into a field marked Pastures New, where hundreds of stallholders are doing a roaring trade selling weird and wonderful food and drinks such as zebra milk and guava smoothies, char-grilled ostrich burgers, organic raspberry ripple gob stoppers and Romanian mung-bean goulash. If the food is weird, the stallholders are weirder; one woman in a long white cloak with a crown of leaves is selling cakes and cookies that promise to give you eternal life because they're blessed by pagan priests.

It's a nice idea, but the LBD are craving something greasy and unhealthful with a pint of coffee, so we join the queue at

Bob's Brilliant Breakfast Emporium and wait impatiently as the aromas of frying bacon and sausages drive us wild with salivation. It's 10 A.M., and the entire site is alive again with hordes of people grabbing breakfast, stretching their limbs and contemplating a day of music and mayhem.

"Shall we eat these by the skate park?" suggests Claude, passing me a gigantic sausage sandwich served by a burly bloke with a buzz-cropped head. Claude nods over to the far side of the field, where *Fireboard* magazine is sponsoring a makeshift skating area with a huge death-defying ramp. From over here, we can already make out several skatey lads on boards shooting through the air, and the obligatory crowd of ditzy chicks lurking about, trying to catch their eyes.

"Yeah, let's go and have a quick gander," I say.

"Er, haven't you seen enough skating for one lifetime?" asks Fleur, who is breaking her fast with a heap of Moroccan falafel.

"Hmmm, true," I mumble as we saunter through the crowds to where around 100 totally hot lads with shaven heads, baggy trousers, ripped T-shirts and various battle scars are hanging about. About twenty of them are darting all over the wooden rink on cool customized boards, while the rest are hanging about in little cliques, posing, posturing and egging each other on to do excessively daft stunts. One guy, with green streaks in his hair and a bleached blond goatee, I recognize immediately as pro skater Tyrone Tiller; he was on the cover of last month's *Fireboard* magazine, which I read in Jimi's bathroom. Tyrone, who is well known for his reckless tendencies, is proving this by attempting to leap over six of his mates' backs on a skateboard. As the LBD slump down with our food on the grass to watch,

Tyrone's followers are all lying down willingly, eager to be hospitalized.

"*Gnnnngnnn!* Why are skateboard lads always so hot?" I say as Tyrone whips off his torn, dusty T-shirt to display a buff, tanned six-pack and a bottle-green scorpion tattoo creeping from the waistband of his khaki combat pants.

All the skating girlies cheer and gasp, including Fleur, who puts both fingers in her mouth and whistles.

"I know," muffles Claude with her mouth full. "It's a bit like Premier League footballers, isn't it? I mean, you never see any proper losers doing that either."

"Or surfers," sighs Fleur. "Or lead singers in rock bands. Or the lad who runs the resort entertainment when you're on holiday with your parents. Or the waiters in Italian restaurants. They're all always hot!" Fleur stops and shakes her head. "So many boys, so little time."

Tyrone shoots toward his friends, hitting the tiny ramp and propelling past five bodies before diving headfirst into the chest of his final victim. Ouch!

The boys both roll around on the floor, screaming in agony . . . before eventually standing up, giving each other a high-five and starting to plan an even more idiotic stunt.

"*Agggggggh!*" I moan. "See? I fancy Tyrone Tiller even more now that I've seen that! What is up with me?!"

"Oh, I reckon that's just normal, Ronnie," sighs Fleur. "I only started fancying that awful Tarrick when he got thrown out of sixth form for fighting. I mean, the second he got that black eye, he suddenly started looking like Brad Pitt! It's ridiculous, isn't it?"

"Errrr . . . anyway . . . maybe it's time to move on," says Claude, suddenly looking a little agitated. I don't think she enjoys the recklessness of the skate park too much. You can tell she's dying to shout, "Stopppppit!"

"What's up?!" I say, cramming the last bit of sausage into my mouth and licking my fingers.

"Ooooh, er, nothing," says Claude, jumping up. "I was just, er, thinking that we should get on with exploring. There's stacks we haven't seen!"

Claude looks a little flustered. She turns around again and looks at the crowd of skaters and assorted hangers-on, then looks at us again and smiles.

"Okay, no worries!" I say as we all stand up to leave.

"Actually, girlies," cheeps Fleur, "I had a fantastic idea this morning! But it would mean us all walking over to the Land That Time Forgot, then Remembered, then Totally Forgot Again field. It's a bit of a trek though."

"Fine by me," says Claude. "Let's go right away."

And so we did. However, you need to remember two things about Fleur Swan and her really fantastic ideas:

1) Her ideas, to the untrained ear, always sound verily fantastic. Take, for instance, the time in Year 7 when she decided to cut my hair into a "raunchy bob cut" in a bid to lure snoggage offers . . . However,

2) Fleur's "fantastic ideas" will get you into more trouble than you could ever imagine. In the case of the choppy bob, I ended up looking like I'd drunk a bottle of tequila, then hacked around a traffic cone with a hedge trimmer. Suffice to say, it wasn't what I'd asked for.

These days, when I hear the term "fantastic idea" spill from Fleur's lips, I tend to book a one-way ticket to Wigan or somewhere else bleak where I know she won't follow me. So, all that said, please don't ask me how the LBD all appear to be lying on our fronts, wearing only pairs of paper panties to spare our blushes, on makeshift treatment tables, in the back of a draughty marquee, coughing away incense smoke, listening to Peruvian nose flute chill-out music . . . and having henna tattoos done!

Nooooooo!

"I'd like a really big, amazing, friendly sun shining out of my bum crack, please," Fleur instructs the tattooist. "And can you put it high enough that my thong doesn't hide it? Oh, and can you make the sun's rays sort of shimmery and dancing and . . . er, have you seen Spike Saunders's tattoo?" she asks.

"Yeah, I know the one!" says the beautiful lady mixing powder and water in an earthenware pot.

"Well, I want it exactly like that, please!" smiles Fleur, who isn't in the least bashful about being virtually in the nude, as she's always being waxed, exfoliated and massaged for birthday treats back home.

"Any other details I should know?" laughs the lady.

"Ooooh, hang on, let me think . . . ," says Fleur. "Yes! I know! Can you write over the top of the sun 'LBD Forever'?"

"LBD?" asks the girl, raising an eyebrow.

"Les Bambinos Dangereuses!" laughs Fleur. "Errrr . . . it's a long story. 'LBD' will do."

"Yeah! Let's all have that done! LBD Forever!" says Claude excitedly. "And I'm going to have this peace dove, please!" she says, pointing at the menu. "Can I have it just above my belly button, please?"

"No problem at all," beams the tattooist, throwing Claude a towel to wrap over her upper half. "And what about you?" she says, gazing straight at me.

I feel a bit sick now.

"Errrr . . . ooh, now that I think about it," I mumble, "I'm not so sure."

"Awwwww, Ronnie!" squeal Fleur and Claude. "Stop being so flaky!"

"I'm not being flaky!" I moan. "How long do they last?"

"Well, up to ten weeks if you treat them well," replies the lady, almost drowned out by the sound of a Malaysian dream-catcher mobile clanging away behind her.

"Ten weeeeeeeeeks! *Gnnngnnn!*" I wimper. "That's the whole summer!"

"Ignore her, she always does this," announces Claude, taking charge, pointing at the menu. "Ronnie would like this fabby Celtic crisscross thing, please. On the nape of her neck, just underneath her hairline. That'll look terrific, won't it?"

"It's a popular choice for petite brunettes," nods the tattooist.

"Claude! Oooooh! You can't make me . . . my mum will go nuts . . . and what if it doesn't suit me? And . . . *phhghhh!*"

I splutter and waffle, searching for words, before finally muttering, "Oh, okay then."

In less than an hour, the LBD are fully clothed again, spat back out into the Field That Time Forgot, then Remembered, then Totally Forgot Again, comparing our wondrous henna designs. Fleur has got the rudest, most raunchy bum graffiti I've ever seen in real life. The sun looks really minxish and feminine. She's even winking! Fleur's thong is perched just underneath it, sticking out an inch or two above her kilt. Paddy will be sooooo pleased.

And me, well, I'm now the proud owner of this weird, punky, ancient Celtic symbol of love, spilling out of the back of my hairline and down between my shoulder blades! It's a bit like the one Amelia Annanova has on her calf. It looks . . . totally incredible!

I look really . . . dare I say it . . . sexy!

"Ha ha ha! LBD Forever!" shouts Fleur after examining my back and Claudette's fabby belly-button dove for the umpteenth time, with such great gusto that festival folk turn round and stare at us like we're crazy. Not bad going, considering we're standing beside a weird performance artist bloke who thinks he's a human grandfather clock and keeps shouting *Boing!* every five minutes.

"These are so cool!" laughs Claude, pulling up her magenta T-shirt again.

The reddish henna contrasts really stunningly with her brown skin.

"This was the most fantastic idea ever!" I chuckle. "Nice one, Fleur!"

That's another thing about Fleur: Sometimes you've got to

give her stupid suggestions a go . . . or you really miss out on some wild stuff.

"Okay, now I suppose we should make some contact with other cosmiverses," announces Fleur dryly, nodding toward a marquee in the corner of the field with a huge fluttering sign written in spiky, silver letters.

It reads:

PEOPLE PODS—MAKING MILES IMMATERIAL IN MILLISECONDS

"What d'you mean?" I say.

"Well, we have to make daily contact with home to prove we're alive, don't we?" says Fleur. "Now, Claudie, you texted Gloria yesterday, didn't you? She relayed the message around Planet Paddy and Magda?"

"Yeah, Mum said she'd give them both a call," nods Claude.

"Er, what? Did you!?" I say, shamefaced.

Ooh, I feel totally guilty now. For all of my promises, I've pretty much forgotten about the Fantastic Voyage from the second I left the city limits. After a few hours here, it feels weird to think that normal life is carrying on outside the gates. Three cheers for Claude! Magda would have been absolutely frothing at the mouth by now. Especially if she'd found my mobile phone.

"So anyway, follow me, ladies," says Fleur, sashaying toward the People Pod marquee, giving a sultry wave to the hunky promotion lads trying to drag people in. Claude and I totter behind, not certain what to expect. Inside the marquee, there's a glass dance floor, with some loud, electro-funk music thumping out of hidden speakers. Behind a raised bar area, a lady with a shaven head and big thick spectacles is shaking bizarre-looking bright green cocktails. More strangely, all around the edge of the dance floor are tall metallic boxes, which look a bit like gambling machines. The contraptions are around the same height as we are, with keypads on the front in the center and cameras on the top that swivel round, following you as you pass them. This is all a little bit eerie!

"Wow! What are they?" coos Claude, pausing in front of a machine and stroking its neon pink keypad.

HELLO! WANNA PLAY WITH ME! flashes up a message across the screen.

"Ooh . . . I don't know about that!" laughs Claude, stepping backward in shock.

"They're People Pods," says Fleur. "Basically, they make a short film of you, then they zip the images through cyberspace!"

"Where to?" I ask.

"Wherever you want!" says Fleur. "You can send them to any e-mail address or mobile phone. I read about them in *ElleGirl.* I thought we could send Paddy one and ask him to do a quick ring around?"

"Yeah! How fab is that?" hoots Claude, tampering with the buttons on the pod again.

STOP TICKLING ME! the pod says.

"Hee hee! Look at that!" dissolves Claude. "Awww, poor Mr. Pod. I don't like being tickled much either!"

"Right, then," says Fleur. "Hey, who's got a couple of quid?"

"Me!" I say, passing Claude the coins as I perfect my most over-the-top pout.

"Insert coins here," points Fleur, grabbing some lip gloss from her bag and smoothing it over her annoyingly plump lips.

THANK YOU! says the pod.

In the blink of an eye, the screen is filled with a huge image of our faces.

It's just like we're on MTV!

"Yee-hah!" squeals Claude, straightening her bunches. "Ooh, guys, this camera makes me look really booby though, doesn't it?"

"Yeah, Claude," I say, rolling my eyes and examining my own deflated balloons. "It's the camera."

"NOW TOUCH ME WHEN YOU'RE HAPPY WITH HOW YOU LOOK!" reads Fleur, examining the screen. "Right, girlies . . . are we happy?"

Fleur throws her arms around our shoulders.

"Fleur! No doing rabbit ears behind my head!" I say, grinning and sounding a bit like a ventriloquist's dummy.

"As if!" smirks Fleur.

"Ooh! Hang on a second! I've got one wonky bra cup!" shouts Claude.

"Say cheeeeeese!" shouts Fleur, pushing the button.

"Nooooo! Stop! Ooooh . . . Cheese!" groans Claude as the camera begins to whir and play a sinister hip-hop tune, eventually slowing to a halt, then emitting a loud trumpet fanfare.

WANT TO SEE HOW GORGEOUS YOU LOOK? asks the pod.

Of course we do! Within seconds the pod is playing the LBD's small screen debut: Fleur Swan, hogging most of the lens, resembling a *Sports Illustrated* cover girl, except for a large lump of falafel jammed in her front teeth; me, grinning like a demonic hobbit, with flipping Fleur making rabbit ears behind my head with one hand . . . *gnnnngnn;* and on the other side, Claudie with one mitt down her own T-shirt, groping her left boob, with her mouth lolloping open and one eye crossed! This is all happening to a 132-bpm, garage-music backing track, so we look like we're in a proper pop video! But we all look sooooo dumb! This has got to be simply the funniest thing we've seen for ages; in fact we're howling so much we have to hang on to the pod to steady ourselves! Fleur sends a copy of the movie to all of our Macs. I'm going to print out a snap from mine and stick it on my wall. Then she quickly types in Paddy's e-mail address with the message "Greetings from Astlebury!!" and presses "send." She also sends a still image to Paddy's and Daphne's mobile phones.

Ping! Gone! Galloping through cyberspace! How cool is that?!

Within seconds Fleur's phone quacks.

"It's Daphne!" says Fleur. "She says ta for the pic and we should meet her and Rex by the Hexagon Stage. Ooh, shall I say we'll give her a buzz when we get down there?"

"Yeah, that would be cool!" says Claude. "So, shall we move on?"

"Actually, I might just do one more," announces Fleur, arching one eyebrow, fishing in her pink sparkly wallet for coins, and setting the pod's timer to send out a picture at 10 A.M. tomorrow. Odd? Quickly the pod pings and the camera is whirring as the blonde minx flips around and pulls up her vest to expose the large henna sun in all its marvelous tattoo glory, as well as, naturally, a generous display of her pink dental floss thong. Fleur begins to gyrate like a demented pole dancer in time to the music, then furiously begins tapping buttons as the camera stops.

"Nooooooo, Fleur! Don't!" gasps Claude. "Don't send it to Paddy!"

"Oh, shut up," says Fleur, typing in Paddy's address again. "I like to keep him on his toes."

"But I really don't think . . . ," begins Claude, but by this point the video of Fleur's tattoo has already hit the little-too-much-information superhighway.

"Now," beams Fleur proudly, "shall we go and see some bands? If we run, we might just catch the Flaming Doozies! And Final Warning play after that!"

"Okay, to the bands!" Claude and I agree as we follow Fleur's body art out of the marquee.

a bit of crash bang wallop

As we spill out of the Land That Time Forgot field, through the hectic crowds, hitting a winding track leading eventually to the Hexagon Main Stage, I immediately recognize in the distance Zander Parr, singer with the Dutch rock band the Flaming Doozies. That bloke can't half screech!? As the crow flies, the Hexagon Stage is about half a kilometer away, but the VIP enclosure separates us from it, and ordinary punters like ourselves have to make a detour around its boundaries.

"Ooh, I wonder what's going on in there?" Claude says, pressing her face up against the mesh fence. From here, all we can see is tour buses, some mysterious marquees and production people dressed in black, darting about with clipboards and radios.

"Oh, just all the most exciting stuff, obviously!" sighs Fleur. "That's where all the stars and their entourages hang out. And the TV crews. I mean, just imagine?! Right now, CeCe Dunston from Final Warning will be knocking back Jack Daniel's and chatting to Jocasta Jemini from the Losers . . . And Lester Ossiah from Color Me Wonderful will be facedown in his macrobiotic vegan buffet getting an aromatherapy shoulder massage. And I bet Zaza Berry and Cynthia Lafayette the supermodels will be chilling out in the Jacuzzi and . . ."

"Erm? You've really given this some thought, haven't you, Fleur?" smiles Claude, examining a huge stern sign above our heads, which decrees:

STRICTLY NO ACCESS PAST THIS POINT EXCEPT FOR PRIVILEGED WRISTBAND HOLDERS

"Just a soupçon," mutters Fleur.

At this instant, a ginormous triple-decker black tour bus with a sleek red flash along the side sweeps up slowly to the gates, followed by a gleaming long white stretch limo. The security guards immediately spring to action, yelling at each other agitatedly while beckoning the VIPs inside.

"Nooooooo! I can't believe it!" squeals Fleur, gesticulating furiously. "It's Carmella Dupris! In there! In the limo!"

Fleur's right!

Claude, who owns every one of Carmella's CDs, as well as all of Carmella's old-school stuff from when she was part of girl group G-String, begins to leap around squawking too. Wow! Can this really be true? I crane my neck to get a glimpse, but now people are surging all around me, knocking me out of the way.

"Carmella!" squeals Fleur, ringleading the riot, slapping

the limo's side windows as it passes. "You rock, Carmella! I love you!"

It is her!

Inside the car, Carmella Dupris, who's about as big as a saltshaker in real life, waves one tiny caramel-colored hand from underneath her huge floppy hat right in our direction. She's teensy-weensy!

"Dolce and Gabbana hat!" screams Fleur to anyone listening. "And Gucci shades! Carmella always has the most amazing wardrobe! She's so cool!"

"And she waved at us! She waved at the LBD!" hoots Claude, touchingly unaware that there are about five squillion fellow looky-loos hanging around us, going equally as berserk with adulation.

"I know! I know!" agrees Fleur. "And did you see Big Benson!? Carmella's boyfriend? The boss of Big Benson Records? He was in the back with her! He gave me a peace sign!"

As Claude and Fleur hyperventilate, I stand with a silly grin plastered all over my fizzog, staring as the back of the limo disappears. The very second the vehicles are safely through the thick mesh gates, they crash shut firmly and a heavy bolt is thrown across, leaving the lowly LBD very much outside of the VIP enclosure.

"Operation complete! Ms. Dupris is inside the enclosure!" shouts a belligerent-looking security guy into his walkie-talkie. "No intruders have entered the enclosure! Repeat: No intruders! Well done, everyone!"

After some persuasion, we drag Fleur away from the VIPs,

floating around the peripheries of the hallowed enclosure, in-toxicated by adrenaline, drawing closer to the Hexagon Stage, where the crowd grows denser and more intimidating. The dry ground is reverberating with a pounding bass line. There must be about 50,000 people gathered here watching the music. Swarms of bodies are screaming and cheering, leaping up on each other's shoulders; dancing and laughing and falling about, while up on stage Zander Parr caterwauls, albeit tunefully, like a cat in a combine harvester.

"This is the band that sets off fireworks, isn't it?" I shout.

"Yeah!" yells back Fleur as a thunderous crash rips through the air, making everyone duck for cover, then rise up again cheering.

On stage Zander Parr is leaping up and down in wild glee. Zander looooves pyrotechnics! He gets banned from every venue he plays at for taking things too far.

"Wow! Look!" gasps Claude as pretty scarlet and ivory paper petals shower the audience; the crowd cheers wildly, pick-ing them out of their hair. On stage, a vast pyrotechnic display is kicking off with all the requisite shooting flames, silver sparkles, bangs, whizzes and crashes. Eccentric Zander, looking practically robotic in his black T-shirt and skintight gold-mesh trousers, is jumping about like a man possessed, setting off Catherine wheels and waving around flaming torches with such abandon that he keeps totally missing his cue to sing lines.

"He's really lost the plot this time!" laughs Claude, pointing at the huge video screens on either side of the main stage.

"Thank you, Astlebury! I looooooooove yer!!" Zander screams while his lead guitarist looks on in mild dismay, shaking his head. At this point I notice Zander literally has no eyebrows left, just singed strips above each eye. Living proof that you really shouldn't play with fire.

"Let's get farther forward!" shouts Claude.

"Cool!" beams Fleur, never satisfied as a spectator to the mayhem.

"Er, okay," I say gingerly.

Traveling anywhere in this field is no mean feat; it's like treading through a maze of bodies, bags, coats, beer cans and burger boxes. Worryingly, whenever you spot a sneaky shortcut and shoot through it, your friends have all vamoosed in the blink of an eye, as they've taken another route entirely. That's a total freak-out. Lordy, I'd hate to get lost here. Astlebury is so unbelievably massive, I don't think I'd ever find our tent by myself.

"C'mon, Ronnie!" says Fleur, linking my arm tightly. "I've got you!"

On stage, the Flaming Doozies are cranking up their biggest hit, "Dead and Dirty," and the crowd is surging forward in response: bodies slamming toward each other, people tumbling over and struggling to gain a foot up again. Some kids are throwing plastic bottles at the stage, narrowly missing Zander Parr, who's retrieving them from behind the speaker stack and lobbing them back. This is so wild! Scary wild, but wild all the same.

"Woooooooow! Look at him!" squeals Fleur, pointing out a hairy lad clad in baggy tartan shorts and a ripped tank top with a blue Mohawk being propelled by the willing crowd, right at the front of the stage. Change is pouring from his pockets.

"Oh my God! A real-life crowd-surfing dude!" says Claude.

Eventually, after twenty minutes of bobbing and spinning through the fuss, we emerge far nearer the front, but at the side where it's a little calmer. By this point, Zander's rolling about on the stage, screaming and sobbing, seemingly in the midst of some sort of total nervous meltdown, which the crowd is really lapping up because, well, let's face it, he always flipping does it. (Whenever Zander is on *Top of the Pops,* my dad always huffs theatrically from behind his *Daily Mirror,* before yelling, "I don't pay my license fee to watch this sweaty pillock jumping around screaming! Gimme that remote!")

Fleur is loving all the drama; she whips out her mobile phone and takes a picture of sobbing Zander to send to Josh in Amsterdam.

"My brother loves Zander Parr! He'll be so jealous!" she hoots, staring at her handiwork on the screen, then frowning a touch. "Ooh, hang on a minute. What's up here?"

Fleur turns the handset off, then on again, the phone booting up with a perky polyphonic flourish of Spike Saunders's "Merry-Go-Round" and a screen saver of Fleur and her gorgeous mum on holiday in the south of France. Blondie pushes different combinations of buttons impatiently, with growing annoyance.

"There's zilch bars on the antennae screen," she shouts. "Stupid flipping phone! I knew I should have pestered Paddy for that upgrade! Claude, you got any signal?"

Claude pulls out her handset, an ancient, rather bedraggled implement manufactured at some point when dinosaurs roamed the earth.

"Oooh, no," shouts back Claude. "We're both on Fusia network, aren't we?"

"Yeah," frowns Fleur, smacking her phone off her thigh, like it will help.

"Errr . . . sorry for butting in, ladies," chirps up an elfin girl with denim dungarees and spiky blonde hair, rocking to the music beside us. "If you're trying to use Fusia, you've no chance. The whole network crashed. Been down for over an hour."

"Oh, for crying out loud!" gasps Fleur. "Again? How?"

"Er, about one hundred thousand folk in a remote field trying to send pics and messages at once probably!" shouts the girl. "People say it might be gone for the whole weekend."

"What!?" gasps Fleur.

"Calm down, Fleur," whispers Claude. "It'll just be one of those Astlebury rumors."

Fleur gets very antsy indeed when her phone doesn't work.

"Well, forget meeting Daphne," says Fleur, sounding genuinely a bit narked. "She's on Fusia too. That'll be my fault, I bet."

"Not much chance of bumping into her here," I say, looking around us. We all look at one another, trying to weigh up how much trouble we'll be in for officially 100 percent losing our "grown-up," but somehow we're distracted by the antics of Zander Parr. The singer has decided to finish the Flaming Doozies' final number by whipping off his clothes, one item at a time, chanting "La! La! La!" to a tune that sounds suspiciously like "Baa Baa, Black Sheep," while the rest of the band struggle to keep up with him, resorting to pure improvisation.

"Zander! Zander! Zander!" chants the crowd, egging him on.

Just as Zander begins removing his underpants, which I'm

sorry to say are a rather saggy, mottled pair of beige Y-fronts that have certainly seen numerous world tours, a posse of flustered security guards rush onto the stage to try to remove him.

"Thank you, Astlebury and goooooood-byeeeeee!" Zander yells in his cute Dutch accent as the microphone is forcefully removed from his person and someone in a headset places a clipboard over his delicate nether regions. "This is the best day of my life!" he yells. "I'm Zander Parr and I am as ne-kked as zee day I was born! Good night! Have a good flight home!"

The crowd goes absolutely nuts as he's carried off stage.

"*Aggghhh!* That was so much better than on TV! It's so wild when you can actually see the fireworks!" laughs Claude.

"And smell Zander's singed underpants," I laugh.

"Hey, and Final Warning are on next," reminds Fleur. "It's their first British gig for two years."

"Yeah, that's going to be huge," says Claude. "We were so lucky to get tickets for this!"

And then there's a bit of an awkward silence as the LBD all know exactly whose total favorite band Final Warning is. Let's not even go there.

"Two . . . two . . . two . . . testing . . . two . . . two . . . okay?" repeats a roadie on stage, sound-checking CeCe Dunston's microphone. "Can you hear that? Two?"

Uggggh . . . , I think. *I wonder what Jimi's doing right now, while I'm here having fun. Crying on his tear-drenched pillow? Counting off the hours till I come home?*

Or doing more normal Jimi activities, like retrieving a wide array of boogers from his nose, then smearing them on stuff? Or staring at pictures of women with massive moshee-moshees in Maxim? *Or finding the hilarious hidden extras on his* Dude, I Sooo Blew Up Your Mom II! *DVD?*

Suddenly a firm hand cups my waist, almost sweeping me entirely off my feet!

"Ooooh," I say.

"Fancy seeing you here!" says a familiar, rather deep voice.

I turn around with a gasp.

"Oh my God! Joel, hello!" I smile as the hazel-eyed hottie stands before me, surrounded by his motley crew. "It's you!"

As I give Joel a small friendly hug, Claudette Cassiera is letting out a big not-playing-it-cool-at-all whoop.

"Damon! You're here!" Claude laughs, then whispering more to him, "I didn't think you'd remember."

"You were pretty specific!" whispers Damon back, giving Claude a sloppy peck on the forehead. Fleur, Nico, Franny and I all pretend not to notice. "You said you'd be near the front on the right for Final Warning."

"Ronnie! Fleur!" cheeps Claude, turning to us. "Look, it's the lads again! Fancy these guys finding us again . . ."

Fleur and I swap "Does this bird think we fell off a Christmas tree?" glances and begin laughing. Soon Fleur's roundly abusing a slightly green Franny about his vomit-regurgitation antics, and Nico is off at the bar getting us drinks, while up on stage, there's a flurry of movement as hairy roadies tape track-running orders to the amps at the front of the stage, and fiddle about, tuning up guitars.

"Er, incidentally, Ronnie," Joel says to me, looking slightly bashful. "Can I point out that I'm not stalking you?"

"Er, yeah, whatever," I say cheekily. "Tell it to the judge, Stalky McStalkerson."

"I'm not!" laughs Joel. "It's just that Damon wanted to . . ." We look across at Claude and Damon, who appear to be having a *play fight,* of all things. ". . . oh, you know."

"Yeah, I'm only winding you up!" I giggle.

"Good," he says, half smiling, poking me in the stomach gently. " 'Cos, I mean, who'd walk out of their way to see you anyhow?"

"Precisely," I agree. "Perish the thought."

But then the emcee cuts in, telling us to make some noise for the one, the only, the legendary FINAL WARNING!

YESSSSSSSSSSSSSSSS!

~~~~~~~~~~~~~~~~~~~~~~~~~~~~~~~~~~

the pit

The next few hours prove to be the most incredible ever.

First, Final Warning crash through a fabulous set, playing all of their most famous songs accompanied by a totally tone-deaf crowd singing along enthusiastically. During one song, lead singer CeCe Dunston, with his trademark floppy, curly black hair and big blue-bottle dark glasses, divides the 50,000-strong audience up into two sections, making both sections battle to be the noisiest! I almost lose my voice yelling. Then CeCe pulls an amazingly lucky girlie out of the front rows onto the stage and serenades her with a raunchy song about her peachy bum! She isn't offended, of course; in fact she pulls out a pen and asks him to sign the washing instruction label in her panties.

By now, the sky is clear, the sun is blazing down and a

soothing breeze is breathing gently through the fields, cooling us all down wonderfully. It's so cool that we met up with the lads. They're a brilliant laugh as well as top eye candy to boot. And just to make matters more amazing, between songs, the verily lovely Joel and I have been giggling and gossiping about life (okay and having a bit of a flirt too!). I've been uncovering some pretty impressive "boy data" on my new friend. Stuff such as he's taking A-levels in physics, chemistry and math next summer (wow?!) and he lives with his mum in a small town called Charlton-Jessop approximately ninety-seven miles from the Fantastic Voyage. I've also uncovered that the scruffy yellow van with the graffiti isn't Joel's, it belongs to Franny (which makes much more sense), and also that Joel drives a black Volkswagen Polo. Hey, but most impressive of all, Joel's biggest ambition is to be a *surgeon*. Oh, and not just any old everyday surgeon . . . a brain surgeon!? Apparently, according to Joel, that takes about ten whole years!

Yes, Joel knows what he wants to do with his life for the next ten years!

I haven't even planned the rest of this summer!

(Jimi wrote "cosmic spaceman" as his ambition on his last career advice questionnaire.)

And if all that isn't enough, Joel also works at Charlton-Jessop's municipal pool on Saturdays as a lifeguard! Gulp! I can only surmise from this information that beneath Joel's combats and T-shirt nestles one of those toned, smooth lifeguard bods that totally distracts the LBD during Blackwell swimming lessons when we're supposed to be rescuing bricks from the bottom of the pool, dressed in pajamas.

My mother would soooo love Joel.

She'd be sizing him up for a bridegroom's top hat the millisecond she set her beady eyes on him. He's totally the type of guy I suppose I should be going out with.

After Final Warning stagger exhaustedly off stage, the Losers, an Australian four-piece band with two boys and two girls, replace them. The Losers play lots of synth, string and flute lullaby-style songs, which seems to lull the audience into a catatonically calm state. Some of the Losers's songs are so sad, they actually make you want to weep, especially when Jocasta Jemini, the minuscule, rather depressed-looking lead singer, plays her flute and sings lyrics about being "lost at sea" and "dying of a broken heart." Some people wave lighters backward and forward during the most maudlin songs; some seriously, as they love Jocasta, others sarcastically, as they think she's a miserable old trout. Oh, and some people just throw plastic bottles at her. I've figured by now that some people just throw plastic bottles whatever the occasion. By the time the Losers finish, then run off stage, then run back on and play all of their biggest hits, then finish properly, the sun has set and the air feels much crisper. It's almost 8 P.M. Where has the time gone? Everyone in our gang is in high spirits, especially Fleur, who's utterly determined that for the next act, Color Me Wonderful, we should all move farther into the center of the crowd, then push to the front, against the stage barrier, where the rowdiest action always is.

"Oh, come on!" Fleur scoffs. "Stop being such wet farts! This band always has the most amazing laser show! We have to get right to the front, so we can really dance!"

Franny and Nico agree immediately. Joel, Claude and I

aren't so sure. It looks pretty rough down there to me. I've already seen kids who've fainted or been crushed being pulled over the barrier by security guards. Saying that, I know that Fleur will go anyway. Then I'm going to miss out on one of those once-in-a-lifetime experiences.

So I agree to go.

"You sure, Ronnie?" asks Joel.

"Yeah, let's do it!" I say, sounding reckless. Fleur lets out a little victorious squeak.

We begin weaving our way through the excited crowds in the direction of the front barriers, Damon with his arm around Claude's shoulder, Franny and Nico forging ahead, clearing our path, Fleur in her black miniskirt drawing wolf whistles and appreciative glances at her henna tattoo as she tiptoes through the bodies. Joel bringing up the rear, being rather protective of me, which is sweet, but feels a bit odd. Soon we're about ten rows from the front, as far as we can possibly go, as by now there's no more room to move. We're all squashed against each other's backs, guarding our spaces territorially. Right then, Joel lifts me up by the waist and turns me around to see the view behind us . . .

There must be about 100,000 faces spanning as far as the eye can possibly see.

Unbelievable.

I feel a little woozy . . .

And then the stage lights plunge to darkness and the audience erupts, whooping excitedly as the familiar opening bars of Color Me Wonderful's "Swamp Song" explode through the speakers, saturating the air with a cacophony of noise, making all the hairs on the back of my neck prickle up. I seem unable to stop smiling. All around us, people are dancing, jumping and crashing into each other in a nonnegotiable frenzy.

"Er, thank you kindly," remarks Lester Ossiah, the meek, one-man music machine during a quieter interlude in the track, the crowd quieting to hear him speak. "I wasn't sure if anyone would turn up," he adds dryly. Everybody laughs and cheers.

A few meters away, the irrepressible Fleur, who's been dancing and cheering wildly with the demeanor of a chick possessed for the last ten minutes, has now persuaded some poor, gullible bloke nearby to allow her to climb up on his shoulders, where she jiggles and joggles and waves frantically at Lester Ossiah, blowing him kisses. Eventually the timid star notices the flurry of hands and blonde hair in front of him and blows her a kiss back! Amazingly, Fleur's elated face fills the huge video screens on either side of the stage. She looks like she's going to cry with total happiness.

Incredibly, Lester then makes "Swamp Song" blend effortlessly into his worldwide number one hit "Looking Glass," an infectious tune that's been used on tons of film soundtracks, sports car ads and video games. *Gahhhh!* I love that tune! The crowd seems to be surging forward more strongly now, there's hardly any room to breathe and the security guards are yelling at us to move backward. This is beginning to get quite scary . . . especially as Fleur has now propelled herself off the guy she was perched on, making her fledgling crowd-surfing attempt.

"Oh my God! Claude! Look at Fleur!" I scream, pointing upward.

"Weeeeeeeee-hah!" squeals Fleur. "I'm flyyyyyyyying!"

"Fleur, get down! You'll hurt yourself!" shouts Claude pointlessly as Fleur travels about on a sea of hands above our heads, supported by numerous partied-out individuals who I don't place a hell of a lot of trust in.

My heart is in my mouth. I'm jealous, but I wish she'd get down.

Thankfully, after a few minutes, Fleur descends gracefully back to Earth, kindly positioned on both feet by a hulking guy with a kindly face and a nose ring who looks like an amiable bull.

"Wooooo-hooo! Rock 'n' roll, baby!" yells Fleur, throwing both hands in the air in devil horn signs. "That was sooooo fantastic! Did you see me?! *Agggh!* I want to go again!"

Claude and I roll our eyes, relieved our daft mate's back in one piece. However, right that instant another faster, louder track known worldwide as "Dead Zone" bursts to life and we're dismayed to see Fleur tapping bull guy on his sweaty shoulder, flirtatiously requesting a leg up.

"Noooooo!" says Claude, but by this point, we're just staring at Fleur's underwear as she climbs aboard.

Claude and I both watch dubiously, fighting to keep ourselves upright as Fleur crowd-surfs past, in her absolute element, squealing and giggling. Occasionally she disappears downward into the crowd, then appears again upon another stranger's shoulders, punching the air riotously. Claude and I try to keep an eye on her, but it's getting more difficult now; she keeps disappearing completely as the crowd surges forward and falls backward.

I'm not certain we're in the same place Fleur left us now.

And the next time I spot Fleur, she's about eighty meters

away, perched on some guy's shoulders, chatting to a girl on shoulders next to her, laughing her head off.

But then the guy carrying Fleur seems to stumble and I see Fleur's face change. She looks scared, then plummets clumsily into the crowd.

I wait for her to surface and for everything to be okay again, but this time it doesn't happen.

Claude, Josh and I fight our way sideways to try to rescue her, but when we reach the spot, sweating and panting, Fleur's just not there.

Or on anybody's shoulders.

Or crowd-surfing.

Or in any of the places that we were standing.

Or back at the tent.

Or even at the missing persons marquee.

Not anywhere.

Fleur has completely disappeared.

Chapter 7

the pits

"What time is it now?" I whisper.

"Er . . . Four fourteen A.M.," whispers Claude, sitting up in her sleeping bag, illuminating her face with her mobile phone's glowing screen.

"*Pggghhh* . . . this is getting ridiculous now," I say, sitting up and placing my head deeply in both hands. "We've got to own up that she's gone."

Claude sighs, nodding slowly in agreement.

"I know," she says. "Let's face it, we should have done it hours ago. Have we made things worse, d'you think?"

"I don't know," I whisper, genuinely confused. "I just don't know."

Outside our tent, the gentle tippy-tap of rain bounces off the tarpaulin. It's drizzled for the best part of four hours now, which means that wherever Fleur Swan is, she's soaked through and freezing cold as well as lost.

Claude peers at the signal bar on her mobile phone for the zillionth time, rattles the handset, holds it up above her head, anything to get a connection. Why can't the flipping Fusia network mechanics get a move on and restore the signal? Then Fleur could give us a call, text or sign of any kind. We're not fussy. But for now, the network is still very much kaput and Claude and I are plummeting into the most maudlin genre of despair.

It's not like we've not tried to find her. We searched for Fleur high and low tonight, the length and breadth of Astlebury, for hours and hours on end, Claude and Damon combing the Hexagon Stage field, scanning every face, tattooed back and long pair of legs for distinguishing Fleur characteristics. Joel and I wandered the various other fields, where I kept "seeing" Fleur, hanging off the arms of random musicians, or holding court elegantly at numerous bonfire parties, or just sitting by herself, sipping a drink in the beer tent.

But I didn't really see her—it was just my mind playing tricks. So then we hunted through every boutique and stall in the main shopping thoroughfare, where I'd have given my right arm to see Fleur just one more time, trying on some ostentatious pair of sparkly stilettos, wrapped in a feather boa, being her usual absolute limit of cheekiness, convincing stallholders she's a celebrity and needs a 40 percent discount.

But we didn't see her there either.

Or in the fun fair, or the skate park, or the casino or the dance tent. Then we climbed up Briggin Hill to Astlebury's makeshift medical center, hoping maybe we'd find her wrapped in a bandage, flirting with the male medics; but when we got there, the nurses showed us a logbook full of lads who'd plummeted over guy ropes, or battered their thumbs with camping mallets, or stage dived off the new-bands stage and found the audience had parted and they were nosediving into the hard earth. But the medics had seen no girls that evening at all.

"Is there any chance that we wouldn't know she was a girl?" asked one nurse. "It can be quite hard to tell sometimes," she smiled.

Joel and I looked at each other and shook our heads.

The missing persons marquee was the worst bit.

As Joel and I began to write Fleur a "Calling Fleur Swan!" note to stick on the board, oodles of people swarmed all around us, reuniting with their friends and family. People were hugging, kissing and even crying. Everyone was blaming the Fusia phone network for ruining their entire schedule, then rushing off as fast as their feet would carry them to catch up on fun. Kids were literally jumping for joy when they spotted their buddies, grabbing each other and twirling each other about in wild elation.

But my friend didn't show up.

I wasn't reunited.

And instead of thinking up something useful to write, I found myself reading some of the more serious "missing persons" posters plastered over the marquee's walls. There were faces of girls, just as pretty and sassy looking as my Fleur, grinning ghoulishly down at me, accompanied with blood-chilling captions such as:

MISSING: IMELDA SMITH, AGED 15, LAST SEEN SIXTEEN MONTHS AGO. HER PARENTS AND FRIENDS MISS HER DESPERATELY. LAST SEEN SPEAKING TO AN UNKNOWN MAN (BROWN HAIR, 6', GLASSES) AT A HOTHOUSE LIZARD CONCERT AT THE SHEPHERD'S BUSH

EMPIRE. DO YOU HAVE ANY INFORMATION AT ALL?
CALL THE CRIMESTOPPERS HOTLINE.

I felt utterly bilious just looking at that one.

Is this how it feels when somebody goes missing forever? It all has to begin somewhere. Those terrible things you see on the news that happen only in other people's lives. When loved ones just go completely missing, and years go by, and still nothing, and eventually other folk tell you to get on with your life, 'cos, hey, it's what they would have wanted, blah, blah, blah . . . yet instead you never give up wondering what became of them. I'd be like that with Fleur. I couldn't ever forget her.

To add to the mood, the marquee was also displaying posters warning festivalgoers about various religious cults recruiting in the vicinity. Twisted freaks who brainwash you, so it seemed, into moving abroad, giving them all your money, and breaking all contact with your friends and family forever.

"Oh, come on," Joel said quietly. "Fleur wouldn't be as totally stupid as to speak to weirdos like that, would she?"

In all honesty, I wasn't too sure. I mean, Claude? Never. Not a chance. But Fleur? Jeez . . . if they had a good-looking lad recruiting for them, then . . . Ugh. I couldn't even think about that.

I was at rock bottom.

But the problem with "rock bottom" is that there's always room left for a few layers of sludge underneath it.

I felt a bony finger jabbing my shoulder blade from behind. "Ronnie!" came the insipid voice. "Fancy seeing you here!"

I couldn't flipping believe it.

One hundred and twenty thousand people standing in a

field, and in my hour of need I bump into Panama flipping Goodyear!

"Ooh, you look a bit shell-shocked!" she rasped. "Weren't expecting to see me, were you?"

Was I hallucinating? No, she really was there, standing in front of me, looking vaguely ragged around the edges after her day in the great outdoors, although still slappably glamorous in camel Hessian trousers, a pale pink vest and open-toed sandals revealing an expensive paraffin pedicure. One small mercy was that she seemed to be alone.

"Uggghh . . . hi, Panama," I said quietly.

"Eh?" smiled Joel, looking at both of us. "You two know each other?"

"We go to school together! Small world, eh?" chuckled Panama warmly, looking deeply into Joel's hazel eyes and holding out her hand. "Sorry, I don't know your name."

"I'm Joel," he told her.

"I'm Panama Goodyear. Pleased to meet you," cooed Panama, shaking his hand, radiating oodles of charm.

She can do that so well when she wants to.

"Have you guys been having a good festival?" she asked.

"Mmm . . . well . . . not at the moment," I muttered, nodding at the Missing Persons sign. I hated allowing Panama the pleasure of knowing the mess we were in, but there was a tiny chance she could help.

"We've lost Fleur," I said. "Have you seen her?"

"Who?" said Panama, sneering ever so slightly.

Panama knew full well who Fleur was. She's known who

Fleur was from the very moment my friend, who's taller and prettier than Panama, walked into Blackwell on day one of Year 7. She's made life uncomfortable enough for Fleur for the last four years. Funnily enough, Panama's memory seemed to be failing her.

"Fleur," I repeated, sighing deeply. *"Fleur Swan."*

"Tall girl?" Joel added, trying to jog her memory. "Blonde hair?"

"Oh, right, *her,*" said Panama, rolling her eyes. "Sorry! Not seen her, I'm afraid."

"Oh, well, never mind," I sighed, feeling even more deflated.

Joel put his arm around my shoulder reassuringly.

"So, er, how long's she been gone?" asked Panama, feigning concern.

"About three hours," I told her through very tight lips.

"Oh, well," chuckled Panama. "Still a glimmer of hope then, eh?"

"Of course there is," said Joel assertively. "It's not been long. She'll turn up."

"Yeah, sure," said Panama insincerely. "But y'know, I'd inform the police before it gets too late. I mean, they'll find her, won't they? Or y'know . . . whatever's left of her."

At this point, Joel glared at Panama, slightly taken aback by her tactlessness.

"Ha ha! Joke!" Panama giggled. "Oh, dear, looks like you both lost your senses of humor in the Ethnic Drumming Zone."

"Er, we've got to get going now anyway," Joel said, grabbing my hand and leading me away.

"Me too," smiled Panama. "Gotta get back to the gang! I only nipped off to use the porta-loo. They'll be sending out search parties for me! They'll think I've been murdered!"

I stared at Panama, feeling a lump begin to form in my throat.

"Oooh!" giggled Panama, throwing her hand to her mouth. "No joke intended there, honest!"

"Good-bye then, Panama," said Joel quite forcefully.

"Bye, Joel!" winked Panama, turning on her heel and flouncing off. "Oh and Ronnie . . . good luck, y'know, finding whatsit!"

"Fleur," I said pointlessly.

"Oh yeah, *Fleur*!" sighed Panama, skipping off. "See ya!"

I wanted to break down and cry my eyes out right there and then. But Joel held my hand tightly and pointed out that I was probably just hungry and tired and getting things totally out of proportion. Then he force fed me sugary doughnuts and sweet tea until I could at least get it together to walk back to meet Claude.

"Fleur will turn up, I just know she will," Joel said, giving me a little cuddle. "She'll have just met some people, ended up at a party and lost all track of time. She'll probably pass by here any minute."

Joel and I waited for another half hour.

But no one showed up.

Eventually, Claude and I met back at our tent in the Magical Glade, feeling mutually defeated. By this point, we just wanted to be alone, so we thanked the lads for all their help and told them to go off and have some fun. It was time to make some tough decisions.

And with hindsight, Panama was probably right: we should have informed the police. Or at least told Daphne her sister was missing the very second we saw her. But stupidly, we didn't do that, because we both had this nagging feeling that we were betraying our friend. Fleur was going to be in so much trouble for getting lost, Daphne was bound to ring Paddy, Paddy would call the police, our folks would find out and make us all go home, what a total nightmare. But the longer we left it, the worse trouble we'd be in for not saying anything. It was a lose-lose situation.

So we did something really dumb. Something, in fact, so retardedly idiotic that there are no prizes for guessing it was my idea. We borrowed Franny's blonde wig from the boys' tent and decided to buy Fleur a little bit more time. Positioning the luscious, rather realistic blonde locks, pouring out of the top of her sleeping bag and stuffing pillows inside to form a body, we made a near-perfect fake bambino. It looked exactly like Fleur was sleeping soundly and had been since not long after Color Me Wonderful came off stage.

At first Claude and I felt like the cleverest, most ingenious young women in the world, but then time passed, and Daphne stuck her head through the tent doors, saw us all "snoozing" and whispered a relieved "Good night, girls" to us. I was beginning to feel virtually satanic. Especially when Daphne placed her hands sentimentally on the foot of Fleur's sleeping bag, then whispered to Rex, who towered behind her, "Aww, bless them, they've been so good! They're so flipping sensible for fifteen-year-olds!" Then she shut the tent door carefully, and we heard her saying, "She's a brilliant little sister, y'know, Rex? I love her to bits, really. Dunno know what I'd do without her."

That totally, completely sucked.

What were we doing covering for her?

"Right, Ronnie, here's the sketch," says Claude forcefully.

"Go on," I say.

"We wait till it's light, that's about two hours away, then we get out there and look for Fleur again. We try all the different places we did last night. If she's not appeared by nine A.M., we go straight to the police. She's had her chance by then—we have to grass her up. Agreed?"

"Agreed," I nod.

Claude was right. We could keep on lying, but we were just making things much worse.

"This is like a nightmare," Claude mutters. "I want to wake up."

I flounder about in my sleeping bag, trying to get comfy and perhaps even grab a bit of shut-eye, but the horrible star-shaped chasm between myself and Claude where Fleur should be is really choking me up. I can't fight my tears any longer so I try to let them out very quietly, wiping them on my sleeping bag. Claude overhears me, sitting up with a start.

"Hey! Come on, Ron, don't blub!" she says, putting her arms around me, her voice faltering a bit. "We'll get through this. It's just another LBD adventure, isn't it?"

"S'pose so," I say, wiping more tears on Claude's shoulder.

And then Claude begins to cry too.

enter the mud people

In the meantime, Astlebury has been transformed into a vast, grotesque swampland. Between 4 A.M. and 6 A.M., the gentle

British tippy-tappy of rain has accelerated into a torrential Goan-style monsoon, meaning that by the time Claude and I crawl from our leaking tent to embark on our manhunt, we have to crawl right back in again and dress for typhoon conditions. Quickly Claude is clad in Wellington boots and one of her mother's huge checkered raincoats, holding a tartan golfing umbrella, while I tie black bin liners around my sneakers, head and body in a bid to make me vaguely waterproof. Sure, I'd planned to pack wet weather gear, but my rucksack was already heavy after I filled it with sunny weather gear, so I, er, *didn't.* Then with the sun beginning to snook its reproachful head from behind Briggin Hill, we set off on our mission—Claude resembling an insane Ghanaian granny, and me waddling behind like a disgruntled polyethylene Big Foot.

Every route we take is soggy and thick with muddy puddles of water. Damp, miserable muddy people are wandering in every direction, trying to keep warm around bonfires, shivering under blankets as an uncharitable wind blows through the forest, dispersing the stench of three-day-old portable toilets through the fields. That said, I'm far from "lemon fresh" myself. In fact I stink like ripe Stilton cheese lost down the back of a radiator. I last showered at 8 A.M. on Friday morning—it's now forty-eight hours later. My nails are filthy and muddy, my hair's formed into huge wild tangles. Thankfully I'm far from home so no one important's going to see me.

"Where do you want to begin?" I sigh to Claude.

"Pastures New?" she suggests, and off we trudge, in and out of the burger vans and coffee carts where hordes of folk are sipping coffee and smoking ciggies to keep warm. We plod past the skate park where depressed skaters are sweeping puddles of water from their beloved ramps and Jimi Steele look-alikes are crawling out of vans, cursing the weather. No Fleur. We wobble through the mud around the back of the Karma Quadrant, checking every face in the toilet queues. No Fleur. Then we soldier on, chatting total rubbish to each other about this and that, trying to keep our spirits up, past the tattoo parlors and the People Pod marquee, and by this point the sun's rising high into the sky, making the fields feel much warmer. Eventually we reach the missing persons marquee, where a kind-looking lady in a multicolored striped jersey is snoozing facedown behind her desk, still clutching her clipboard. Behind the lady's head a large poster warns girls about freaks who drug drinks:

MIND YOUR DRINK! IT MIGHT NOT BE WHAT YOU THINK!

Uggghh! I didn't see that one last night! What's with this marquee? That woman must just sit there, thinking up new and imaginative demises to scare me with. What sort of twisted ghoul would actually drug your drink? *Aagggh* . . . I don't even want to think about that! After checking the medical center again (no luck, although we did meet a guy who was getting treated for a form of trench foot), we wander back through the sea of muddy litter, which now is the Hexagon Stage field. Claude and I are just communicating with each other in grunts by now.

God, I really wish I was at home in my bed. Whose flipping dumb idea was it to come to Astlebury?

"Right, it's three minutes to nine," announces Claude as we rest by the VIP enclosure gates and its obligatory posse of black-shirted security guards. As the sun tries its utmost to dry the fields, Claude strips off her raincoat, revealing a mud-splattered magenta T-shirt, damp jeans, filthy arms and a very grimy golden wristband.

"I feel disgusting," she sighs, staring at her phone yet again.

"Me too," I say.

We both pause and look nervously at each other.

We both know fine well what the agreement was.

"So, who do we inform first?" I say.

Claude thinks for a second, eyeing one of the burly VIP guards with some trepidation.

"Well, I suppose we just tell one of those guys that we have an urgent police matter, then, well, that will be it, won't it?" she says. "They'll set the ball in motion. The police, Paddy, the media . . . all that . . . I mean she's fifteen, Ronnie, she's blonde and pretty, from a good family . . . the whole of flipping Britain will be looking for her by midday. It's going to be really heavy."

"It's already really heavy, Claude," I sigh.

"So let's get it over with," Claude says, pointing toward a seven-foot-tall guard who looks a bit like a sofa with sunglasses. "He'll do."

Sorry, Fleur. We really have to do this. It's for the best.

We tread gingerly over to the guard, Claude waving slightly at him as we approach. "Er, excuse me, sir," she says.

The guard peers down at us suspiciously, chuckling a little at my bin-liner haute couture before bending down to examine first Claude's golden wristband and then mine.

"Er, yes, excuse me," begins Claude again. "We seem to have got ourselves into a spot of trouble . . ."

But the guard's not listening one little jot. He's turning round, shouting to a crowd of other security men and women standing on the other side of the fence.

"We've lost our friend, you see?" continues Claude, raising her voice a bit, but I can barely hear her, because the massive metal VIP enclosure gates are sweeping open with a mighty thrashing of metal.

"Well, we've more than lost her," shouts Claude. "She's been gone for fourteen hours . . . And, er, I know that you're busy, and it's not really your job, but do you think you could contact the police for us?"

The guard, who has totally ignored Claude's little speech, gives a "thumbs-up" sign to his colleagues before staring back at us with a perplexed look.

"Eh? I beg your pardon, ladies? Missed all of that," he smiles, nodding at the open gates. "But you're free to go in now. Make it quick, though, 'cos we have to get these gates shut pretty sharpish."

Claude and I stare at each other in utter confusion, then gaze in mystification at the open VIP gates.

"What!?" we both squeak in stereo.

"What? What do you mean, *what*?" says the guard. "You're free to go in now."

"We . . . we . . . can go through, into there?!" I gasp. "Into the VIP?"

"Errrrr . . . duh . . . yes!" says the guard as if he's dealing with complete simpletons. *"You've got gold wristbands.* Look, you do want in, don't you?"

We both stare at him with our mouths agog, just catching flies.

"Have you girls been taking drugs?" says the guard.

"No, we haven't!" squeaks Claude.

Just this second a bloodred tour bus looms up behind us. The guard grabs his walkie-talkie and begins barking, "The Annanova crew are here! Repeat! Annanova crew are on their way in. Can you inform hospitality?" He turns to us and chivies us through the gates, less patiently now. "Look, shift your bums, girls, you're going to get run over!"

It all happens quick as a flash. Within seconds, Veronica Ripperton and Claudette Cassiera are standing inside Astlebury's legendary Very Important Person enclosure, totally gobsmacked, staring at our wristbands in overwhelming disbelief.

It's surreal—no, it's more than surreal. I feel totally dizzy.

"Claude," I shriek, *"we've . . . we've got . . . VIP wristbands!"*

"I . . . I . . . er . . . ooh, I know!" yells Claude as the gates slam shut behind us, making us officially part of the "beautiful people."

"It was Spike! Spike Saunders!" I splutter. "He must have sent us VIP wristbands! And we didn't even know! We didn't even notice. None of us sussed that our wristbands were different from the other zillion folks' who are here! I mean, did, d . . . d . . . d . . . did you notice? I didn't! Did you?"

My head is spinning now.

Claude is shaking her head, hopping from one foot to the

other, half smiling, half crying. "So . . . we've been VIPs all along!" she cries. "We could have met Carmella Dupris! We could have been hanging out backstage. Oh my God, Fleur would have been so happy. God, if we'd known about this, we'd never have been in that stupid crowd! We'd never have lost Fleur in the first place."

"But what do we do now?" I say, feeling totally bewildered. "I really want to have a look around! But should we just call the police like we agreed?"

Claude bites her lip, eyeing the VIP marquee ahead of us. "Well . . . I really need to use the bathroom," she says, biting her lip nervously. "So I suppose we could use the VIP ones and freshen up a bit first, eh? And then call the police straight afterward?"

"Okay, that sounds fair," I say, my stomach doing somersaults. "Oh, noooo, Claude! We're going to use the VIP toilets! I won't be able to pee if there's anyone famous in there."

"Me neither!" says Claude.

We drag each other up to the door of the marquee, where two excessively tall, fresh-faced, salon-coiffed blondes are standing, dressed like they've fallen off a catwalk wearing customized denims, funky silk vests and kitten-heel sandals displaying perfect pedicures and ankle jewelry. The girl with the whitest hair drawls heavily on a Marlboro Light, gossiping in a clipped Eastern European brogue.

"It's bad en-uff that you've got to put up with that seelly beetch Hazel inviting Curtis to be front row with her at the Versacci collection," huffs the girl, "but now she turns up here too!"

"Oh, tell me about it!" snaps the other tall, terrifyingly pretty blonde. "That Hazel Valenski is cruising for a kick up the ass if she even so much as lays one more finger on my Curtis!"

Claude and I sneak past, nudging each other furiously.

"Claude! Wasn't that . . . Tabitha Lovelace . . . y'know, the *supermodel!?*" I say under my breath.

Claude spins around to double-check, letting out a little squeak.

"Yes! And that was Zaza Berry! The face of Helena's Boudoir underwear!"

"They were slagging off Hazel Valenski!" I say, feeling extremely honored to have heard such high-level tittle-tattle. "That is all sooo *Red Hot Celebs!*"

"I know!" gasps Claude, but by this point we're turning into the VIP enclosure, instantly forgetting about Zaza and Tabitha, because what lies before us is even more terrifically, awesomely wonderful.

We're now standing in a vast black marquee, with a floor made out of black rubber and a raised DJ box in the corner. People are milling everywhere, but not muddy bin-baggy folk like me and Claude; oh, no, beautifully kept, heavily styled, zingy-clean people with gleaming skin, fresh breath and laundered socks. Oodles of folk hang around the bar area guzzling espressos, smoothies, Bloody Marys and straight bottles of Jack Daniel's. Others feast on a vast buffet of delicious-smelling croissants, eggs Benedict and smoked salmon bagels served by chefs in large white hats. Vast plasma TV screens fill the entire back wall, playing highlights of last night's Astlebury Hexagon Main

Stage. As we pass by, Zander Parr fills every screen, stripped down to his underpants, victoriously waving a flaming torch at the audience.

"Look!" gasps Claude, nudging me. "Zander Parr! I don't believe it! He's there!"

I spin around, spotting Zander Parr, not merely on TV, but asleep on a sofa right beside us, looking all small and delicate, wearing the aforementioned underpants firmly on his head, wrapped in a Union Jack flag to spare his blushes.

"Oh, wow!" I say. "It's really him."

We peer at him, mesmerized by his famousness for a moment, before moving on to a bistro-style seating area where TV and radio crews are holding meetings about their day ahead. Men and women are lugging bundles of heavy cameras, wires and lights into the marquee, while TV presenters such as MTV's Lonny Dawson and Chloe Kissimy are rehearsing their lines for today's live links as well as making up questions to ask the bands.

"So, how have you been enjoying Astlebury so far?" Chloe Kissimy is reading off a piece of paper, over and over again, trying to commit the difficult question to memory.

In a small clearing in the chairs, kicking a soft football, are some lads we recognize straightaway as the hip-hop squad Blaze Tribe Five. They're the first band on today. God, they are all so lush! Meanwhile, over in a quieter corner, slumped on a set of plush leather couches, SmartBomb, the three-piece Cornwall electronic dance act, are being interviewed by the *Midnight Mayhem* girls, Britain's premiere tabloid gossip columnists. Fleur reads that page every day! Those girls are her heroes.

On an adjacent sofa, Mick Monroe, the editor of *Red Hot Celebs* magazine, is quaffing back champagne cocktails flanked by a flurry of beautiful girlies who are either a girl band, some more random models . . . or simply a passing Swedish volleyball team, sent by God to make girls dressed in bin bags and raincoats feel inferior.

I don't really know what to say by this point.

I'm suffering from celebrity overload! No one at school is ever going to believe this, and I'm far, far too cool to go up and ask for autographs. Claude is also beginning to walk funnily, as she's totally desperate to pee and there's no toilet sign anywhere. Asking anyone is out of the question. These people look like they've never pooed or weed in their entire lives.

"Okay, this is just too weird now," I say to Claude. "It's beginning to freak me out."

"I know," says Claude, picking some mud from her hairline. "I think we're a tad underdressed."

We look at each other, knowing that although it's tempting to hang about and grow "acclimatized" to a VIP lifestyle, we've got a far bigger drama to handle.

One of us is missing.

And that's when we spot the most freaky sight of all.

Commandeering the entire far corner, which boasts several squashy burgundy sofas, is a posse of people who just compel you to stare at them, as they're all so impossibly, funkily, glamorous and "in-crowdish." There must be more than two dozen of them, I'd guess, slumped together, like they've been up all night but want to carry on partying. They're giggling and gossiping and playing guitars. The guys all seem to have long scruffy locks and a variety of facial hair, and they're dressed in faded denim and kooky T-shirts. They look like male models attempting to look like normal Joes and failing, wonderfully. Several women are lounging among the clique too, all of them out of exactly the same angelic mold as Zaza Berry: tall, bronzed, willowy, vaguely bohemian, either lying with their pretty doe-eyed heads on the laps of a rock star, or sitting cocooned in a pair of strong arms, wearing beestung pouts of indifference.

You'd have to have lived on Jupiter for the last year not to recognize their ringleader, the legendary Curtis Leith, singer with the Kings of Kong. He looks like Jesus in blue jeans, chairing the Last Supper.

"Claude! It's the Kings of Kong!" I splutter far too loudly, which thankfully no one hears, as the DJ has begun spinning some tunes.

"No, it can't be," says Claude. I don't know who she's arguing with, me or just the laws of reality.

"It's them, Claude! It's them!" I persist. "Over there, lying on the burgundy sofas, look! Curtis Leith! And Lorcan Moriarty, the lead guitarist, is there too."

"You're right!" shudders Claude. "And Benny Lake, the drummer!"

I home in on the tableaux more carefully, trying to pick out faces. There's a chick I recognize from last winter's Gap campaign . . . Lilyanna someone? She was married to Zander Parr for, like, about five minutes. Beside her a brunette woman applies red lip gloss in a small heart-shaped mirror as a coffee-skinned model type regales everyone with a story about something fabulous she did last year in Cannes. And in the eye of the storm, chatting, giggling and looking supremely minxish, wearing this incredible pair of indigo jeans and an off-the-shoulder stripey top, is a blonde girl who might well be Tabitha Lovelace's little sister. She's pretty and slim, with slightly flushed cheeks. Maybe she's an actress or a pop star or something. She looks really familiar.

Uh-huh. Hang on.

"Claude!" I gasp, placing one muddy hand over my mouth. "You're not going to believe this. I think that's Fleur."

Friends reunited

The next few seconds are an absolute whirlwind. Claude and I let out huge screeeeeeches, all the music and chatter seems to pause, and the entire room turns and gawps at the fuss. At the same time, Fleur Swan, for it truly is the little madam, sees us, emits an even more piercing euphoric eruption, then proceeds to charge at us, arms and legs and hair flapping, before scooping us both up and hugging us tightly.

"It's yoooooooooou!" she squeals. *"You've found me! Oh, hurray!"*

I'm so relieved to see her safe, well and not dismembered by the local neighborhood serial killer, I feel like collapsing.

"Fleur!" I say, getting a bit choked up. "We're so pleased to see you!"

"Me too!" laughs Fleur. "Hey, and isn't this all so great? We're in the VIP!"

Claude, by contrast, is not letting Fleur off so easily. Propelling herself up to about seven foot, three inches of pure anger, she begins jabbing Fleur away with both hands, shouting, "Well, we can see that, can't we?! You're in the VIP!" stamping one foot, with eyes as black as a raging bull.

"I know!" coos Fleur. "Spike sent us VIP passes! Isn't it wonderful?"

"Wonderful!?" thunders Claude. *"Wonderful, Fleur? You brainless, selfish, vacuous, idiotic bimbo. I could almost punch your lights out, you silly mare! How is it wonderful?"*

"Er, it's a bit wonderful," I mumble, realizing the entire Blaze Tribe Five collective have pulled up seats to watch.

"Oh, and you can shut up, Ronnie!" yells Claude. "You've been worried out of your mind!"

Fleur's not looking half as perky now.

"You are so out of order!" shouts Claude. "Who exactly do you think you are, putting me and Ronnie through all this worry?"

"But I was fine! I was partying with the Kings of Kong in here!" Fleur says.

"Oh, you were fine, were you?" growls Claude. "Well, while you've been being *fine,* we've had police sniffer dogs looking for you! Oh, and Sky News has been showing your Year Seven Blackwell school photo since six A.M.!"

Fleur's face turns green. "Not the one where I've got a wonky fringe and a sweaty forehead!" she whispers.

Claude glares at her, torturing her for a few seconds.

"You're kidding, aren't you?" says Fleur anxiously. "You didn't call the police really, did you? Or Paddy?"

Claude flares her nostrils a little, making her sweat a tad longer.

"Okay, Fleur, we didn't," she says. "But we very *nearly* did. We covered for you instead. We've even lied to Daphne and that's not on!"

"Oh, mmm, yeah . . . Daphne," Fleur says sheepishly, as if it's beginning to dawn on her what she's put us through. Fleur's eyes begin to fill up a little. "Look, I'm really, really sorry, girls," she says. "Truly, I am. I got a bit carried away, you know, once I got in here and met everyone. And the phone network's broken so I couldn't call anyone. And then I met the Kings and . . ."

"Oh, just button it, bimbo, and give me a hug," tuts Claude, fighting to suppress a small smile. "I'm so flipping relieved you're alive, Fleur!"

Fleur gives Claude a big warm hug and a kiss.

Thank God they've made up—that was going to be one long, silent car journey home.

"So anyway," says Fleur, untangling herself from Claude's muddy raincoat. "I take it we don't have to rush right back to Daphne, do we?"

Claude and I look to each other for consent.

"Well, maybe we could stay just a little while longer," I suggest, eyeing the buffet. "I'm famished."

"Me too," says Claude, licking her lips.

"Hurray!" says Fleur. "But, er, before that, I was just thinking maybe you two could fit in a quick restyle."

"A restyle? What do you mean? What's wrong with us?" says Claude awkwardly.

"Er . . . not much," begins Fleur. "It's just that right now you remind me of that old lady who used to live in the hedge behind the tennis courts. And, well, we all know what happened to her, don't we?"

"No," says Claude.

"She got locked up, Claude," says Fleur seriously.

i'm ready for my close-up

In less than an hour, I barely recognize the Veronica Iris Ripperton standing before me in the mirror.

Trust Fleur to have not only ingratiated herself with the Kings of Kong and all of their girlfriends, who seem to view her as a tiny protégé, but to have infiltrated the enemy camp too, becoming all chummy with the fashion stylist Hazel Valenski. Hazel, who's been flown over to the UK by the Kings of Kong's New York record label to style them for tonight's gig, is hiding away from her enemies in the wardrobe marquee next door to where we found Fleur. Hazel was surrounded by racks of expensive designer dresses, astounding hats, fabulous shoes and handbags you'd probably slit your own throat for. As Fleur dragged us into Hazel's lair, the fashion legend was sucking a jujube and echinacea smoothie through a twirly straw and grumbling about the "demented skeleton" Tabitha Lovelace, who she'd heard was in the VIP "bustin' her chops about Curtis Leith."

"Jesus! I am so over her freakin' ugly boyfriend!" Hazel yelled to a passing makeup artist. "The papers just made all that rubbish up anyway!" she moaned. "But hey, if Tabitha pops in for a touch-up, you better get that antiseptic concealer stick out. Her acne looks set for another flare-up. That's quite an unfortu-

218

nate situation for the face of La Rivess cosmetics, don't you think?"

The makeup artist cracked up, laughing at Hazel's bitchiness.

"Hey, Hazel!" shouted Fleur.

"Hey, Lost Girl! What's new?" smiled Hazel, the platinum blonde streak in her curly brown Afro reverberating as she spoke.

"Ooh, I'm not lost anymore!" laughed Fleur. "I found my friends! This is Ronnie and Claude. They sort of need a bit of Hazel magic on their look though. Could you help them out too?"

Hazel stared at our bedraggled clothes, raised an eyebrow, then began to roar. "I'm a stylist, not a magician!" she hooted, standing up and browsing through a nearby rail. "But I'll give it a shot."

"Great!" smiled Claude.

"But first of all, you both need showers," Hazel said, throwing us towels. "I don't even put trash that smells like you two outside my apartment, because it lowers the tone of the neighborhood."

Claude and I blushed furiously.

"Hey, and you girls better bring this stuff back! Or I'm gonna be in trouble! If I lose any more clothes, Venus Records will fly me back to New York cattle class. And Hazel Valenski does not do cattle class! What does Hazel not do?"

"Cattle class!" we all yelled as Hazel began passing us armfuls of incredible outfits. I had my eye on some black Dolce and Gabbana trousers with silver studs and an emerald green Gucci vest with a silver butterfly on the shoulder, verypopstarrish.com!

After a hot shower (bliss!) and a snuggle in some extra-fluffy dressing gowns, the LBD grabbed our outfits and moved into the makeup area, where tons of dancers, backing singers and TV presenters were begging the makeup girls and boys to disguise last night's partying with under-eye concealer gloop and light-enhancing lotions.

We grabbed seats and waited our turn on the beauty conveyer belt, bristling with glee as first one lady dabbed us with foundation, then shooshed us with a massive brush festooned with shimmery glitter. Then a hairstylist appeared, back combing and straightening various sections of our hair. My hair was titivated into a sort of 1950s quiff with funky bunches!

It looked totally marvelous! I'd never be able to do this myself at home!

And while all this went on, a manicurist gave me a neat French nail transformation with a tiny red heart inset into each cuticle!

So when I finally reach a full-length mirror, I can barely believe my eyes.

I look really . . . WOW!

Not that I'm one to blow my own trumpet but . . . hang on just one moment . . .

(gets out LBD trumpet)

HONNNNNK HONNNNNK!

I look flipping marvelous! We all do!

Claude resembles a mini Carmella Dupris, clad in black suede trousers, coordinated snakeskin ankle boots and a fitted purple top, while Fleur's made another costume change because she's fallen in love with a pale pink, sparkly girlie frock with a lacy skirt and spaghetti straps.

Of course, all the way through our restyle, Fleur nattered away, filling us in on "the lost hours" about how she tumbled off a biker dude's shoulders headfirst during Color Me Wonderful's set and nearly got trampled to death in the mosh pit. Apparently, the crowds seemed to rally together and pass her over the safety barrier, where she wound up in the VIP medical area with Zander Parr, who was getting burn treatments on his nether regions. Finally, after the nurse certified her well, Fleur found herself in the VIP marquee, where she sat quietly for ages (no, I didn't believe that part either), waiting to be forcefully ejected. But nobody threw her out. In fact, everyone was really friendly! "So then I started chatting with some executives from Big Benson Records in L.A.," Fleur told us, "and I confessed to them that I was an intruder, because, like, they were all big and tough and gangster-rap and I felt like a bit of a wuss. But they said I wasn't an intruder at all! I had a VIP pass like everyone else! *I was a VIP, for crying out loud!* That's when I realized what Spike had done."

"And did it occur to you at any point, you great twit, to come and find us!?" nagged Claude.

"Of course!" sighed Fleur. "I planned to! But then things got really, really crazy. I mean, first Carmella Dupris had a little private after-show party right here in the marquee. And Million Dollar Mark DJ'd!"

Claude scowled at Fleur.

"And then there was a huge rumpus because some boring

bods from the Astlebury Parish Council in tweed jackets with corduroy patches on the elbows tried to have Zander Parr arrested for being nude on stage. We all had to argue with them to let Zander stay."

"Oh, that's fine then," grumped Claude.

"Claude, stop sulking!" protested Fleur. "I was just about to leave right then. But then the Kings of Kong's Winnebago showed up and the whole entourage piled out and the party really kicked off!"

I had to laugh. Fleur was really trying hard to do "humble" and "regretful."

It was not working.

"Anyway, what did I have to come back for?" Fleur scoffed. "Claude, you were copping off with Damon. And Ronnie! You were with that Joel. I was a total gooseberry!"

Ouch . . . I knew that was coming.

"Hah! Well, you soon put a stop to that, didn't you?" snapped Claude, slightly guiltily.

"And I wasn't with Joel," I protested. "I didn't even snog him!"

"What . . . really?" gasped Fleur. "You haven't snogged him? Well, you should have by now, you total clot! He's totally gorgeous and obviously fancies you like mad!"

I wanted to argue with her, but I couldn't. Joel is totally gorgeous.

"For heaven's sake, Ronnie!" squealed Fleur, shaking her head. "How have you not snogged him yet? What is wrong with you, woman?"

I pondered Fleur's words for a second, but the truth is, I don't really know.

vera the Pearless

A tremendous buzz is growing in the VIP enclosure.

Makeup artists and stylists are jittering around, whispering and giggling. Dancers and singers are ladling on extra lip gloss and perfecting their man-catching pouts. Everyone's nudging each other, eyes as wide as saucers, ogling the door expectantly.

"He's here!" gibbers a young waitress excitedly to her pal.

"He's walking in now!" barks an MTV producer to Chloe Kissimy. "Make sure you get that exclusive!"

"Yes, it's definitely him getting out of the helicopter!" shouts a *Midnight Mayhem* columnist to her colleague. "Which supermodel flew down with him, Fifi or Lily? We need it for tomorrow's headline!"

"Talent walking through!" yells a burly security guard into his mouthpiece.

"Hee hee!" beams Fleur, grabbing our hands tightly. "Spike Saunders is here!"

Claude and I freeze.

Spike Saunders, the guy who is responsible for us being here, is going to be in this very room any second. We hadn't bargained on having to actually meet him again!

We haven't planned our "spontaneous" small talk!

Agggghhhh!

And we're not going to get a chance either, because right

that second, a plethora of pretty people, most of whom are regulars in *Red Hot Celebs* magazine, roll into the marquee. There's Fenella Tack, Spike's hard-as-nails manager; Tasha, his makeup artist; Krafty, his hairstylist; Bobby Bean, Spike's wardrobe mistress; and more than a dozen different bouncers. Walking behind them is Spike's little brother Caleb (who played one of the lead zombies in *Zombie Killer IV*). Caleb's chatting with Spike's personal assistant, Lewis, and Spike's personal helicopter chauffeur, Parker Hendry. Somewhere in the middle of the madness, moving far more slowly and with strikingly less self-importance than his staff, is Mr. Spike Saunders, looking even more fabulously scrummy and swoonsome than last time we met him!

"Oh, wow!" says Fleur, 101 percent bedazzled.

"Ahhhhh!" sighs Claude as Spike's entourage flounces snootily past.

Security guards are busying themselves ejecting lesser mortals from the sofas, claiming that it's all reserved for Spike's crew. Lewis, Spike's P.A., slumps down on one, clicking his fingers at a waitress. "We need water here! Now!" he says, brimming with arrogance. "Not sparkling or still, mind. I need gently carbonated Peruvian mountain water. It was on Spike's hospitality prerequest form. And make sure it's chilled to no less than ten degrees!"

Lewis roots around in his . . . well, it's a handbag, to be honest. "Here, take my thermometer!" he says.

The waitress scurries away as a *Midnight Mayhem* girl sidles closer to the sofas, attempting to have a word with Spike, who's sitting quietly, playing a game of Snake on his mobile phone.

"Er, excuse me, Spike," begins the reporter, brandishing her notepad, "how was the helicopter flight down here today?"

"Don't crowd the artist!" screams Spike's manager, Fenella. "And no unsolicited questions! All press requests must be faxed to Spike's management in Los Angeles and approved by Selena Kanchelskis, head of artist relations at Silver Shard Records! Move away, please!"

"Oh, for God's sake, he's sitting right there!" huffs the columnist, stomping off.

Spike gazes upward, sees the altercation and slumps farther down into his seat. The whole room is pretending not to stare, as it's sooo uncool to rubberneck, but frankly, it's dead fascinating watching him breathe. The bloke sells out 100,000-seat stadiums from London to L.A. to Sydney. So why does he look so depressed? He must have more money than he knows what to do with!

Just then an additional figure staggers into the VIP room, shedding some light on Spike's sad countenance.

"It's Twiggy Starr," says Claude behind her hand, "and he looks absolutely wrecked."

If gossip columns are to be believed, Twiggy, Spike's lead guitarist and childhood friend, is on the brink of being fired. *Red Hot Celebs* ran a story only last week saying he's been cutting sound checks, arguing with Spike and showing up for gigs so inebriated he's unsure which end of the guitar to strum. And now that I've seen him, it's pretty believable.

"Kari, where's the bar?" slurs Twiggy to the blonde-haired American girl propping him up. Not only does Twiggy have cornflakes and chocolate sauce in his curly black hair, but his nose is bright red. Kari, who sent us the tickets, seems to be supervising him.

"Sorry, Spike," mouths Kari. "I took my eyes off him for ten seconds and he did a runner. I'll get him some coffee. Lots of coffee."

"It's not your fault, Kari," sighs Spike. "You're doing your best."

Spike's manager, Fenella, eyes Twiggy with a glare of unadulterated revulsion.

"Hey, we should go and say hello to Spike!" says Fleur, gleefully missing the palpable tension.

"Nooooo, Fleur!" I tut. "Leave it! Let's just be glad we're here. We don't need to hassle him."

"Ronnie's right, Fleur," agrees Claude, as Twiggy crashes backward from his spot at the bar, taking out two coffee tables behind him with a tremendous crash. The *Midnight Mayhem* girls grin deviously, grabbing their notebooks.

"Pick him up now!" Fenella barks at the security guards.

In the ensuing chaos, Fleur shoots through the fortress of Spike's staff, pitching up right in front of the pop star with her hands on her hips.

"Spike!" she says. "It's me, Fleur! Do you remember me?"

Spike Saunders looks up and squints at Fleur. He looks a little confused.

Claude and I hold our breath, bracing ourselves for the most humiliating knock-back of all knock-backs.

Gnnngnnn!

He stares for a few excruciating moments longer, then

chucks back his head and howls. "Ha ha! It's you! The BDL girl, isn't it?" he roars.

"The LBD! That's right! You remember us, don't you?!" laughs Fleur.

"Do you want me to remove her?" barks a security mutant. "I'll have her thrown out."

"No, I don't want you to remove her. I want you to find her friends!" laughs Spike. "You've brought the other two trouble-makers, haven't you?"

"Yeah, Ronnie and Claude! They're over there!" points Fleur. Hurray!

In a show-biz blink, we're on the sofas, sitting with *the* Spike Saunders! Everyone in the room seems to be whispering, "Who are they? Are they a girl band? Who are the LBD?"

Hee hee hee!

"Well, helloooo, young ladies," chortles Spike Saunders. "Long time no see!"

"It's been a whole year," I giggle.

"A whole year already?" he laughs, displaying rows of freak-ishly perfect white teeth. "We toured America all winter and the Far East all spring, so the time's just really flown by for me."

"Wow! So have you not been home at all?" says Claude.

"No. Not really," he says a tiny bit sadly.

"Like, not even to change your pants?"

Spike laughs heartily. "Well, I've got an underwear roadie," he winks, "so don't worry. Even if I get hit by a truck in Arlington, Virginia, my underwear will be fresh for the emergency room staff."

"So, are you, like, still nervous about stuff like the gig

tonight?" I ask, trying to think of a sensible question not involving Spike's pants.

Spike glances apprehensively at Twiggy, sighing a little. "Well, not about my role in it, Ronnie," he says. "It's the *random factors* I worry about. We're playing all of our new tracks for the first time tonight, you see."

"Oh," we all say.

Does Spike really think that Twiggy is fit to headline Astlebury?

"So how's school going, then?" says Spike mischievously. "Did things ever get back to normal after that summer fête you had? That was pretty, er, wild, wasn't it?"

"Our principal's still on medication over it all," says Fleur. "He's still really mad about the police needing to be called."

Spike meets thousands of people every year. I can't believe he actually remembers any of this stuff. Maybe he doesn't meet many people he can chat to.

The next thing Spike says, however, absolutely floors me:

"And what about that Jonny, Jimi, Timmy bloke?"

"Jimi Steele?" I squeak. "How do you know about him?"

"Er, because Fleur sends e-mails to my fan club telling me what you're all up to." Spike laughs.

Fleur bristles with pride, mouthing at me and Claude, "See! I told you Spike reads them!"

"And you, Ronnie, posted some messages on my web boards last summer saying you'd been making out with 'the skater dude' a few months after I met you last time," Spike says.

I've gone crimson!

"You sounded really loved up!" teases Spike. "It really cheered me up!"

"Ugghh . . . I just wanted to keep you up to date on the LBD gossip after, y'know, you were so kind to us." I smile. "I didn't actually think you'd read your own web message boards!"

"Oh, I don't just read them," whispers Spike, mock-solemnly. "I post on them too! In fact I got so bored during the last stadium tour of Southeast Asia that I stole Lewis's laptop and began posting messages slagging myself off. I pretend to be a mother of three in Doncaster called Vera."

"Hang on a minute!" gasps Fleur. "I had an argument with you a few months ago! I'm Blondie101!"

"I'm Vera the Fearless!" whispers Spike, tapping his nose. "Hey, just don't tell the *Midnight Mayhem* girls!"

And then a grand cheer erupts right through the VIP room: The Fusia phone network has been restored!

What a relief! Fleur's phone begins to buzz furiously, her first greeting being from an apoplectic Paddy Swan, who threatens to "drive down to Astlebury and rip the arms off the joker with the tattoo gun." Oh, dear. Next along is Daphne sounding pretty cross indeed that we left this morning without telling her where we were going.

"If only she knew the half of it!" tuts Claude.

I decide to leave Fleur alone to make some apologetic phone calls.

I think I'm suffering from a celebrity overdose.

I sneak off to the VIP bathrooms. I need a break from all this craziness. Standing in the loo, in front of the mirrors, soaping my hands in the metallic sinks, I can't stop ogling the all new, improved, über-babe Ronnie Ripperton.

Ooh, y'know I almost fancy myself! And to think that three short weeks ago, on Blackwell Disco night (or Black Friday, as Dad calls it) I was *this close* to shooting myself repetitively with a nail gun.

Look at me now! With my va-voom celebrity hair and makeup! And I'm hanging out with the Spike Saunders entourage! I'm on top of the world!

So why do I feel like there's just one teensy-weensy-eensy thing missing?

"Cool tattoo," remarks a girl beside me, drying her hands. "Is that real?"

"Er, wah . . . eh?" I say, snapping out of my trance.

"The tattoo?" repeats the girl, clad in navy cut-off trousers, sports jacket and a yellow baseball hat. Her long brown hair is swept into a ponytail.

"Ooh! Ta," I say, remembering the artwork on my neck. "It's not real."

"Ah . . . well, good for you!" she smiles, taking off her cap and displaying a red streak in her gilt-tipped hair. "It's a crazy concept, isn't it? Drawing stuff on your body, like, permanently? 'Cos y'know, things change, don't they? You end up feeling different about stuff, you know, like tattoos, music, boyfriends. No feeling lasts forever, does it?"

"Hmmm, I know what you mean," I smile, letting out a little groan. I used to think Jimi and I would last forever.

"Oh," cringes the girl, "I've put my foot in it, haven't I?"

Don't even ask how I wound up telling a total stranger the

entire story of Jimi Steele, Blackwell Disco and the curse of the flaky buttmunch. And all about Joel, who began sounding a bit like Superman when I described him. It all just spilled out. What is it about the ladies loo that makes you do that? It just felt good to get it off my chest.

"And Jimi's never even told me that he loves me," I sigh, scooshing myself with complimentary perfume.

"Ooh, that's cold, man," says the girl. "Well, you're right to teach him a lesson."

"S'pose," I sigh.

"We have to go now, Ammy," instructs a fierce lady with a clipboard looming impatiently beside us. "We're totally behind schedule."

"Fine," the girl says, turning to me. Her eyes are astoundingly green.

"Well, better split. Gotta go to work . . . hey, but if you ask me, sounds like the Jimi one needs another chance."

"D'you think?" I say.

"Well . . . yes and no!" She laughs. "Probably yes. I mean, he sounds like he's being a real doofus . . . but it's all pretty regular guy stuff. Guys do stupid things. They forget about parties they've arranged to take you to sometimes. Cut him some slack, eh?"

"Hmmm, maybe you're right," I say, noticing the Celtic tattoo spilling out of the bottom of her trouser leg.

"Hey, actually," she says, "forget that, don't listen to me. My man problems are world famous," she groans, sweeping out the door. "See ya, kiddo!"

"Bye!" I smile.

Of course, I don't feel one iota clearer about my love life. But she was lovely, whoever she was.

totally over the top

It's almost 10 P.M. on Sunday, and we're standing in the wings of Astlebury's world-famous Hexagon Stage. The Kings of Kong went down like an absolute storm. I've never heard people cheer so loud and stamp their feet for an encore. The LBD got so wrapped up in the Kings' post-gig celebrations (and yes, Curtis really is just as lush up close, even if he does need to use stronger deodorant) that we ended up missing Amelia Annanova's set completely! I never even set eyes on her! *Aggh,* never mind . . . it was worth the sacrifice just for the pleasure of seeing the Kings' drummer, Benny Lake, striding into the VIP area, stripping his T-shirt off and then asking us ever so kindly, batting his big brown eyes, if we'd mind finding him a beer. *Phwoaaar!*

But now it's time for Astlebury's star attraction. There must be well over 100,000 people waiting for Spike's performance. Back here in the wings, Spike's been pacing nervously back and forth for the last twenty minutes, praying, crossing himself and sticking his head round the side of the stage, to sneak a glimpse of the crowd, before leaping up and down excitedly, retching with nerves. On stage, an army of hairy technicians fiddle with mike stands and snare drums. As well as Spike's entourage, Lewis, Fenella et al., we're also in the pleasant company of Daphne Swan and Rex, who seem totally starstruck and more than a little bewildered by the events of the last hour.

Incidentally, Rex isn't an evil giant after all. He's just a rather nice, overly tall hippie dude from Brighton who must have terrible trouble getting trousers to fit him. Never mind, though, he's never stopped grinning since the second we called to say that not only was Daphne a VIP, but we'd found a spare gold wristband for her new beau if he wanted to come along too. It turned out that Caleb, Spike's brother, had been chucked by his girlfriend the night before so she'd not be using hers.

"What a piece of luck!" Fleur said mischievously, eyeing the gorgeous Caleb before nicking his extra gold band and running off to find Daphne.

"How do you girls do it?" laughs Daphne, gazing at the crowd, utterly flummoxed.

"It's just a fluke," giggles Claude. "Every time!"

I feel totally chundersome just looking at this huge crowd. How Spike manages to walk out there and actually sing with a zillion sets of eyes drilling into him beats me; he certainly earns that gold turbo-bubble button.

"Hey, look, Ronnie, Twiggy's getting a right telling off," whispers Claude, pointing over to the corner where Twiggy Starr's being slapped, poked and thoroughly harangued by Fenella.

"Just do your job like you're supposed to!" Fenella is barking. "You're not irreplaceable, y'know. I could find nine other clones who look pretty with a guitar by the end of the week, if I chose to!"

"Oh, pur-lease, Fenny-wenn," Twiggy smirks. "Shut your trap, will you? You're all gob. Just try getting rid of me. I'm part of the furniture around here, dear."

Fenella twists on her crocodile-skinned stiletto heel and goose-steps away, leaving Twiggy's best mate Spike to have a quieter word.

"Look, you have got all those chords for 'Lost' straight in your head, haven't you?" asks Spike. "You didn't exactly nail it in rehearsals, did you?"

"It's all fine," says Twiggy, quite believably.

"And what about 'Windmill'—you've rehearsed that bridge again, haven't you?"

"S'all up there," sighs Twiggy, tapping the side of his head.

"It better be, Twiggy," warns Spike. "We're going out live on BBC1. And we're getting syndicated worldwide by MTV2! And . . ."

"You worry too much," scoffs Twiggy, then belches loudly.

Spike wanders away, shaking his head.

"Five minutes, Spike!" yells Fenella. "C'mon, people, let's start moving! Where's Foxton? Where's the drummer?"

"Ere," grunts a wide-eyed guy with a bald head who's been in and out of the loo seven times in the last half hour. He must have a weak bladder.

"And where are the backing singers! Are they still in wardrobe?" screams Fenella. "Lewis, round everyone up now! Now!"

Suddenly, the entire Spike Saunders road show emerges, guitarists, backing singers, synth players, percussionists, all swigging from bottles of water, practicing scales, pacing about nervously, hugging each other and wishing each other the best of luck. They all look quite terrified as they gather around Spike for a little pep talk.

"I just want to say good luck to everyone," Spike says. "There's no need to be nervous, they sound like a friendly bunch. Let's just do what we always do and we'll be more than okay. I've got every faith in you lot . . . that's why I pay you so much!"

Everyone groans at Spike, albeit highly affectionately.

"We can do this, can't we?" he says. "Right?"

"Right!" choruses the gang.

"So, let's do it then!" he grins, and behind him the vast audience begins to chant an unmistakable rowdy chorus.

"One Spike Saunders! There's only one Spike Saunders! There's only one Spike Saaaaaunders!"

Gulp! I'd be out the back gate hiding in a hedge by now.

Spike gives Fenella a small nod. Fenella winks, then gives a thumbs-up to a woman in a headset, who nudges an old rocker who's acting as emcee. Taking a deep breath, the emcee picks up his silver microphone and begins yelling in an excitable, raspy manner, *"Well, helllllloooooo, Astlebury!"*

The roar almost knocks me off my feet!

"You've all been very patient," he says. "But here's the person you've all been waiting for! Let's make some noise for one of the biggest-selling recording artists this side of Jupiter! Are you ready for Mr. Spike Saunders?"

The noise is deafening!

"Well, here he is!"

Spike's drummer takes the stage first, running out and jumping behind his kit, kicking off with a rather terse, forceful beat on his foot pedal. The crowd immediately begins clapping above their heads, in syncro, as Spike's entire band rushes onto the stage, finding their positions, gradually adding voice and texture

to the noise. Wow! Then, just as things can't get any more elec-
trifying, Spike Saunders sort of swaggers onto the stage, raising
the biggest, most rapturous cheer of the weekend, punching the
air to the beat as he goes.

"Where's Twiggy?" shouts Claude.

"Over there!" I scream as Twiggy stumbles out of the shadows, swigging from a bottle that doesn't look much like gently
carbonated Peruvian water to me.

"Rock 'n' roll! Twenty-four seven!" shouts Twiggy to, well, no
one in particular really. With around five million folk worldwide
watching with growing horror, Twiggy slings his guitar over his
chest and begins a clumsy sprint to the center of the Astlebury
stage, strumming the opening chords of "Lost" as he goes. The
audience roars as Twiggy makes a grand entrance, dropping theatrically to his knees and skidding right across the waxed floor
with his tongue hanging out . . .

. . . grossly misjudging the size of the stage and plummeting
headfirst fifteen feet into the space behind the safety barrier, almost squashing a *Rolling Stone* photographer as he falls.

Oh my God!

A morbid silence sweeps across the crowd. The large screens
on either side of the stage are showing images of Twiggy, lying
in a lifeless heap as the *Rolling Stone* photographer sits up, looking dazed, before attempting to resuscitate the guitarist. The guy
checks the pulse on Twiggy's neck, looking panicked as he yells
across in horror to the oncoming medics, "I think he's dead!"

Chapter 8

situation vacant

Of course Twiggy Starr wasn't dead.

He was just concussed.

But he probably wished he was dead, because if Fenella Tack's expression was any measure of her incandescent rage, she was clearly going to beat the last remnants of life from him with a Miu Miu clutch-purse the second he reached the medical tent.

"Get that stinking carcass out of my sight, and fetch me another guitarist noooooooooow!" Fenella screams as three security guards wrestle Twiggy's floppy torso away. Spike watches on in utter dumbfoundment, all his cocky swagger drained away.

"Find the stand-in guitarist!" bellows Fenella, looking like a velociraptor in Chanel lipstick.

"But there isn't a stand-in guitarist," shouts Spike.

Fenella's eyes narrow to slits; if her brow was indeed capable of movement despite the high levels of Botox administered to it, it would certainly be very furrowed.

"What do you mean no stand-in? Have you gone berserk!?" squeals Fenella. "You better be kidding me, Spike. This fiasco will cost our insurers twenty-eight million dollars to cover if we pull the gig after ten minutes!"

"I know . . . but . . . ," shouts Spike.

"This is Silver Shard's premier chance to promote *Prize* to an estimated two hundred and twenty-three million people worldwide! And you're telling me we've got no guitarist?"

"Yes, that's what I'm telling you," says Spike, practically blubbering. "Twiggy's the only person who knows the new songs."

"I'm not hearing this!" explodes Fenella. *"You put your entire trust in that washed-up, bourbon-addled burnout! Are you out of your tiny mind, Spike?"*

Fenella looks like she's going to leap on Spike's chest and rip his heart out with her bare hands.

"Yes, I trusted him, Fenella! He's my best friend," cries Spike. "He's been having a rough patch, but I didn't think he'd do this. I'll get him into rehab! I'll sort him out!"

"That doesn't help us now!" squeals Fenella.

As the pair squabble, the sounds of growing unrest sweep the crowd.

"Spike! Spike! Spike!" the crowd is beginning to chant, accompanied by the obligatory throwing of bottles.

"We'll be back as soon as possible!" shouts the panicked emcee, appealing for calm, as Lewis the P.A. pushes Spike and Fenella into the wings where the LBD are all standing, watching the events in dismay. In seconds the yelling, posturing pair are joined by an army of sweating technicians and suited and booted record company executives, screaming about losing amounts of money so vast that Spike looks like he's going to vomit.

"But there isn't a replacement guitarist!" screams Spike for the seventy-fifth time at a rotund toadish record company exec who is sucking on a Cuban cigar. "Nobody else knows the flipping new songs! Can't anyone hear me?"

And that's when I have one of those eureka moments.

"Claude! Fleur!" I shout. "Come on! We have to speak to Spike!"

Both girls stare at me in horror, but I grab their hands, dragging them with me into the growing dogfight, fighting my way closer and closer to Spike, although every time I get close enough to speak, one of the many record execs grabs me by the waist and chucks me back out of the circle again.

"It's not autograph time, little girlie!" shouts Fenella, clicking her fingers for assistance. "Security, chuck these three girls out!"

"Noooooo!" I scream as loudly as my lungs will let me, stamping the foot of the black-shirted ogre who's lifting me up by my thong. "Spike! Listen to me just for a second! I know someone who can play!"

Spike freezes and stares straight at me. "What?" he says, his face softening. "How? This isn't a joke, is it, Ronnie, babe?"

"No! It's not a joke!" I persist, trying to remove my thong from my butt crack. "I met a guy who knows the whole of your album *Prize* off by heart!"

"That's impossible, Ronnie," argues Spike. "It's not released for weeks!"

"It *is* possible! He ripped it off RippaCD.com!" I say. "Please believe me, Spike!"

"It's true, Spike!" shouts Claude, jumping up and down. "I've heard him too!"

"He's dead good!" says Fleur, nodding wildly.

"Er . . . okay . . . ," says Spike, his eyes widening. "I mean . . . wow! Where is this guy? Can I meet him?"

"Yes! He's . . . he's . . . er, out there somewhere," I say, pointing ridiculously to the umpteen squillion people in the baying crowd.

Talk about finding a needle in a haystack!

Spike looks at us like we're insane . . . but we're also his only chance.

"Don't worry. We'll find him!" shouts Fleur, pointing at the emcee, who is floundering in the corner with his microphone. "But we need that guy's help."

Fleur darts across and begins whispering in the ear of the emcee, who raises one eyebrow, takes a deep breath and begins to yell into his mike.

"Hellllloooo, Astlebury! Errrr, we now have a vital announcement for one special audience member this evening! Could a Mr. Joel . . . er, Joel what"—The emcee turns and shouts to us, "What's his second name?"

We don't know!

"Joel . . . who drove here in a yellow van with graffiti on it!" says Fleur.

"And he's a lifeguard. A lifeguard who wants to be a brain surgeon!" I add.

"And he's got a best friend called Damon with a shaven head!" shouts Claude helpfully.

All this surreal info reverberates around the fields as the mystified crowd dissolves in giggles before looking to see if mystery man Joel is standing beside them.

"So, er, right, if that's you, Joel, please make your way to the VIP enclosure. Spike Saunders needs you!"

"Just give us five minutes!" I shout to Spike, praying with all my heart that Joel heard the call-out. But let's face it—he could be anywhere.

Claude, Fleur and I sprint down the stage steps, then spill through the VIP enclosure and out of the marquee down to the main gates. As we run, Claude's attempting to call Damon using a phone number she has scrawled in lipstick on an old paper cup in the bottom of her handbag.

"*Agggghh,* it's going straight to voice mail!" she yells.

"I can't believe we're doing this!" I shout. "Is there, like, any chance he heard?"

"Don't fret, Ronnie," screams Fleur. "Look! There are people at the gate already!"

Fleur's right. There are tons of folk at the gate already. About fifty chancers trying to blag their way into the VIP area.

"But I'm Joel! It's true!" a guy with buck teeth and blond dreadlocks is shouting. "Let me in now!"

"Ignore him," a guy with a purple turban rants. "I'm Joel! Spike needs me to play! I've just been parking my yellow van, that's why I'm late!"

"Right, everyone, butt out," a black guy in camouflage trousers and a trilby hat is yelling. "I'm the real Joel, you're all just imposters!"

"Oh, no!" I groan. Now we're really done for.

As we approach the rumpus, a hulking, ginger-haired security guy with hands like La-Z-Boy armchairs and a nose like a strawberry is keeping the interlopers at bay.

Haven't we seen him somewhere before?

"It's Hagar!" gasps Claude. "Hagar, the really quite Horrible! The guy who took our tickets on Friday!"

"The one who chose not to point out that we had VIP ones!" growls Fleur.

But just as Fleur opens her gob to say something ungracious, we spot someone who makes our spirits soar. Floundering among a sea of fake wannabees is the real Joel! Joel, with hazel eyes, brown hair and perfect teeth, flapping his arms and jumping up and down! Beside him, a highly irate Damon is trying to tell Hagar the truth.

"Joel!" I shout, but he can't hear me.

"We're here, Joel!" shouts Claude.

"Oh, hurray! You've arrived!" squeaks a rather bedraggled girl looming up beside us. "Everyone, look! Ronnie and Claude are here! They'll sort this mess out!"

"Er, yes, I suppose we will," I say, slightly confused, turning to shout at Joel again. "Joooooel!"

"You look great, by the way. Love the outfit!" simpers the girl, who is covered in mud and grass stains.

Hang on a minute. I'd know that sickening voice anywhere!

"Panama . . . er, Goodyear?" gasps Claude. Panama looks virtually unrecognizable! The elements have not been kind to her.

"Yes! It's me! Hello!" squeals Panama, spotting Fleur glowering at her. "Oh, and you've found Fleur too! What a relief! I was really worried!"

Things are now getting far beyond weird. I take a step back from Panama, who smells exactly like the porta-loos.

"What do you want?" I say, rather unkindly. I've got bigger priorities than chatting with Panama Bogwash.

"Well, I saw you girls up on stage," smiles Panama, "and, y'know, heard the call-out for Joel . . . and I just wanted to swing by and say hello!"

"Hmmm . . . nice of you," growls Fleur, pulling me away. "Come on, Ronnie, we've no time for this."

Panama keeps on smiling, occasionally gazing past me into the VIP area where she'd no doubt kill for a hot shower, a Hazel Valenski restyle and a chance to hang out with the Kings of Kong, Amelia Annanova and Spike.

Not a snowball's chance in hell! I think.

"C'mon, Ronnie! Hagar needs to know who the real Joel is!" shouts Claude.

In the middle of the scrum, Joel is pleading with the ginger giant from the bottom of his heart. "But I drove the yellow van! And I'm a lifeguard!" Joel is shouting, flashing his Charlton-Jessop municipal swimming baths ID card. "Please believe me! I know all of Spike's new songs off by heart!"

" 'Course you do, kiddiewink," chuckles Hagar cruelly, putting his fingers to his mouth theatrically. "So do I. In fact I'm playing one right now . . . on my invisible pennywhistle!"

Hagar blows his invisible instrument sarcastically as Damon pulls Joel away.

"Come on, Joel, man," grumbles Damon. "We're wasting our time."

"You're not!" I squeal, summoning up superhuman strength and elbowing my way into the center of the group.

"Ronnie! Ronnnnnnnie!" beams Joel, throwing his arms around me. "Is . . . is . . . this for real?"

"Yeah, it's for real!" I say. "You have to come and meet Spike now! Come with us! And you too, Damon, you've got to come and give him some support!"

"Oh, hurray!" says Panama, clapping her grubby hands. "A happy ending!"

"Oh, no you don't," sniggers Hagar, shaking his head. "No, no, no, no! It's not happening. Not on my watch. You know the rules: no VIP passes, no entrance. No exceptions."

At this point I almost collapse into a heap on the ground with frustration, but Claudette Cassiera isn't playing ball at all.

"Right! Ooooooh, this is just about the flipping limit!" Claude yells. "Now then, Mr. Hagar . . . Hagar . . . What is your second name, incidentally?"

"It's Windybottom actually," growls Hagar, daring anyone to laugh.

Jeez, no wonder he has issues, I think.

"Rightio, Mr. Windybottom, sir," continues Claude. "Now, just you listen to me. I've about had my fill of your antics!"

Hagar sneers at her, but it's definitely a fake sneer, because he actually looks quite shocked.

"Now, I don't suppose you remember me and my friends," continues Claude, "but on our way through the gates on Friday you did us three ladies a heinous disservice!"

"*Pgh*, I've never set eyes on you before," shrugs Hagar, but a small flicker of recognition passes his face and he looks sheepish.

"You knew we had special VIP tickets! You just didn't tell us, did you?" hollers Claude. "I ended up missing Carmella Dupris's after-show party and hanging out with the Kings of Kong till this morning! You ought to be ashamed of yourself, Hagar. That was one low-down dirty trick!"

Hagar looks more than a soupçon guilty.

"And now, I am appealing to you," says Claude, "as a fellow human being, to redeem yourself in the eyes of the LBD and God, *and do the right thing!*"

It's one of Claude's Jedi mind tricks again, I think to myself.

"You know full well Spike Saunders needs these boys up on stage now," Claude screams, poking Hagar's chest. "We need to save Astlebury. And it's within your power to do it!"

Claude takes her voice much quieter now. "Because what I think you need to ask yourself now, Mr. Hagar Windybottom, is, Are you a sinner or a winner?"

"What?" asks Hagar.

"Are you a goodie or a baddie?"

Hagar thinks for a second. His eyes look a little red rimmed.

"I'm a goodie," Hagar says petulantly, seeming to have shrunk by about two feet during Claude's verbal onslaught.

"Well, that's what I wanted to hear," whispers Claude, reaching upward and placing one hand on his plump shoulder. "So will you let the boys in?"

Hagar takes a deep breath, then signals for the VIP gate to be opened. The boys run past, whooping and cheering.

Hurray! We've only gone and done it!

Of course, we're forgetting one small hiccup. We seem to have acquired Panama Goodyear, who has spotted her chance at the open VIP gate and is beginning to stride past.

"Not her!" Claude shouts at the guards, pointing at Panama. "That girl is not with us!"

"But I'm their friend!" squeaks Panama, just as her friend from Gate A, Boris the raven-haired guard, appears from nowhere. Boris picks Panama up with one hand, by the back of her filthy trousers. Panama's legs and arms are flapping as she's carried away.

"Put me down this instant! I'll sue you all! Do you hear me?" Panama squeaks. "They're my friends over there. I need to go in the VIP too!"

"You've never been our friend, Panama," Claude says firmly. "See you around sometime, eh?"

"Yeah, ta ta for now, Panama!" I wave.

As the VIP gate begins to swing shut, Panama's face turns to pure venom. "You little weasels!" she's screeching. "As if I'd be seen dead with you anyhow."

"Yeah, *whatever*, Panama," laughs Claude, clapping her hands excitedly. "Right, Joel, Ronnie, Fleur, Damon, come on! Now! We've got to get back to the stage!"

"Yeah, you certainly do! Get a move on!" yells Hagar, waving one huge hand at us reproachfully as we run off. "Hey, and guys? You all have a good show now, won't you?"

With less than a microsecond to spare, we race up the stairs to the stage. Quickly, Spike and Joel are embroiled in a stern negotiation, Joel gesticulating wildly, Spike shaking his head, looking like he's going to cry. I haven't a clue what Joel says to convince Spike, but it must be something fantastic, because all of a sudden he turns around to the band with a winning smile plastered right across his face.

"So it's a yes?" shouts Joel.

"Yes, you're on," shouts Spike, waving across at a guitar roadie to fetch Joel something to play. Fenella surveys the whole scene with utter horror as Spike picks up his microphone once more and yells above the impatient, roaring crowd, "Right, ladies and gents, on behalf of everybody on stage, I'm very sorry about that little impromptu interval! Now, who says we forget all about that and have a little song?"

Hurray!

Fleur wraps her arm around my shoulder. "Well saved, Ronnie!" she laughs.

"Hey, Betty, Tonita, Marie?" yells Spike to his backing singers. "Can you all shift up a bit? We've got three extra bodies we need to squeeze on stage tonight. Now, everybody give a loud Astlebury cheer for the girls who saved Astlebury—Ronnie, Claude and Fleur! I want you to make them feel at home!"

"What?! Now?!" I splutter as Fleur kicks me onto the stage, dragging Claude behind her. Eeeeeek!

I try to hide behind the drum kit and the bassist, but to no avail. The whole crowd can see me!

Aaggghhh, I'm up on the video screens too!

Hellllooooo, Mum!

"And let me introduce our new guitarist for this evening . . . Joel!" shouts Spike.

Joel, who's clearly spent a good ten years in his room with a tennis racket practicing for this moment, takes a modest bow while simultaneously rooting a guitar pick from his back pocket.

"And this one's called 'Lost'!" shouts Spike, as Joel replicates every note of the opening bars perfectly.

Spike exhales audibly as he realizes Joel's stunning talent.

This is one of those wondrous, scrummy stay-in-your-heart forever moments. A veritable ocean of faces is watching me as I smash my tambourine against my thigh and howl into a mike that I dearly hope is turned right down. Beside me, Fleur Swan shimmies, shakes and squeezes herself into every BBC1 camera shot, while Claudette Cassiera improvises the lyrics to every verse, wailing harmonies that just don't fit without giving a hoot 'cos she's having fun. In the wings, Daphne and Rex are dancing and cheering, accompanied by Tabitha Lovelace, Zaza Berry and the whole of Blaze Tribe Five. On the other side Hazel Valenski, SmartBomb and the *Midnight Mayhem* girls are grooving wildly. Damon's telling anyone who'll listen that Joel is his best mate, and the Kings of Kong are gazing on jealously as Spike wins the loudest cheers of the entire weekend. In the shadows, I see Fenella Tack take a tissue from her clutch-purse, quickly dabbing her eyes, then checking to make sure no one noticed.

Aggghh, this is so much fun!

How can we be on our seventh song already? Where's all the time gone to?

I don't want to get off stage yet! I can see now why this show-biz lark is so addictive.

As Spike gently warns the crowd that it's nearly curfew time, people begin pleading for "Merry-Go-Round," the song without which no Spike Saunders set could be complete.

"You know that one, don't you?" shouts Spike to Joel.

"You're kidding me, right?" smiles Joel, as the familiar moving opening bars bring a lump to a million throats.

Spike chucks back his head and laughs.

"Okay! You guys know all the words," he shouts at the crowd. "I'll just have a rest while you do the work!"

After two encores (well, we have to keep our public happy!), the LBD tumble off stage, sweating, giggling and panting, where we're passed warm fluffy towels and Peruvian mineral water by Lewis. Lewis quickly escorts us all back to the VIP marquee. En route, we pass by some mesh barriers separating us from the Astlebury crowd. Bizarrely enough, people begin bashing on the fence as we go past, trying to touch. People are begging for autographs! Just like we're real superstars! Of course, Fleur is quickly scribbling huge swirly signatures for her fans, while Claude has been dragged away to do an impromptu interview with Radio One. Staggering along with me and Joel is Spike Saunders, giggling like a maniac at what's just occurred.

"Thanks, Ronnie! You really did me proud," he says.

"You're very welcome," I say, brimming with happiness.

"And as for you, Joel, well, what can I say?" says Spike, shaking his head. "I'm speechless."

"Anytime," says Joel proudly.

As Fenella sweeps Spike away for a press conference, Joel and I are left alone in the walkway. Joel looks down at me slightly mushily, placing his arm around my shoulder.

"You've . . . you've changed my whole life, Ronnie," he says. "I don't know what to say."

"Oh, well, y'know." I blush. "Anybody would have done the same."

Oh, dear, I think he's going to go all sloppy on me!

"No, shh . . . listen! You're special, Ronnie. You're amazing!" he says, sounding quite choked. "You're beautiful as well as amazing!"

"Ugghhh *gnnnggn*!" I blush. "Well, I've got a lot of makeup on today."

"Not just beautiful on the outside, Ronnie. On the inside too," Joel says, looking a bit misty eyed.

Right, I have to shut him up now.

"Woooh now! Hold yer horses, Joel!" I laugh nervously. "You're beginning to sound like a Spike Saunders song."

"Flipping heck!" says Joel, catching himself. "I am, aren't I? Things have all gone to my head a bit, haven't they?"

We both stand, staring at each other. Joel's arms are wrapped around my neck. My head's resting on his chest. I can feel his heart thumping.

Okay, I suppose this is the point where we're meant to snog, just like Fleur Swan has instructed me. Somehow, it doesn't feel quite right, but I look up, closing my eyes anyhow and wait for the "power of love" to overcome me.

And I wait . . . and wait. But Joel's got his eyes closed, waiting too!

"Joel!" yells Claude, springing from somewhere to unintentionally ruin the moment. "Fenella says she wants you at the press conference now! E! News Live and Fox want to ask you some questions!"

"Me? Really? Wow!" says Joel, rushing away, leaving me loitering under the clear moonlit sky, not quite sure what happened.

"Ronnie? Are you okay?" asks Claude, blissfully ignorant as to what she's just interrupted.

"I'm beautiful, Claude," I say. "In fact, I'm beautiful on the outside as well as in."

"What?" she says.

"Oh, nothing, Claude, just a load of old bobbins I've just heard," I laugh. "Hey! Shall we go back in the VIP and lord it up a bit?"

"Just try to stop me!" says Claude, grabbing my arm and whisking me along. "We need to celebrate . . . and I mean celebrate big style! We, like, totally saved Astlebury! The dangerous bambinos came up trumps yet again!" Claude natters on and on breathlessly. "I mean, how do we top this one, Ronnie? It seems like you and Fleur and I can do absolutely anything when we put our minds to it!"

But then Claude's face drops, changing in a flash to total and utter dumbfoundment.

"Oh . . . My . . . God!" she groans.

"What?" I say.

"It *was* him," she splutters. "It really was him after all! I thought I was seeing things at the skate park yesterday . . . But it was him!"

"Who? What?" I say. Claude looks quite startled.

"Him!" Claude repeats, swinging me around to see who's behind me. As I spot his piercing blue eyes, staring at me through the mesh, I almost feel my knees buckle right under me.

"Jimi Steele?!" I shout. *"What in the devil's name are you doing here!?"*

~~~~~~~~~~~~~~~~~~~~~~

barriers

No, I'm not hallucinating.

It really is Jimi.

Yes, "my" Jimi.

Staring at me through the fence, reminding me slightly of when Mrs. Perkin from our local store placed lost teddy bears in the shop window, hoping owners might pass by and reclaim them.

Abandoned and vulnerable.

Oh, and mud caked and exhausted looking too. It's safe to say Jimi Steele has not gleaned the benefits of a Hazel Valenski restyle. He looks like the Wildman of Borneo.

"And who was that?!" emerges as Jimi's opening gambit. "That guitarist dude! The brown-haired Clark Kent looky-likey! Have you been snogging him? What's going on there?!"

Oh, well, this is just the absolute limit, this is!

"What do you mean?" I shout. "What's it got to do with you, mud-boy?! And what are you doing here anyway!?"

"I followed you here! Because you wouldn't speak to me. You stupid woman!" he yells.

"You *followed* me? *Gnnngnnnn!*" I roar. "Well, you've found me now, haven't you? I was singing on stage with Spike Saunders! What have you got to say to that? Anything you've thought up yourself . . . or stuff Naz and Aaron have told you to say?"

"Er . . . I'm . . . just going to . . . ," mumbles Claude, scurrying away quickly, "go and get that thingie from the . . . er, whatsit . . ."

"Oh, that's very rich coming from you!" singsongs Jimi back. "Yeah, I'm the one who puts my friends first, aren't I? Hey, why don't we get Fleur Swan out here? She'll be gutted we're having this argument without her!"

That shuts me up . . . well, for about three seconds.

"It wasn't Fleur who told me you're a no-good waste of flip-ping space, Jimi Steele!" I say. "I figured that little concept out all by myself. You proved it to me. You stood me up on Blackwell Disco night! You left me at the Fantastic Voyage all dressed up like the Trafalgar Square Christmas tree and went out with Naz and Aaron instead! How could you do that to me?"

Jimi blushes, rattling the mesh railings crossly.

"*Gnnngn* . . . and I'm sorry about that, Ronnie! You don't know how sorry I am!" sighs Jimi. "I am so, so, so flipping ashamed of myself! I've thought about what I did every day for the last three weeks. And every night!" Jimi starts rattling the mesh even more now.

"You're the most important thing in my whole world, you annoying, stubborn woman. You are my world!"

I raise my nose primly in the air, sneering slightly at him. "Skateboarding is your world, Jimi!" I mouth furiously.

Ha! That shut him up!

"I've sold my skateboard, Ronnie," replies Jimi.

"You've . . . you've what?" I gasp.

"Sold it," he mumbles. "I've sold Bess."

That totally floors me.

"I got a hundred pounds for her. Then I hitched here with an old bloke in a Volkswagen, bought a ticket off a scalper and started searching for you. But the campsite was bigger than I thought."

"Where have you been sleeping?" I say, trying to sound like I don't care.

"In the back of Tyrone Tiller's van," says Jimi, "with five other skaters."

Jimi looks at me sadly. "But I got up every day at dawn to search for you."

"Oh," I say, letting out a small sheepish smile. That is one of the sweetest things I've ever heard. Darn him.

"Well, you've found me now," I say in a small voice. I twinkle my hand at him. "Hello."

"Hello," Jimi replies, doing this daft wave and scrunched-up face he always does whenever I turn up to meet him. It always makes me pee laughing.

"I love you, Ronnie," he suddenly blurts out.

"Oh, shut up," I say, shaking my head.

"I do!" he says, looking rather hurt. "Look, I know I don't often say it . . ."

"You've never said it," I say. "Not once."

"Haven't I? But I thought you knew that I . . . *gnnngnn!* Well, I'm saying it now," says Jimi. *"I love you."*

I gaze at him, really, really wanting to believe him. He really is so gorgeous and funny and lovable.

And useless. And a terrible timekeeper. And bound to break my heart.

"Look, this is stupid," says Jimi. "I know you're one of the beautiful people now, but can't you come out of your little VIP enclosure for a while and talk to me properly? We could go for a walk on Briggin Hill. It's amazing up there when all the bonfires are blazing."

I ponder that for a moment. It couldn't hurt, could it? Just one little walk?

"Okay," I say frostily. "But don't get your hopes up, Jimi. I'm not promising you anything."

Chapter 9

homeward bound

"So what does everyone fancy singing?" asks Fleur Swan, drumming her fingers excitedly on the Mini Cooper's dashboard as Daphne Swan indicates left, heading out of Astlebury's main gates into the narrow country lanes through Marmaduke Orchards.

"Haven't we sung enough this weekend?" giggles Claude.

"No!" hoots Fleur. "And today I really feel like it! Hey, what about 'You Canny Kick Yer Granny Off the Bus!' "

"No!" I groan from the backseat. "Anything but that one!"

" 'Jimmy Crack Corn'?" suggests Fleur. " 'Five Hundred Green Bottles'?"

" 'Alice the Camel'!" shouts Claude. "We used to sing that one on the way to Brownie camp!"

"Yeah! But we'll only do twenty verses!" says Fleur. " 'Cos after that, y'know, it gets a bit repetitive."

Oh, dear.

Everyone in the Mini Cooper is in thoroughly jubilant spirits.

After an epic Damon and Claudette farewell scene, involving fervent sobbing and promises to call, text and e-mail each other the very second they reach home, if not before, Daphne and I finally forced Claudette Cassiera into the Mini. Meanwhile, Damon, who hasn't really mastered playing things cool, was hugging the side of the Mini, quacking stuff like, "I can't believe you're leaving me!"

Claude, who was equally distraught, was pushing her face against the window, moaning, "I'll ring you later! I miss you already!"

"Oh, pur-lease!" sighed Fleur, rolling her eyes and climbing into the front seat.

Obviously, I'd packed all of Fleur's clothes and makeup for her, as she was too busy speaking on her mobile phone to journalists from both *Shout!* and *Scream!* magazines.

"I can't tell you journalists everything you need to know!" Fleur was telling one of them as she sat on a tree stump watching me wrestle her damp sleeping bag into Daphne's trunk. "I need to retain a little part of my privacy, y'know, just to remain grounded."

"Hmmmph," said Daphne, rolling her eyes.

"And just for the record," Fleur bleated starrily, "I am not dating Spike's brother Caleb Saunders! We are simply *just good friends.* I did sit with him at the after-show party last night, but it was purely platonic. Put that in your newspaper, if you will, please!"

"Platonic snogging?" remarked Claude dryly. "Whatever next?"

"Of course, you do realize," I groan as we descend the access road to the motorway, "that we've broken every single rule, without exception, on that behavioral contract we signed. That's pretty bad, isn't it?"

We'd have probably got away with losing Daphne, forgetting to call, talking to weirdos, canoodling and hanging out with hedonists, but there's not much we can do about the photographs plastered all over the *Daily Mirror* of the LBD draped around Spike Saunders, sipping flutes of chilled Cristal in the VIP enclosure.

I had only one glass! And it was a celebration, after all! (It tasted a bit like fizzy feet, if you ask me.)

Fleur thinks for a while, counting off all the rules on her fingers, "Champagne? Snogging? Weirdos? Hey, wow! You're right, Ron," she says, bristling with pride. "Ooh, I'm rather proud of myself. Lifetime best!"

Just then Fleur's mobile rings once more and she starts giving yet another interview about how, single-handedly, she saved Astlebury with her wit, guile and lightning brains.

"So then I turned to my friend Ronnie," Fleur brags, "and I said, hey, we know someone who can play all the new Spike Saunders songs, don't we?"

I can't help but chuckle.

In the driver's seat, Daphne Swan seems soporifically smug, but of course, her farewell to Rex was far from final too.

"We've decided to put school on hold for another year and go off traveling again," coos Daphne dreamily. "You see, Rex has heard about this patch of rain forest in Guatemala that's being depleted at the rate of ten square hectares a month. We're going to fly out and help the indigenous people save it."

Ahh! Paddy will be thrilled, I think, resting my exhausted head against the back window.

I'm trying to make sense of the last few crazy days, but too many wild and crazy images are cluttering my brain. I'm remembering Joel, gallantly helping me with our numerous bags and boxes to the Mini before tucking his phone number into the back pocket of my denims. "Look, Ronnie," he said, "I know your head's a bit mixed up about that, y'know, Jimi guy . . . but if you ever, like, wanted to see me, just pick up the phone and give me a call. I'm two hours away. I'll jump in the car and drive across. Just say the word."

Then I think about me and Jimi last night, walking up over Briggin Hill, with a cacophony of fireworks exploding overhead and a huge smiling full moon above us. Thousands of festival-goers were flocking all around us, enjoying their last night of Astlebury craziness as Jimi jabbered on, ten to the dozen, trying to prove that he'd learned a lesson by messing up so badly. And that he knew he'd been a flaky buttmunch, but that he was determined to change things, and think more about how I feel about stuff. He said he wanted to change, he wanted to be the best boyfriend in the world ever.

But people never really change, do they?

Then I think about Mum, Dad and Seth and realize that I'm actually absolutely dying to see them. I'm actually craving my dad's terrible jokes and my mum nagging me about the mess in my room. I'm dying to give Seth a cuddle, then have a long bath with tons of bubbles and a night in a real bed, under my squashy duck-feather duvet.

It's nice to get away for a while, I think to myself, *but sometimes it's even nicer to go home.*

home

As I fall through the doors of the Fantastic Voyage, a massive cheer erupts. Somehow, Dad's amassed all of the pub's regulars: Toothless Bert, Travis the Aussie bartender, Muriel from the kitchen and various other social misfits who call our pub a second home. Good old Dad is boring them all senseless with tales about his wonderful, hyper-intelligent, superstar daughter. Even better, behind the cash register, ripped from this morning's *Daily Mirror,* is a photo of the LBD cuddling Spike Saunders, hiding the old one of me, aged six, dressed as a sunflower. Good fortune really is abundant at the moment!

"Hurray! The wanderer returns!" laughs Dad, giving me a stubbly smackroonie on the cheek. "Y'know, I couldn't keep those media hounds at bay much longer!"

"What d'you mean?" I say.

"That Fun Time Frankie from Wicked FM's breakfast show wants you to do a phone interview at six forty-five tomorrow morning!" Dad says.

"Oh, and the *Local Daily Mercury* wants you to write some sort of piece about live music."

Me? A music journalist? Wow!

"Y'know, I'm thinking of giving up this pub game and beginning work as your agent," Dad says as I look around the pub for the character most conspicuous by her absence.

"Hey, what have you done with my mother?" I say.

"Who? Oh . . . right, your mother," says Dad, wincing slightly. "Now, that will be that very poorly lady over there in the corner . . . but go easy on her, Ronnie . . . she's a bit *delicate* today."

Over on the sofas, my green-gilled mother is sipping water, bravely managing a smile and a small wave at me.

"Hey, Mum!" I yell. "I'm home!"

"I can see. It's my famous daughter! The one off the television!" she whispers, giving me a cuddle. "Do me a favor, though, Ronnie, eh? Stop shouting, will you?"

"Are you sick?" I ask.

"Self-inflicted, Ronnie. Give her no sympathy," butts in Dad, plonking down beside us, clutching my beautiful little mushed-banana-covered brother. "And don't even ask how Paddy Swan is," he mutters under his breath.

"Mother? What *exactly* is up with you?" I say.

"Something I ate," moans Mum. "Ghanaian food clearly doesn't agree with me."

"Ghanaian food?" I frown. "What have you been up to?"

"Oh, right," begins Mum sheepishly. "Well, since you girls were all away, Paddy Swan decided to have a little, er, gathering. Y'know, just to console ourselves, as we were bereft of our teenagers for the weekend."

"Your mother was especially distraught," says Dad, fake-solemnly.

"A gathering? What sort of a gathering?" I say, suddenly recalling Paddy's "letting off some steam" comment from weeks ago.

Mum opens her mouth to explain, but she simply burps, then grimaces, clutching her head in her hands.

"It started off as just Paddy's James Bond Society cronies," Dad says. "They were all around at Disraeli Road, playing roulette and drinking martinis . . ."

"But then your aunty Susan offered to baby-sit Seth, so we went along too," mumbles Mum. "You know, just to be sociable."

"And then Gloria popped by on her way home from evensong and she brought a dozen of the Ghanaian Methodists with her," says Dad. "And Lord, do they like to let their hair down!"

"Gloria Cassiera?!" I say, shaking my head.

"I blame Gloria!" groans Mum. "She was the ringleader! And once that Pastor Jones fella got control of the barbecue and that woman Winnie with the hat started mixing rum punch, well, it all went downhill from there . . ."

"I don't believe this!" I say. "You people are all over forty years old! Geriatrics! You should be tending your begonias and sipping chamomile tea. Not drinking rum and cavorting! This is all extremely wrong."

"Oh, Ronnie, calm down," laughs Mum. "You're such a stress-head! You'll end up at that anger management group before long, with all those guys we met at the party!"

"Oh yeah, I forgot that bit. The anger management group showed up too," explains Dad, rolling his eyes. "They were all quite cool guys . . . well, until the fight broke out."

I stare at Magda and Loz with my mouth wide open for well over a minute.

"I'm going to go to my boudoir now," I say. "I need to try to erase these shocking images from my brain."

"But I haven't told you about when your mother fell over backward trying to limbo-dance yet!"

Aaaagggggh!

Parents having parties? It's a world gone mad, I tell you.

Upstairs, I change into fresh sweatpants and a baggy sweater and lie down on my fabulously soft bed.

Bliss.

What do I do now?

I pick up a copy of *Red Hot Celebs* and begin to leaf through, but I can't seem to concentrate on any of the features. Something else is playing on my mind.

So I switch on the radio, but every song reminds me of the problem I need to solve.

So I turn on my TV and try to engross myself in some cartoons, but all I'm doing is goggling the box while thinking about another more prevalent issue.

Eventually, I realize that I've just got to see him. I can't fight my feelings anymore.

I pick up my mobile phone from the bedside table, where I left it, draining the last remains of battery with the call I've got to make.

"Look, I've been thinking about what you said," I blurt out when he answers. "How long will it take you to get here?"

"Ronnie! It's you! Excellent!" he says, sounding over the moon to hear from me. "Yeah, of course I can come over. I'll be right there."

"Open it," I say.

"What is it?" he says.

"You have to *open* it to find out," I say. "That's the point of wrapping paper, bozo."

"It's not wrapping paper," he says, nitpicking. "It's newspaper."

"Well, I didn't have much time!" I tut. "Look, do you want it or not?"

He unwraps the hastily wrapped item, then looks at me in utter shock.

"It's a skateboard!" he says. "It's . . . like a brand-new version of Bess."

"Yes, well done," I say sarcastically, trying to conceal my delight.

"Ha ha!" Jimi hoots. "Ronnie, babe, I can't believe this! You are totally amazing!"

"Well, it's been said before," I say mischievously.

"Ronnie, look, I can't accept this. It must have cost a bomb!"

"No, Jimi, you must accept it," I say. "I can't live with the guilt. You know, you love skating; therefore you're a skater boy, therefore you're going to look pretty idiotic just running along the road beside Naz and Aaron making wheel sounds."

Jimi picks up the skateboard with eyes as wide as saucers.

"Oh, and I want you to have it, of course," I say. "I got paid cash in hand for some of those magazine interviews I did last night, so I can afford to be a bit spendy."

Jimi puts the skateboard down on my bedroom floor, then stands on it. "*Gah!* Have a go, Ronnie! Just stand on it!" he says, hopping off. "It even feels expensive! It's amazing! Oh, I love you so much, Ron! What a woman!" he says, welling up a bit.

"Yeah, well, you've said that eighty-two times now," I say, welling up a bit too.

"I'm making up for lost time!" he laughs, brushing away a singular eyelash on my cheek. "So, er, do you love me too?"

"Hmmm, s'pose so," I smile. "Annoying though that is."

Jimi looks at me, biting his lip a little. "You know, Fleur's not going to be happy about this," he warns.

"Uggh . . . let me worry about her. I'll talk her around . . . and my mother," I say, pausing to savor that lovely prospect.

"So . . . like, are we, er, okay now?" he asks gingerly.

I stop to consider that option. "Well, I'm okay," I say eventually. "Are you okay?"

"I'm okay," he grins.

"Well, okay . . . we're okay then," I smile.

Jimi cups his hands around my cheeks and kisses me gently on the lips. It tastes all familiar and gorgeous.

"So . . . cool, that's that sorted then . . . ," he beams, looking a lot more like his old scampish, confident self. "Hey! How's about sojourning to the beer garden for a game of ridiculous man-sized chess then?"

I look at him, letting out a small ecstatic snortle. "Oh, what the heck," I say. "Go on."

APPENDIX
MAGDA RIPPERTON'S OBSERVATIONS ON BOYKIND

1. You can tell when a boy feels comfortable in any given space, as he'll begin leaving small piles of loose change around. This is an offering to the Great Small Change God. It's a girl's right to pocket this money and spend it on mascara.

2. Boys truly believe they become invisible once inside a car. That's why we girls totally cannot see them excavating their noses at traffic lights.

3. All boys secretly like the smell of their own flappy bum explosions. They pretend to look sheepish and shoo the smell away only when girls are present.

4. Important: When canoodling, boys will always go as far as YOU allow them to. Don't expect a boy to say, "Oh, noooo, I couldn't possibly feel your boobs—that's a bridge too far! Please button your top back up!" They're chancers, the lot of them. You've got to police your own body.

5. If you ask a boy to help you with something boring, e.g., washing the dishes, tidying your bedroom, etc., there's a strong possibility the crafty dog will do it very badly on purpose so you never ask him again.

6. If a boy you're dating suddenly springs the "I need some space" line on you, I suggest changing your phone number, burning all of his possessions that are at your house in a large bonfire and then inviting his best mate to the cinema. I usually find that's as much "space" as a boy requires.

7a. *Never* date boys who hate their mother. Mothers are fabulous; therefore he's quite clearly a serial killer and will have a collection of human heads in his freezer.

7b. On the other hand, if his mummy is still choosing his outfits in the morning and spooning boiled eggs to him in bed, get rid of him, as he's clearly a total sap. Avoid at all costs.

8. You won't believe this now, but no matter how much you cry when you're a teenager about being dumped by someone, there will be a time in distant years to come when you can't even remember his second name. Or why you split up. You'll definitely be relieved you split up though. Especially when you run into him, aged thirty-five, in Wal-Mart and he's got a receding "Temple of Doom" hairline and beige slip-on shoes. Believe me.

9. Boys will always get in the way of your friendships. The thing to remember is that boyfriends come and go, whereas great girlfriends last forever. Take your aunty Susan. I've been trying to get rid of her since kindergarten.

10. The recklessness of a boy's behavior and how badly he treats girls will always be in direct correlation with how unbelievably desirable womankind finds him. Somehow, any boy who mothers would detest on sight will always be the one girls will lose their marbles over. I have no idea why this is, but forsooth, it has been the law since the dawn of civilization.

11. Try to date boys with roughly the same size feet as you. Then if you get married someday, you can steal his socks.